PETER C
THE STAR'

REGINALD Evelyn Peter Sc
born in Whitechapel in the East Enu ...
as a lieutenant during the First World War, he wo...
a police reporter and freelance investigator until he found
success with his first Lemmy Caution novel. In his lifetime
Cheyney was a prolific and wildly successful author, selling, in
1946 alone, over 1.5 million copies of his books. His work was
also enormously popular in France, and inspired Jean-Luc
Godard's character of the same name in his dystopian sci-fi
film *Alphaville*. The master of British noir, in Lemmy Caution
Peter Cheyney created the blueprint for the tough-talking,
hard-drinking pulp fiction detective.

PETER CHEYNEY

THE STARS ARE DARK

DEAN STREET PRESS

Published by Dean Street Press 2022

All Rights Reserved

First published in 1943

Cover by DSP

ISBN 978 1 915014 23 8

www.deanstreetpress.co.uk

"Pale ghosts tread softly
when the stars are dark."

CHAPTER 1
ASSIGNATION WITH SHADOWS

I

A FILM director, seeking a ghostly scene for some *macabre* film, would have acclaimed the location of the Box of Compasses.

It stood, set back fifty yards from the deserted cross-roads, one arm of which dwindled away past the wooded crest of the hill; turned itself into a footpath and disappeared amongst the scrub on the cliff top. One arm ran into the moorland; the other wound past the inn and broadened on its way to the town. There was no shelter from the wind. The ramshackle building stood on a bare plateau surrounded by scrubland. On the other side of the woods the cliffs descended steeply, disappearing into sand-dunes running down to the long shelving beach of the bay.

Either there was fog or rain or wind—sometimes all of them. This night was stormy. The wind howled in from the sea, through the woodland, swept down to the cross-roads to vent its fury on the Box of Compasses. It rattled the old-time shutters, banged unsecured doors, set window frames and hinges creaking, and swung the inn sign backwards and forwards, creating in the process a rusty dirge as a set-off to its own shrill voice.

The lorry came from the direction of the town at a good thirty miles an hour. The canvas flap at the back was open, whipped against the side, making a noise like a cracking whip.

When the inn came in sight, Greeley, who was sitting in the cab beside the driver, said: "Look, run up the road till you come to the side of the wood. There's an open space there you can turn in and park."

The driver said: "All right." He spoke in a cultured voice and the hands that gripped the steering-wheel were white—unused to manual work.

Greeley looked at them. He thought: "Jesus, they're givin' us some fine proper boys these days. I wonder where this one came from." He put his hand into the side pocket of his leathern wind-jammer; brought out a crumpled cigarette. He lit it; drew the smoke down into his lungs, opened his mouth and let it come out again. The cigarette was stuck artistically to his lower lip. Greeley was one of those men to whose lower lips cigarettes always stuck. He undid two of the buttons of his leathern jacket; put his hand inside. Under his left arm, in a soft holster, was a .45 Webley Scott automatic. He pulled the holster a little forward, so that his right hand could close easily on the butt. He buttoned up his jacket, put his hands on his knees, sat looking through the windshield.

He began to think about the girl at Kingstown. Jesus . . . there was a girl. When they were serving out nerve—and when he said nerve he meant *nerve*—she'd got herself a basinful. And she had one of those pale, wistful sort of faces and fine blonde hair, and a figure that made your fingers tingle. . . .

She looked sort of weak and helpless, and she would look at you with big blue eyes, and you would think that somebody had taken her for a very rough ride and you would feel sorry for her.

Weak and helpless. . . . Greeley, his sharp eyes looking at the windshield in front of him and not seeing anything except that wistful face, began to grin. Weak and helpless. . . . Like hell she was! He remembered the do in the cellar of the Six Sisters on the Meath Road when she'd shot Vietzlin when he was nearly through the window . . . a lovely drop shot . . . with a forty-five that she'd grabbed out of Villier's coat pocket and a pull on it that weighed all of two pounds.

Greeley wondered who she was; if he would ever see her again. He wondered where the devil Quayle had found that one. Quayle certainly knew how to pick them. He certainly had some method. He never made a nonsense of picking people. . . .

Greeley conceded that Quayle knew what he was doing. Nearly all the time he knew what he was doing. A cool, hard-headed one, Quayle . . . one who knew when to be tough and when to play it nice and soft and easy; who knew how to look like a big kind-hearted one and who could talk you into or out of anything, but who could do other things beside talk.

Greeley wondered what Quayle was getting out of it. Pretty much the same as the rest of them, he thought. Sweet nothing . . . sweet Fanny Adams . . . sweet goddam all . . . except maybe the kick. Perhaps Quayle was getting a kick out of it.

Massanay, who was driving, said: "I feel damn' funny. I feel as if my stomach's cold inside. I wonder what's going to happen?"

Greeley grinned. He said: "You should bleedin' worry! You take a tip from me—don't you ever think of what's goin' to happen before it happens in this game, see? It don't do, you know, and it don't get you any place. Just take things as they come. The other thing you can remember is that nothing is ever as bad as you think it's going to be."

Massanay said: "You ought to know."

"You bet your life I ought to know," said Greeley. "When you've been kickin' around in this racket as long as I have nothing's going to make you feel funny; nothing's going to surprise you. If a couple of burnin' fiends dropped out of hell in a flash of blue flame, you wouldn't even blink."

There was a pause. Then Greeley asked: "You know what you've got to do?"

Massanay said: "Yes." He went on, talking like a child who's learned a lesson: "I'm going to park the lorry round in the clearing of the woods. I'm going to wait ten minutes; then I'm going down to the saloon bar of the Box of Compasses. I'll have a drink. There are going to be three other men there—yourself and two more. I know what the other two will look like. All right. By the time I've had my drink it ought to be time for people to start moving. First the tall man will go; then the man of medium height with very wide shoulders. About two minutes after he's gone I shall leave."

Greeley said: "That's all right. Where do you go to?"

"I follow the path along the top of the cliff," said Massanay. "Down the other side, about a hundred yards down, there's a cut in the cliff. The cleft runs down to the beach. I'm to turn down into that cleft. Somewhere there I'll find you three."

"That's all right," said Greeley. "All right. Well, you do it." He grinned. "All you got to do is to pull your belt in one hole, if you've got a belt on. That'll stop your guts from turnin' over. And the second thing is try and keep your teeth from chatterin'. Every time there's a lull in the wind you sound like a bleedin' typewriter workin'."

He grinned suddenly in a friendly manner. He dug Massanay in the ribs. He said:

"Don't worry, kid. You'll be all right. I was like you the first time. You can drop me off here."

Massanay slowed down. Greeley opened the door and stood on the step of the slow-moving lorry. He said:

"When you park this lorry, tie up that flap at the back. There might be some nosy fellow hangin' around—a cyclist policeman or a Home Guard. Maybe they'd want to know what you're doin' with four six-foot boxes in this outfit."

Massanay said: "Why should they worry?"

Greeley said: "Why? Because they look like coffins, don't they?" He grinned again. "Because they look like coffins nobody would believe they were fruit boxes. And the joke is they *are* fruit boxes but they *ought* to be coffins. So long, chum."

He dropped off into the road. He stood watching the lorry as it went up the hill towards the wood.

II

Fells finished his whisky and soda as Greeley came into the Box of Compasses. Greeley looked casually around the bar, showing not the slightest sign of recognition when he saw Fells and Villiers.

Villiers was sitting at the little table on the left of the fire, drinking Guinness. He was wearing a bowler hat perched rather incongruously on the top of a round head. Villiers looked like the sort of man who would be a coal agent or an insurance agent or anything like that—the sort of man you wouldn't notice.

Fells, leaning against the bar, lit a cigarette. He was thinking about Greeley. He was thinking Greeley was pretty good—a funny, odd fellow Greeley—a regular Cockney—but with a peculiar sense of something that you couldn't put your finger on—utterly reliable. He drew the cigarette smoke down into his lungs.

Fells had a long thin face, and when you looked at it the first time you thought that it was a very sad face. The deep ironic lines about the mouth, the bony structure of the jaw and the peculiar thinness at the side of the eyes gave you an odd impression of asceticism. When you looked again you noticed the groups of finely cut humour lines at the edge of the eyes. When he smiled—a rare occurrence—his eyes lighted up. Then it seemed as if, for a moment, he had forgotten something—something that he wanted badly to forget—as if he had obtained a few seconds' respite from a ghost that haunted him. He was tall and thin. He had long legs, slim hips. His shoulders were good, and underneath the superficial appearance of laziness you could sense a great energy—an energy born of frustration or impatience or something. Fells might have been anything, but first of all he might have been an actor. He had the ability to blend into a background, and here in the tap-room of the Box of Compasses he seemed to be completely a part of the scene.

Villiers, with his bowler hat, drinking Guinness at the far side; and Greeley, his drink ordered, leaning against the bar counter, casting an appraising eye on the buxom barmaid—all of them somehow, and in some strange fashion, blended into the atmospherics of the Box of Compasses. An odd process, but one which is possible to men whose nervous system is finely attuned to atmospherics.

Massanay came in. The barmaid, who was wiping the zinc counter, looked at him for a moment. She wondered at the influx of business. She thought Massanay looked nice. Then she looked at Fells in the quick, appraising manner of her kind. She thought Fells looked a little odd and sad—the sort of man who has been pushed around by life and doesn't know what to do about it.

Fells thought. He thought that he would like to go to the Palladium; that he would like to see Tommy Trinder. He had seen a poster earlier in the day. Mr. Trinder's face gazed at him invitingly from the poster. Mr. Trinder was saying: "Oh, you lucky people!" The suggestion conveyed itself into the mind of Fells that by going to the Palladium, by seeing Tommy Trinder, he could be lucky! He might secure for a little while happiness. He might be amused. Definitely, he must go and see Tommy Trinder. Then he thought that when he had the chance he would speak to Greeley about it. First of all Greeley was certain to have been there. Greeley went everywhere. He had an extreme ability for enjoyment. Only Greeley could enjoy things such as—Fells sighed. Then he smiled a little whimsically. After all there was only one Greeley.

He ordered another whisky and soda. He began to think about Tangier. The process was pleasurable. Not always did he allow himself to think about Tangier—just occasionally. When things were a little bad, or getting to be a little exciting, or there was a chance of any particular unhappiness in the near future, then Fells would think about Tangier.

A picture of her would come to him. He would visualize the soft chestnut hair framing her beautiful oval face. He would think about her face, of the carved beautiful lines of her mouth. Thinking about

Tangier brought a sense of peace or exhilaration, whichever was required at that moment.

The barmaid brought his drink. Fells drank it slowly. Then he turned his wrist over and looked at his watch. It was ten o'clock. He wore his wrist-watch on the inside of his wrist because it had a luminous dial and if it were worn on the outside of the wrist it might be seen in the darkness. Fells and Greeley and Villiers and the rest of them always thought of little things like that. They realized they weren't little things; they realized they were very big things. Important things like life—if it *was* important—sometimes depended on such little things.

He put his cigarette stub in the ashtray on the bar. He said good-night to the barmaid, put his hands into the pockets of his old navy-blue raincoat. He went out of the bar.

Greeley ordered another half-pint of bitter. When it was brought to him he looked into the tankard rather as if he were expecting to read something in the brown surface of the beer. He was thinking that it would only be necessary for him to allow Fells a couple of minutes—that would be enough. He turned his head slightly as Villiers—his empty glass in his hand—came to the bar. Villiers put his glass down on the bar. He said:

"Ten Players, please, miss!"

The girl brought the cigarettes. Villiers put the shilling on the bar and turned away. As he did so his foot touched Greeley's accidentally.

Greeley was inclined to be artistic. He said: "Go easy, that's my blinkin' foot."

Villiers said: "Sorry!"

Greeley said: "That's all bleedin' well, but I got a corn on that foot. I've tried everything for that corn that a man can think of—plasters and Gawd knows what. But it's still there. Funny thing is, on a night like this, when it's a bit cold, and there's maybe a spot of rain hangin' about, that corn starts sproutin' like hell. The slightest thing and the pain goes right through me. It's useful in a way though—it always tells me what the weather's going to be like."

Villiers said: "Does it? That must be very nice for you."

Greeley said: "You're not being sarcastic, are you?"

Villiers shook his head. "I wouldn't be sarcastic about a man who's got a corn," he said. "Have a look at me—do I look the sort of person who'd be sarcastic about a thing like that?"

Greeley said: "Well, I can't say you do and I can't say you don't."

Villiers said: "Well, that's all right."

Greeley drained his tankard. He said: "If it's O.K. with you it's O.K. with me."

Villiers opened the packet of cigarettes; took one out. He lit it and looked at the glowing end for a moment; then he said casually: "Well, good-night." He went out.

Massanay, who had ordered a gin and tonic, put the empty glass down on the mantelpiece. He held out his hands to the fire for a moment; then walked over to the door. As he pushed aside the black-out curtain he said to the barmaid:

"I take the left fork for Halliday—don't I?"

She nodded. "Over to the right of the copse," she said. "An' take care you don't fall in the sewage pit."

Massanay nodded. Greeley, lighting a cigarette, heard the door close.

After a minute he said: "I suppose you shut at ten o'clock."

The barmaid nodded. "That's right," she said. "It's a good thing too. There's very little business doing around here these days."

Greeley said: "I should think so. Funny sort of place to have a pub—sort of deserted, isn't it?"

She said: "It used not to be. There used to be a lot of traffic on this road before the war was on. Most of the lorries found it easier to come round this way. We used to do lunches." She sighed. "I wonder if those days will ever come back," she said.

Greeley said: "I wonder! Well, I'll be goin'."

She said suddenly: "You'd better be careful if you're going over the cliff path. The wind's strong to-night. Two years ago a man was blown over."

Greeley said: "Ah! But I'm not going over the cliff path."

"Well, you'll have a long walk to the town," said the girl.

He said: "I know. I like walking." He thought: "To hell with this woman. Now I've got to walk down the road to the town just in case she's looking out of the window, and it's a clear night so I'll have to walk quite a way." He put the box of cigarettes in his pocket. He said: "Well, good-night. Sleep well." He went out.

III

The wind howled dismally round the cliff edge. On the top of the cliff amongst the scrub where the cleft began, a little shower of stones and dry twigs descended and rolled down into the gully. Half-way down the cleft where the cliff walls were twenty feet high, where there was protection from the wind, Greeley, Villiers and Massanay sat, their backs against the cliff wall. Villiers was whistling softly to himself.

Massanay said: "It would be funny if they didn't come!" He took a packet of cigarettes from his pocket.

Greeley looked at him sideways. He said, with a not unkind grin: "Maybe the wish is father to the thought, hey? And I wouldn't light a cigarette if I were you—just in case they *did* come."

Villiers said: "They'll come all right. They're consistent bastards." His voice was bitter.

Greeley said: "Yes, they're consistent enough. Whatever else you can accuse 'em of you couldn't say they were inconsistent. They make up their minds to do something and they go on doin' it." He grinned in the darkness. "They haven't got the bleedin' sense to stop doin' it even when they get knocked off."

Villiers said: "Well, the boys behind 'em don't know they're knocked off, do they—anyway not for a long time?"

Greeley said: "That's as maybe. The thing is they keep on comin'."

He got up. He began to walk down the cleft towards the seashore. In spite of the darkness he walked surely. He made no noise. Almost at the bottom of the cleft, standing behind a ledge in the cliff wall, was Fells. He was looking out to sea. He had a night glass to his eyes.

Greeley said: "You won't see much. There's a mist comin' up. It's bloody bad visibility."

Fells said in a soft, almost disinterested voice: "So much the better. They'll have to come in close before they signal."

Greeley said: "They'll be goddam good if they find the place on a night like this."

Fells put the night glasses back into the case which hung round his neck. He said: "If they're coming they'll find it—that is if they've got so far."

Greeley ran his tongue over his lips. He said: "I hope they do come." There was silence for a minute; then Greeley asked: "How are you goin' to play this?"

Fells said: "I don't know whether the people coming in know the party who were supposed to meet them—the people whose place we're taking. We might have to think quickly. If they didn't know this Apfel, who's the contact man here, we shall be all right."

Greeley said: "I see. That means to say you're goin' to meet 'em and give 'em the old schmooze."

Fells nodded. "My German's good enough for that," he said.

Greeley said: "Well, that's all right. And supposin' they do know what this Apfel fellow looks like, and they take a look at you and see that you are not Apfel. So what then?"

Fells smiled. He looked at Greeley. He said:

"That's where you'll have to be very quick."

Greeley said in a matter-of-fact tone: "All right. You go down towards the beach but not too far. I'll stick around here in the shadow. Villiers can be on the other side of the cleft behind me. We've got to know where each of us is going to be, see?"

Fells said: "That all sounds very nice. What do you propose to do with Massanay?" He was still smiling.

Greeley said: "I think we'll leave him out. He can stick up at the end of the cleft and watch the cliff top. I think he's feelin' a little bit cold in the stomach. Don't get me wrong—there's nothing wrong with Massanay. He's a nice boy, but we can't afford any slip-ups."

Fells said: "Definitely not." He sounded quite disinterested. He was thinking, in fact, that he really must go up and see Tommy Trinder at the Palladium. The words on the poster—"Oh, you lucky people"—for some reason or other passed through his mind with monotonous regularity.

Greeley leaned up against the cliff wall. He was relaxed, indifferent, poised. Fells thought: "Greeley doesn't give a damn for anything." He liked Greeley just as much as one man can like another one.

Greeley said: "What's on your mind? You're thinkin' of something, aren't you?"

Fells's smile broadened. He said: "Yes—the oddest thing. I saw one of those Palladium posters about Tommy Trinder. For some weird reason the words—'Oh, you lucky people'—keep going through my mind. When I've got time I must go and see that show."

Greeley said: "That's a good one." He spat artistically. "Oh, you lucky people!" He looked about him, shrugged his shoulders humorously. "Are we lucky or are we?" he said—"on a bloody picnic like this!"

Fells asked softly: "Do you mind it?"

Greeley said: "What the hell! I should worry!"

There was a silence. No one spoke. Suddenly, from out of the mist on the other side of the waves that broke gently up the shelving beach, there came the sound of a sea-gull screeching three times.

Greeley said between his teeth: "For crissake . . . the boy friends."

Fells said: "Well, here we go!" He moved a few steps towards the beach, took a flash lamp from his pocket and, standing up against the cliff wall, began to flash the lamp out to sea.

Greeley moved back a few paces, cuddled his shoulder against an overhanging boulder, slipped his hand into the pistol holster under his left arm, brought out the pistol. He moved back the safety catch; stood, his right arm hanging straight down by his side. He whistled very softly between his teeth.

Villiers came down. He said: "So they've made it?"

Greeley said: "That's right, chum. Look, the boss is keepin' over to the right, so he'll be on the right-hand side of the cleft where it runs down to the sand. That's where the talkin' will be. I'm goin' to be here on the left. You be a little higher up on the other side. That way we don't give it to each other, see?"

Villiers said: "I see. Look, if they're leery, you wouldn't miss, would you? If you did, it wouldn't be so good for Fells."

Greeley said: "You go and teach your bleedin' grandmother to suck eggs! Have you ever known me to miss?"

Villiers grinned. "No," he said. "But everybody's got to start some time." He moved back up the cleft.

The nose of a boat grated on the shingle that edged the sand. Two men jumped out. They came through the water up the beach. Fells made a movement towards them. He stopped, still in the shadow of the cliff. He stood there waiting, the flash lamp in his left hand. The leading man out of the boat was by now only a few feet from Fells. He was peering forward in the darkness.

Fells said quietly: "*Güten Abend. Ich hoffe Sie hatten eine güte Überfahrt.*"

The man from the boat said: "*Ja, es war nicht zu schlecht.*" Then, suddenly, as he saw Fells's face, he began to shout. Three words were out of his mouth when Greeley fired.

The bullet hit the leading man in the stomach. He made a horrible noise, crumpled up in the sand. He was trying to get at his coat pocket. By this time Fells had dropped the lamp and fired through the right-hand pocket of his raincoat. He shot the second man. Three shots came from the direction of the boat. Immediately Greeley, followed by Villiers, both of them bent double, ran down the beach towards the boat. Greeley fired three times—Villiers twice.

There was silence.

Fells took his hand out of his pocket, bent down, picked up the flash lamp. He put it into the left-hand pocket of his raincoat. The man in front of him lay quite still. He was dead. Fells began to walk down the beach. He could hear the noise of the sea lapping against the sides of the motor-boat. He heard Greeley's voice:

"It's O.K. There're three of 'em here. We've got 'em all."

Fells asked: "Wounded?"

Greeley said: "No, they're all dead all right."

Fells said: "All right. Get them out and get the boat round and start the motor. Let it be washed in somewhere else. We don't want it here."

Greeley said: "O.K."

Villiers stood beside Fells. He said: "Well, that's all right. This is the part I don't like. We can do with a little help from Massanay. I'll go and get him."

Fells nodded. He went towards the boat. Greeley was already throwing the bodies over the side into the shallow water. Fells dragged them up the beach in the shadow of the cliff.

Greeley, cursing and swearing in the darkness, up to his thighs in water, swung the motor-boat round. He climbed in over the stern; started the motor. He jumped back quickly, finding himself in deeper water than he had anticipated. He scrambled out up the beach, blaspheming under his breath.

Fells was standing at the opening of the cleft.

Greeley said: "Of course I had to go into that bleedin' drink up to my neck. One of these fine days I'm goin' to get pneumonia. I always did have a weak chest." He lit a cigarette. He said: "Where do we bury 'em—here?"

Fells said: "No, not in the sand here. The tide may come right up as far and uncover them. Half-way up the cleft would be a good place."

Greeley said: "All right. I'll tell Massanay to get the quicklime."

As he turned, Villiers came up to them. There was an odd expression on his face. He said: "Don't look now, but you can't think what's happened."

Greeley said: "What?"

Villiers said: "One of the shots fired by those three bastards got Massanay. He's a goner. It must have been a ricochet. He walked down the cleft, see? He was curious."

Greeley said: "For crissake! What do you know about that?" He sighed.

Fells said softly: "That isn't so good, is it?"

Greeley said: "No. Well, it's no good talkin' about it. All we have to do is to make room for another one." He said to Villiers: "Look, there's more of these so-and-so's than we thought were comin'. If we're goin' to get 'em underground we've got to work good and quick. Go get the lorry and bring it up on to the top of the cliff."

Villiers said: "Is that chancing anything? Supposing somebody came by?"

Fells said: "Nobody's going to come by this place on a night like this. That's the best thing, Villiers."

Villiers said: "All right. Isn't life wonderful! Everybody else gets the fun and I carry the spades and quicklime." He went away.

Greeley said after him: "What the hell's eatin' you? You could be worse off. You could be Massanay."

Villiers grinned. He said over his shoulder: "You might be right. I never thought of that."

IV

Quayle was half asleep. He lay on the outside of the bed underneath the eiderdown. He was wearing crimson silk pyjamas and his hands were folded behind his head, which was almost entirely bald except for a fringe of hair, giving him the appearance of a tonsured monk.

He stirred uneasily as the clock struck three; realized vaguely that he was not asleep; realized simultaneously that he seldom slept properly; that most of the time his rest was like a cat's, with one eye half opened, one ear cocked. He stirred again; then lay looking at the ceiling.

The bedroom was large and comfortable. The electric fire was burning and the bedside lamp was shaded by a red shade, tilted so that the light fell on Quayle's face, the idea being that even if he wanted to go to sleep the irritation from the lamp would keep him awake.

Outside the bedroom was a passage, and leading off it on both sides were the five other rooms that constituted the flat. At the far end of the passage was a kitchen; leading off the kitchen was a small scullery. Against the far wall of this scullery was a cupboard which, when you opened it, gave access to the flat next door, a flat which, whilst supposed to be empty, was in fact Quayle's office.

The telephone by the bedside began to ring. It made a harsh jangling noise. Quayle swung his feet onto the floor. He got up; picked up the telephone.

He was very tall; he moved easily and quickly. His face was round, intelligent, and could look weak or strong as he willed. Quayle was a character. He had been all sorts of things; done all sorts of things. It was once said of him that like George Moore he had no enemies but his friends weren't particularly fond of him. This was possible because Quayle was too busy to spend time being charming; because he found himself continuously driven to do things which he didn't want to do; to be things which he didn't want to be. Yet if you had asked him to do something else, to turn his life into a quiet routine set in some backwater where the days flowed easily by, he would have refused. He was fascinated by the web in which he was a central point; fascinated by seeing the things he wanted to happen happen; in watching the wheels go round.

He said: "This is Mr. Quayle."

The operator said: "This is a priority call. Will you take it on that line, sir?"

Quayle said: "No. Put it through to the private line. Hold it for a minute."

He hung up. He went out of the bedroom, down the corridor, through the kitchen into the scullery, through the cupboard into the flat next door. He turned into the first room off the hallway. It was austerely furnished as an office—a big desk, a small typing table, a row of steel filing cabinets. On the desk were three telephones with special mouthpieces. Quayle picked up one.

He said: "Hello."

Fells's voice came through. It was soft and tired. Quayle thought Fells's voice always sounded the same. No matter what happened it had the same timbre, the same quality of boredom. Quayle wondered just how bored Fells was.

Fells said: "I thought you'd like to know everything's all right."

Quayle said: "Then you met your friends?"

"Yes," said Fells. "We met them."

Quayle asked: "Were they glad to see you?"

"Not particularly," said Fells. "Apparently they expected someone else to meet them."

Quayle grinned. He said: "They weren't too glad when they found it was you?"

Fells said: "No, they weren't glad—not afterwards."

There was a moment's silence; then Quayle asked: "Anything else?"

"Yes," said Fells. "Massanay . . . not very good. . . ."

Quayle asked: "How bad?"

"Very bad, I'm afraid," said Fells.

Quayle said: "I see . . . I'm sorry about that."

Fells said: "Yes, so am I. . . . Is that all?"

Quayle said: "Yes, for the moment. But I think there'll be some more business in a little while—something perhaps not very exciting or important, but something that ought to be done. I'll get in touch with you. Good-night."

Fells said: "Good-night." Quayle heard the receiver at the other end click. He put down the telephone. He sat for a few seconds looking at the desk.

He got up. He went across to one of the filing cabinets and opened it by pressing a spring in the side. Inside the cabinet were half a dozen folders. They were labelled with the names of different trading concerns. Fells took one out. The jacket of the folder was labelled "Anthracite Co-operative." He took the folder back to the desk, opened it. Clipped to the sheaf of papers inside were a dozen cards—the sort of cards one used in a card index—each one bearing the name of a man or a woman.

Quayle extracted the last card. Typed on the top line was: "Massanay—Charles Ferdinand Eric." Beneath the name were details of Massanay's career. Quayle noticed vaguely that he had served as a Pilot Officer, Flying Officer and Flight Lieutenant, for eighteen months in the Royal Air Force; had shot down eleven of the enemy before being invalided out. Quayle put the card in the breast pocket of his scarlet pyjama jacket. He put the folder back into the filing cabinet; shut it. He went back into the hall, through into the scullery, back to his bedroom. He went over to the fireplace and stood for a moment looking into the imitation coal fire.

He opened a box on the mantelpiece; took out a cigarette and lit it. With the same match that he used to light the cigarette he lit the corner of Massanay's card. He watched it burn slowly. He held it until the embers burned his fingers. He dropped the ashes into the fireplace. He stubbed out the cigarette; got into bed. He put out his hand and switched off the red-shaded light. He was grateful that he could go to sleep.

His last thought was that it was rather a shame about Massanay.

CHAPTER 2
FELLS

FELLS sat in the twelfth row of the orchestra stalls at the Palladium. His eyes were on the stage and were aware of the presence of Mr. Tommy Trinder, but if they realized Mr. Trinder's presence only vaguely, it was because, hovering about the scene, were shadows not included in the cast—shadows and figures and scenes which existed only for Fells.

Now he knew that the experiment of coming to the Palladium had failed. The business of being amused did not exist—not for him. Hearing the laughter that came from all around him at Mr. Trinder's cracks, Fells told himself that there must be something wrong with him; began to think that he could take an interest only in practical, exciting things—things which demanded so much of his nervous system that his brain must perforce concentrate on them to the exclusion of those insistent shadows which persisted in hovering about the Palladium stage.

And he had made up his mind to enjoy himself; had tried to concentrate on what was going on; had joined automatically in the laughter. But now, with a complete sense of failure, he sat, looking straight before him, his hands buried in the pockets of his old blue raincoat, his chin sunk a little forward, his eyes dim under the frown which persisted on his forehead; looking at the bright spot that was the stage, dimly seeing the figure of Mr. Trinder in the centre of it.

Once or twice the woman seated on his left hazarded a quick glance in his direction. The first glance was due to mere curiosity—the second, to interest. After that, in spite of the fact that she wanted to look again, she was careful to keep her eyes away from him. She decided to enjoy the show; to dismiss Fells from her mind. She had thought that his face was very attractive, very sad. But she concluded that war was a sad time. Perhaps he had lost a near relative, or some other unhappy thing had happened to him. She felt rather annoyed with herself for wanting to think about him.

Fells, who had given up the struggle of fighting between the desire for happiness ("Oh, You Lucky People"), and the almost permanent miasma in his mind, allowed the stage of the Palladium—the personality of Mr. Trinder—to disappear. Into its place came the scene which he had seen so often in his mind's eye that he knew every square inch of it by heart; every shadow cast by the latticed blinds, every reflection of the sun on the brass objects on the desk, every small thing.

He hunched his shoulders a little farther forward and looked and saw himself.

He went back nine years—to 1933.

It was late afternoon, but the hot sun came through the latticed blinds and threw dark shadows on the floor. In the centre of the room, just on the left of the chair before the desk, stood Fells. But he was not Fells. He was someone else. He was Major Hubert Eric somebody-or-other—it didn't matter who—wearing a uniform but no topee and no Sam Browne belt, because they had taken the Sam Browne belt away when they put him under close arrest. Major Hubert Eric somebody-or-other, of some regiment, looked across the desk and felt very sorry for the man who sat behind it. The fact that the man was his Commanding Officer made Major somebody-or-other even more sorry for him.

Fells, sitting in the twelfth row of the stalls at the Palladium, felt the long silence that had happened in that room—a silence which had only lasted for a few seconds, but which to the minds of the two men had seemed interminable. Then it was broken. Major some-body-or-other's Commanding Officer had said in a voice which he made as taut as possible:

"In God's name why . . . ?"

The figure in the drill uniform on the other side of the desk smiled. He said:

"I don't know, sir. It isn't any good asking me. It was just what they call 'one of those things.' "

The other man had said: "Was it?"

Fells went on: "Yes, sir. One doesn't explain it very easily. Candidly, I can't find any explanation, excepting of course I'd been on a binge. You remember, sir, I won a little money on the sweepstake. Possibly that was the reason. I got a little excited about winning the money. The binge followed automatically. The other thing seemed to come just as automatically after the binge—if you understand. . . ."

The Commanding Officer said: "I *don't* understand. There have been other binges without *this*."

Fells saw himself saying: "I agree, sir. Perhaps this was a special kind of binge. You see, I'm not fearfully used to women. I thought she was rather attractive, sir. In my state of mind at the time it seemed right to do the things I did. Of course now it all seems rather odd. I don't understand myself."

The older man said: "Understanding isn't going to do us any good. You realize what you're up against, don't you?"

Fells said: "I've been thinking so much about it, sir, during the last four days whilst I've been under arrest, that I am afraid I'm a little confused. That is to say, I don't realize exactly what it means. I realize *some* of the things it means."

The Commanding Officer opened a drawer. He took out a box of cigarettes. He passed the box to the man on the other side of the desk; then he took one himself. Fells leaned over the desk and lit his Commanding Officer's cigarette; then his own. He sat down in the chair.

The other man said: "Of course there'll be a court martial. You'll be cashiered. It's rather terrible to think that a man with your record and your service should be cashiered, but there's no doubt about it, we can't afford to have things like . . . like this happening in India—not now. They'll have to make an example of you." He shrugged his shoulders. "Not that you don't deserve to be made an example of."

Fells said: "Quite!"

"That's pretty bad of course," said the other man, "but it's not all there is to it."

He looked at Fells. His face was drawn. Fells felt sorry that his Commanding Officer should be so unhappy. He tried to help. He said:

"Well, sir, I asked for it and I've got it. I might as well know the rest of it."

"The worst thing is," said the Commanding Officer, "about the cheque. And it isn't as though you'd written a cheque out and couldn't meet it—that might be carelessness—but you had to forge a name. And, my God, did you pick a good one! You picked the name of a man who was out to make every bit of trouble he could for the British Government in India—the one man who would love to publicize this business—the one man who will. Do you think he's going to be satisfied with a court martial?"

Fells said: "No, I shouldn't think he would, sir."

The older man said: "He's going to have his pound of flesh. You'll be court martialled on the military charges, but he's insisting that you're dealt with in the Courts on the other charge—the Criminal Courts. They tell me you'll probably get two years."

Fells said: "I see."

There was another silence; then the Commanding Officer said, rather quickly as if he were saying this in order not to say something else that he wanted to say—that he thought was better left unsaid:

"That's the worst of your type. You're not normal. You don't drink and smoke and womanize when you're young like every other soldier does. You're idealistic. You go about carrying the picture of some woman in your mind—somebody who's going to turn up one day—someone who's going to make life the most wonderful, beautiful thing. You suffer from delusions. You believe that this paragon is actually going to appear—so you wait for her. And then what do you do? After years of this you get drunk. You go off and you raise hell in a city like this with a woman who's tied hand-in-glove with a group of people who'd pay anything, do anything, to kick us out of India. That isn't enough, by God; you have to turn yourself into a forger too—such a silly stupid thing. The devil of it is that only we people who *know* you, realize that you ought merely to be smacked for it all. Instead of which . . ." He shrugged his shoulders again.

Fells said: "There isn't very much to do or say about it, is there, sir? You've been very kind. Everybody's been kind." He smiled wryly. "So now there isn't anything else to do."

The other man said: "No." He got up from his seat; walked over and looked through the lattice. Fells leaned forward, stubbed out his cigarette end in the ashtray on the desk. Then he got up. He said:

"Is that all, sir?"

"That's all," said the Commanding Officer.

Fells went over to the doorway. He had his hand on the door-knob. He was about to open the door when the other man said:

"There's some fellow wants to see you. Probably it's irregular, but I've said it's all right. He'll see you some time to-morrow. I don't know anything about it; I don't know what he wants to see you about."

Fells said: "Do I want to see this person, sir?"

The other man said: "Why not? You're in so bad that nothing that could happen could make it any worse."

Fells went out. On the other side of the door his officer escort, wearing the prescribed sword and revolver, awaited him. He looked apologetically at Fells.

They walked out of the long white building, across the hot square towards the officers' quarters.

On the way Fells thought about the woman. And himself. He supposed the Commanding Officer was right. He supposed he'd been a fool about women. Idealized them and all that sort of thing. He supposed he'd idealized *her*.

Fells began to grin. It was an odd grin. His escort looked at him sideways—uncomfortably. Fells began to think of "*The Green Eye of the Yellow God*." . . . "*There's a broken-hearted woman to the north of* . . ."

Really it was all rather funny and stupid. At least it would be if it were not quite so grim. And when you came to think of it it *was* definitely rather grim . . . at least it was going to be. . . .

She had seemed such a nice woman. But then all women had seemed nice to him. He started off with the idea that all women were nice. And she had a pale face—very pale, and she spoke delightfully with just the suggestion of a catch or something in her English, and he had felt very much at home and safe with her.

Well . . . it seemed that he had been wrong. Life was like that. You made a mistake and you paid. His mistake—his original mistake—had been to drink too much; to get very drunk. If he *had* got drunk. Perhaps the pale lady had put something in the liquor. You never knew with women . . . apparently . . . especially if you were like him and idealized them. . . .

If you didn't idealize them, what the hell were you to do about them? He supposed you had to think about them differently. It seemed that if you thought they were nice they were nasty. Perhaps if you started off by thinking them nasty they might be nice.

He sighed to himself.

The officer escort thought Fells was an odd one. He thought he'd be damned glad when Fells was safely in his quarters and he, the escort, could go and get a drink.

He was damned sorry for Fells.

But then old Felsy-Welsy had always been such a mug about women. And you could slip up—damned easily in India, you could.

The officer escort registered a mental vow to be careful about women.

He remembered it for quite five minutes.

The man came in the afternoon. Fells, who was standing by the window of his room, saw the figure crossing the compound. The man was dressed in a white linen suit and wore a topee a little on one side of his head. He was tall and big, but moved easily.

Fells, glancing down towards the door that led to his quarters, saw that the sentry was gone. He wondered why. He walked away from the window; sat down in the chair by the table, looking rather dully at the ashtray that was almost filled with half-smoked cigarette stubs.

Quayle came into the room without knocking. He had his topee in his hand. Fells saw that he was very bald but with a well-shaped head that made his baldness look almost suitable. For a moment Fells forgot his own misery because he was interested in the man. The tall figure, with the composed, almost smiling, face, radiated something that might have been confidence or cheerfulness. Fells wondered if this was some clever lawyer that the old man had got hold of—somebody who might make things a bit easier. He said:

"Good afternoon. . . ." He stopped then, because there didn't seem anything else to say. In any event, Fells thought, he wasn't going to be interested.

Quayle said: "I won't waste a lot of your time—not that time means anything to you at the moment. The point is I haven't a great deal of time myself and I want to make myself particularly clear to you. In other words, I don't want there to be any misunderstanding. Do you see?"

Fells looked at him in surprise. There was something very matter-of-fact about his visitor. He said, in the rather cold manner of his kind:

"Well, that's very interesting, I'm sure. Who are you?"

"My name's Quayle," said the other. He produced a cigarette case from his jacket pocket, lit a cigarette. Fells was on his feet by this time, looking at Quayle, wondering what it was all about. Quayle held out his cigarette case. He said:

"You have a cigarette and sit down in that chair and listen."

Fells took the cigarette, lit it and sat down in the chair. Quayle went over to the window. He draw aside the lattice and looked out; then he let it fall back into place; stood leaning up against the wall, looking at Fells. He said:

"I know all about you. It's my business to know things. You're in a bad spot. You're faced with a court martial, to be followed by a civil trial. It's pretty certain that you'll get a couple of years at least. Well, that doesn't matter. Lots of other men have done two years. So we won't worry about that part of the job. And we won't worry about your being cashiered from the Army because you won't be the first officer who's been cashiered. So we'll get down to essentials."

Fells began to be bitterly amused. This, he thought, is definitely good. It didn't matter about being cashiered because other people had been cashiered, and it didn't matter about doing two years' imprisonment because other people had done that. These things didn't matter, but Mr. Quayle, the large gentleman with the bald head and the round pleasant face, which at this moment was suffused with a certain energy and attractiveness, was going to get down to essentials.

He said, with a touch of sarcasm: "Do let's get down to essentials. I'm very curious to hear what the essentials are."

Quayle went on: "You'll find it very difficult to argue with me. I'm essentially logical. I have the ability to put facts in their right perspective. Don't think I was being rude or funny when I said that the things I mentioned aren't essentials. They are not. They pass with time. But some things don't pass. They're the ones I want to talk about."

Fells said: "All right. Talk about them."

He had smoked three-quarters of his cigarette. Nervously, he stubbed out the end of it. Quayle watched him; took another cigarette from his case and threw it across the room to Fells, who caught it and lit it.

Quayle continued: "These are the essentials. People like you—professional soldiers who haven't very much money of their own—live most of their lives in watertight compartments. They live in their own little worlds. They have their own rules and standards. Mostly they're good rules—good standards. Well, a man like you is all right so long as he doesn't blot his copybook. If he blots his copybook as you've blotted yours, there isn't a chance in hell for him. His background's gone.

"When you come out of gaol after this job you won't have any friends—not because they'll avoid you, but because you'll take damned good care to avoid *them*. You'll understand perfectly well that it wouldn't be playing the game for an officer who's been cashiered from the Army, who's done a couple of years in the choke, to run around looking up his old friends, or to walk into the Club and order himself a large whisky and soda."

Quayle smiled suddenly. It wasn't a smile of exultation, but one of complete understanding.

"In other words," he said, "you're finished and you know it."

Fells said bitterly: "It's damned nice of you to tell me that. Did you think I didn't know it?"

Quayle regarded the end of his cigarette. After a moment he said: "I told you I was logical, and being logical to me means just that. When most people talk about being logical, in other words thinking and telling the exact truth, they take themselves for a ride. They face up to every fact except the main one. They duck the fact that really matters because it hurts. I never do that. If I did I shouldn't be any good at this job. Being logical to me means, invariably, being tough, because in any truly logical situation somebody has to get hurt. In this case the person is you. Unfortunately—or fortunately—whichever way you care to look at it—it's my business to make you aware of facts, and whether the process is unpleasant to you or to me doesn't matter one damn. See?"

"I see," said Fells.

Quayle grinned. He went on: "Well, I've stated the case pretty well, haven't I? I've made it as bad as possible, not because I'm trying to crow over you, but because both you and I have got to realize that we're through with feeling things—I for one set of reasons and you for another set."

Fells said: "There's something behind all this—something you want?"

"You bet there is," said Quayle. "All right. Let's get back to the essentials. We have realized that when you've finished with this imprisonment business you'll have no friends. All right. What are you going to do? Some men would take to drink. Others would go and bury themselves in some odd spot as far away from civilization as possible, develop a liver and get acid in their old age. They'd call themselves something else and hate themselves for the rest of their lives. That seems to me to be non-constructive."

Fells said: "It may be non-constructive, but it's logical. When a man comes out of prison he's got to do something."

"That's the point," said Quayle. "I've got a proposition to make to you. It's one that I think you're going to like."

He stopped talking suddenly; walked over to the table, stubbed out his cigarette. He moved quickly, almost noiselessly. He went back and leaned against the wall. He was still smiling. He said:

"I think you'll agree with me that the most important thing as far as we ourselves are concerned is what we think. A man's thoughts make his life. Well, on that basis, you're going to have a pretty bad time when you come out of prison. You're going to spend the rest of your life wondering why you made such a damn' fool of yourself over that woman—a woman that a man like you wouldn't normally touch with a barge-pole. You're going to spend a whole lot of your time in wondering how she pushed you into forging that cheque—

because she *did* push you into doing it; I happen to know that. She was put in to do it. Why? The reason doesn't matter, but it's a fact."

Fells said: "I see. So somebody was behind that?"

"That's right," said Quayle. "Somebody was behind it. But don't let that excite you. It won't do you any good. Now listen. I can present you with an alternative to all this misery that is not very nice but it might be a little more attractive, inasmuch as it would give you something much better to think about."

Fells said: "I'm listening. I think you're a most refreshing person."

Quayle grinned suddenly. He said: "You'd be surprised! Here's the proposition: Some people have got the idea that we're on the threshold of another war—the biggest, nastiest war that the world's ever seen. Whether they're right or wrong isn't my business. I don't care. I'm a person who prepares for eventualities—a person who sees things through to their logical conclusion. All right. I'm looking for one or two people I can trust—people like yourself—people who've got brains and imagination and nerve and discipline. In fact, you're the ideal case."

Fells said: "I'm glad to hear that I'm an ideal something. But I wish you'd get on to the alternative."

"Here it is in as few words as possible," said Quayle. "The present situation is that you're going to be court martialled on the usual military charges. Then you're going to be tried by the civil courts. You're going to be tried for forgery—not very nice. I'm going to suggest to you that you're court martialled and tried for something worse. But you won't be tried in the civil courts. You'll merely be court martialled."

Fells said: "My God! This is becoming *quite* interesting. I think I ought to tell you, Mr. Quayle, that you're a most extraordinary person."

Quayle said: "You don't have to tell me. I know that. I can offer you this: In consideration for certain things which you may be able to do in the future, it might be arranged that you were court martialled on an entirely different charge. It might be arranged that I could somehow square all this other business. Then you could be court martialled on a rather sensational and dramatic charge."

"Such as what?" Fells asked.

"Such as stealing secret military documents for the purpose of selling them to a foreign country," said Quayle amiably. "You'd be found guilty. You would be sentenced to be cashiered and to five years' imprisonment. You'd serve the sentence in England and you'd be let out of prison after three or four weeks. In other words, you'd come out by the back door. And," said Quayle with a sardonic grin, "you'd find me waiting for you. See?"

Fells said: "I see. And what happens then?"

Quayle drew on his cigarette. "You'll have a lot of training to do," he said. "You'll have to keep very quiet, but I could find some unobtrusive work for you to do. Remember, officially you'd still be in prison. Well, it's 1933 now. Officially you'd be out in 1938. I should think that would be about right."

"Right for what?" Fells asked.

Quayle lit another cigarette.

"There'll be a war before 1940," he said. "Germany's preparing for it night and day. A hell of a war! If there isn't, it still doesn't matter. If there is, there'll be all sorts of work to be done by people like you and me. Work that isn't perhaps particularly nice, but work that would be very necessary. See?"

Fells nodded.

Quayle went on: "And that's where you come in. Work it out for yourself. Directly the news of your court martial and sentence gets into the papers, German Intelligence will be on it like a cat on a mouse. If I'm not very much mistaken, when you come out of prison—officially, I mean—they'll try and get in touch with you. Well, you'll be ready for them. You'll present to them a picture of a broken-down, dissolute, ex-officer who wants nothing but money. Got it?"

Fells said: "I've got it."

"All right," said Quayle. "That pose might be very useful to me. You realize, don't you, that my alternative is a sound one? You'd still have no background. You'd still have no friends. But you'd know you'd done something decent instead of wandering about odd spots in the world for the rest of your life doing odd sorts of jobs—because you haven't much money—and cursing yourself and wondering why you ever fell for that woman, why you ever forged that cheque. You'd have the satisfaction of being able to tell yourself that you'd make things even worse for yourself; that you'd allowed yourself to be court martialled for about the vilest charge that could be brought against an officer; that you'd sacrificed yourself—for your country!"

Quayle produced a silk handkerchief from the breast pocket of his drill coat and tapped his brow. "My God!" he said. "I get carried away with these dramatic perorations." He put the handkerchief back into his pocket. "Well?" he asked.

Fells said: "Do you really mean this? How do I know that what you say is true?"

Quayle put the cigarette back into his mouth. "Don't be a bloody fool," he said. "How do you think I got in here? You're under close arrest and allowed to see nobody. Why do you think the sentry's taken off the door downstairs? Use your brains."

Fells said: "I see . . ." There was a pause; then: "Supposing I said yes to all this," Fells went on. "And I was sent to England and put into prison and was let out a fortnight later and began to work with you—to begin this period of training for the dirty work you think is to come. Supposing all that. How do you know you could trust me?"

Quayle raised his eyebrows. He presented a picture of hurt surprise. He said casually:

"Don't *you* worry about that. *I'll* worry about that. If you work for me you'll be trustworthy. Why? Well—except for this business you've never let anyone down in your life. Even now you've only let yourself down. But you wouldn't let *me* down—not even if you wanted to. I'd see to that!"

Fells said: "Tell me something—my Commanding Officer told me that nothing could be done with this Indian bloke who insists on bringing the forgery charge; that in any event he was going to have his pound of flesh. He doesn't like the British. But you told me that if I agree to your proposition he won't press that civil charge. Why?"

Quayle smiled. "A fair question," he said. "But obviously you don't know my methods."

Fells said: "I don't know your methods. I'd be very interested to know how you can stop our Indian friend proceeding in this business when apparently everybody, from the Commander-in-Chief downwards, has tried to stop him and failed."

Quayle sighed. He said: "It's not my habit to explain things to people like you, but I'm not divulging anything very much because even if you told somebody they wouldn't believe you. If you are awfully interested in the position as regards our Indian friend, I can make it clear to you. The Commander-in-Chief, and anybody else, can only use the ordinary normal process to bring pressure to bear on him, and if he wants his pound of flesh—his legal pound of flesh—he can have it, but"—he smiled again—"with my methods, however, he *won't* want his legal pound of flesh."

Fells said: "That's what I was interested in—your methods."

Quayle grinned a little. He said: "Your family came from Ireland originally, and they were a very close clan. I've got a young Irishman who works for me. His story *might* be that he was distantly related to you. His story *might* be that the honour of the family was at stake. His story *might* be that if our Indian friend insisted on pressing those charges, something might happen to him one dark night—something not very nice." Quayle smiled again. "And I don't think one of our Indian friend's qualities is bravery," he said.

Fells said: "I see. You can be quite forcible, can't you?"

Quayle said: "You'd be surprised!"

Fells thought for a moment; then he said: "Supposing I agree to all this business; supposing I believed this fairy tale and found it to be true; supposing I allowed this other charge to be brought against me? Well, you say I should only do two or three weeks in prison—when I come out what should I have to do?"

Quayle said: "That's my business. Take it or leave it. I'm offering you quite a lot, you know."

Fells said: "Do you think so? Do you think that not doing the two years matters to me a lot?"

Quayle said: "No, I don't think that; that's just it. But I know you—I know your type. You'll take my offer because that way you'll still be able to think something of yourself. The other way you won't."

Fells nodded. "The devil of it is," he said, "I believe you're right." He got up. He shrugged his shoulders.

Quayle said: "What have *you* got to lose?"

"You're right," said Fells. "I've nothing to lose. I accept."

Quayle smiled happily. He picked up his topee and put it on slightly over one eye. He said:

"I shan't see you again until you come out of prison. When this court martial business is over you'll be sent to England to serve your time there. You'll go to Maidstone. I'll have you out of there in two or three weeks. When you come out we'll have to find another name for you. Then, five years afterwards—because officially you'll have to serve *all* your sentence—there'll be no remission—we'll put you back again so that you can come out officially. And when you do come out officially we'll see that our German friends know where to find you."

Fells said: "You really think they'll try and get in touch—try to pick me up and get me working for them?"

Quayle nodded. "It's just a part of their system," he said. "They'll try anything once."

He went to the door. He said: "We're going to have a lot of fun together."

Fells heard the door shut. He lit a cigarette, walked over to the window, and looked out.

Quayle, his topee slightly over one eye, was walking across the compound.

Fells stretched. He thought that he was beginning to feel a little better. He began to think about Quayle.

He began to admire Quayle—just a little. Quayle had something. He pushed into the background and almost wiped out something you'd done that was not so good, and pushed you into consenting to plead guilty to something that you had not done and which was infinitely worse. Knowing that of the two mental evils you'd naturally choose the lesser. . . .

A clever one, that one, thought Fells.

Almost he could hear the voice of Quayle saying: "You'd be surprised!"

Fells realized suddenly that people were standing up; that the orchestra was playing "*God Save the King*," and the Palladium Company with Mr. Tommy Trinder in the centre was standing on the gangplank built in front of and above the orchestra pit, singing with their friends the audience; that it was 1942.

He moved towards the exit in the crowd. Mr. Trinder, standing on the stage, sent some cheerful wisecracks after his departing fans. As he moved into the corridor, Fells heard the last one: "Oh, you lucky people . . . !"

CHAPTER 3
FODEN

I

FODEN came out of the scrub and stood on the track that ran down the hill, widening as it went, presently turning itself into the dirt road to Suera. After a moment he began to walk again. He was limping and so he walked slowly. He stopped suddenly, sat down and began to curse. His language was terrible. He explored the uttermost recesses of blasphemy, but very quietly and with a certain concentration, giving due attention to the pronunciation of each word.

Although the humidity of the evening had turned into the coolness of a Moroccan night, Foden was covered with sweat. His drill trousers were torn and filthy. His shirt stuck to his body. His face and arms were burnt almost black. His fair tousled hair stuck to the sides of his head. The dust on his face was streaked where the sweat had run from his forehead into his eyes and down his cheeks.

He took off the offending shoe; found the tiny projection of leather which had rubbed a blister on his heel; bit it off with his teeth. There was a large hole in the back of his sock. He removed the other shoe, took off his socks, rolled them into a ball, threw them away. He put on his shoes. He got up; began to walk towards Suera.

A lousy, stinking country, thought Foden—more lousy, more stinking than he had ever known it to be. In the old days you had known what to expect in Morocco. Now whatever you expected it was a goddam sight worse. People, women, climate and drink were lousy—especially the climate and the women. He wiped the sweat from his forehead with his hand; then fumbled in his trouser pocket; produced a broken piece of cigarette. He lit the stub.

On the edge of the foothills about four or five miles from Suera, or Mogador if you like to give it that name, three palm trees stood together. Foden saw them. He began to walk in that direction. He slowed down his pace, thinking.

He was wondering about Suera. He was wondering just what the situation was going to be like there. After a few minutes he came to the conclusion that wondering never got anyone anywhere. He gave it up.

Foden was very tough. He was five feet eleven inches in height, with broad shoulders, muscular arms. The palms of his hands were large, his fingers short. They were the hands of a practical man, and very strong. In spite of the blistered heel, when he put his feet on the ground he did it in a definite and practical manner. His face was thin, with a good jaw line, his eyes blue and steady. A tough proposition was Foden, as many people on the Moroccan coast had discovered.

Because he had not eaten for some time the cigarette tasted bitter on his tongue. He would have liked to have spat, but his mouth was too dry. Now and again he looked casually towards the three palm trees. Most men would have looked hopefully in that direction; but odd things like hope and luck and circumstances—good, bad or indifferent—were not allowed to enter into Foden's calculations. He believed essentially in Foden. If this or that happened that was good so much the better. If it didn't, well, you played it differently—that was all.

Women liked Foden—very often in spite of themselves. There was something cruel—something sadistic—in his attitude. Yet he could be very nice if he wanted to be. He could be very coarse or he could present a picture of almost refinement. He was no fool. If, most of the time, he had not got what he wanted, that had not been his fault and he did not complain, but this time . . .

A figure detached itself from the three palm trees; had come out into the dusty roadway and stood looking towards Foden; then it went back and leaned against one of the trees. Foden saw the match as he lit a cigarette. When he arrived at the palm trees he saw the man.

The man was leaning up against the tree in an indolent attitude, the cigarette—a Turkish cigarette, Foden smelt—hanging from the corner of his mouth. He wore a fez and Foden thought his face reminded him of a chameleon. Beyond this he was merely filthy.

Foden said: "My name's Foden. I take it you're Aked?"

The man said: "Oh, yes. I am Aked." His voice was rather high, strangely sibilant, and Foden wondered if he were a eunuch. He thought it might be possible. Anything was possible.

Foden sat down by the side of the road. He said: "Have you got any cigarettes?"

The man produced a tin. He took the lid off. He did it with a certain flourish. Foden had a fleeting mental picture of, people being shown round bazaars or being sold dirty post cards. He took the cigarette and lit it. It was a good one.

Aked said: "I am ver' glad to see you. I expect you yesterday. I was sorry when you did not arrive. Eet was mos' inconvenient."

Foden drew the cigarette smoke into his lungs.

"Blast you . . ." he said. "So it was inconvenient. I suppose it would be still more inconvenient if I was to get up, hold you against that tree trunk and paste your face into a jelly, you son-of-a-bitch."

Aked grinned. He said: "I am sorry eef I have offended."

"Don't you worry about offending," said Foden. "Any time I want to stop you offending I'm going to do it. I hate your guts."

Aked said: "That ees perhaps unfortunate."

"It just doesn't matter," said Foden. "But you might get it into that dirty head of yours that I've travelled a hundred and thirty miles in seven days—most of it on foot—from Marrakesh. You got that—most of it on foot through this goddam country?"

Aked said: "That ees almos' unbelievable. With all thees Army lorries—French, American, British—maybe you could 'ave got a ride."

Foden said: "Maybe—but I'm not quite certain who this goddam country belongs to yet. I don't know whether it's Vichy French, German, American or British. I've taken enough chances. Well . . . ?"

Aked said: "Please . . . eet ees not good to be rude. I find you rude. Eet ees good to be rude when you don' want somethings. But you want somethings. You should be polite."

Foden said: "Fine! I should be polite. All right. I'll be polite. What have you got to tell me, you bastard? Is that polite enough for you?"

Aked said: "I was told that you would have some monies. I am a good business mans. First of all I require some monies."

Foden said: "Don't worry about the money. I wasn't taking a chance when I came down here. My haversack is up on the hillside there in the scrub. The money's there. You know damn' well I've got it. I haven't had anything to spend it on, have I?"

"No," said Aked, "I don' suppose you have." He looked at Foden. Foden's lips were cracked.

Aked smiled suddenly. He said: "You would like some drink. I bet you don' have some good drink for days. I've got some drink for you."

"Bloody civil of you," said Foden. "What's that going to cost me?"

"Nothings," said Aked. "I give eet to you." He dived into his filthy shirt, produced a bottle. He handed it to Foden.

Foden pulled the cork out with his teeth. He smelt it. It was brandy. He put the neck of the bottle into his mouth and drank the lot. He waited a minute; then he began to feel very good inside. The brandy was working quickly on his empty stomach.

Aked said: "I trust you like anything. I trust you because I always trust everybodies."

Foden said: "Like hell! That's how you've made such a success of life, isn't it? So you're going to trust me. All right. Go ahead."

Aked said: "What you do ees thees: Suera ees in a ver' funny condition jus' now. Nobody knows who's what. You know the Americans landed on the coast ten days ago. Nobody's quite certain if they'd better be polite to Vichy or the Germans or the Americans."

Foden raised his eyebrows. "Germans?" he said. "You're not telling me there are any Germans in Suera with Eisenhower's army about?"

Aked laughed. "My good fren'," he said, "you take it from Aked that there are Germans everywhere. Of course they do not always tell they are Germans. They say they are everythings else. They are Norwegians and Poles and Americans and English. They are Moors and Ethiopians, Jews—but they are never Germans."

Foden said: "Don't they have to have passports? Even people in Suera have to have papers, don't they?"

Aked smiled patiently. "There ees a lovely trade in papers and passports in Suera," he said. "I have made a lot of moneys. I have a fren' who had made a fortune. His trade was quite disreputable—he was a pickpocket. He made a lot of moneys stealing passports and selling them to other people. He ees quite rich. He was quite happy until somebody killed him."

Foden said: "What has all this got to do with me?"

Aked said: "Listen, my fren'. You must listen to me. The advice I give you is ver', ver' good advice. Suera ees not a healthy place at thees moment for an Englishmans. It ees not a healthy place for any mans at all, but for Englishmens especially it ees unhealthy. There ees a certain amount of business goes on—funny business. People disappear. Odd things happen everywhere. There are German spies and Intelligence people. I tell you Suera ees not healthy for an Englishmans."

"I heard you," said Foden. "Well, do you think I want to stay in the goddam place? I want to get out of it. Incidentally I think it was your business to arrange that."

Aked said: "Always I carry out my part of the bargain. First of all, what I do get?"

"What you were promised," said Foden, "and not a penny more. You get a thousand dollars American. And don't think you're going to raise the ante because you're not. I've got three thousand dollars in that haversack up in the scrub. You get a thousand—no more."

Aked said: "That ees all right. That suits me well." He flicked his cigarette end away artistically. "You walk down the road to Suera. There's a street there—the street of the Two Fish. You go down the second street past the old British Consulate, and when it gets narrow you turn down the alley on the left. That ees the street of the Two Fish. At the bottom of that there ees a night club." He sighed. Something in the thought of the night club seemed to touch Aked. He continued: "Thees place belongs to a womans—Mrs. Ferry. Mrs. Ferry ees supposed to be an American. She's not. She ees English. Between you and me," said Aked with a leer, "I don' think Mrs. Ferry has been a nice womans in any country she has been in except Morocco. She ees a nice woman in Suera because everybody else is so God-awful that it makes her look damn' good. See?"

Foden said: "I see."

"All right," said Aked. "Mrs. Ferry ees English. Thees club is called Persimmon Club, and the drink ees terrible. Eet's lousy. But I expect Mrs. Ferry will give *you* some good drink. The bad drink ees only for the customers. You tell her who you are. You tell her you've seen me. She'll look after you. You'll be all right."

Foden said: "What has she fixed—if she's fixed anything?"

Aked said: "I don' know. It ees not my business. When the mans come to me and tells me you're coming he tells me to see you. I get a thousand dollars to fix up with Mrs. Ferry about you. So I fix it. After that I don' do anything and I don' know any more. What about the moneys?"

Foden said: "All right. Let's go and get it." He got up. He said: "Give me another of those cigarettes, will you?"

Aked produced the tin. Foden began to walk up the road towards the scrub on the hillside. He was drawing deep breaths of tobacco into his lungs. He felt good. He swung along the road almost with a certain joy of living. In spite of the night cold which he was now beginning to feel; in spite of everything, he didn't mind life. He thought the feeling was due to the brandy, but behind this thought he knew that he felt good because he could see his way ahead. There were one or two small things to be done of course, but what the hell! Behind him, almost running in his efforts to keep abreast with Foden, came the diminutive Aked.

They turned into the scrub. After a moment Foden stopped in a little clearing. The sand was soft. The moon shining brightly, made it glisten.

Aked said: "I don' see the haversack. You wouldn't tell me some lies?"

Foden said: "I wouldn't tell you a lie."

He put out his left hand. His fingers closed round Aked's throat before the scream that was generated could issue through the dirty teeth. Foden squeezed with his left hand. The muscles on the upper part of his arm stood out. Aked clawed at the wrist and arm in front of his face, kicked and lashed out with his feet. Foden never even moved. It was not even necessary for him to use his right hand. After a little while he let go. Aked subsided in a crumpled heap. Foden turned him over with his feet. He reached down for the tin of cigarettes. He put them in his pocket; then he walked out of the scrub down the hill towards Suera.

II

That Mrs. Angelica Ferry was a "card" was a fact that was generally admitted by one and all. There were other facts about this lady which were not so generally admitted, mainly because it might have been dangerous to admit them. No one knew whence she had come, and it seemed unlikely that anyone would go to the trouble to find out, because Mrs. Ferry was one of those people you did not investigate. It was said that one or two of the more curious spirits had essayed slight attempts in this direction but had decided to give up for health reasons.

Once on a time the lady may have been attractive. Walking behind her in the street, you might have thought that her figure still had possibilities, but her back view was definitely more attractive than the front. Possessed of an amazing bosom out of proportion to the rest of her body, Mrs. Ferry had a certain appearance of top-heaviness which, whilst being attractive to the oriental mind, was quite alarming to those who approved normal types of occidental beauty.

Her face was large and heavily made up. It would seem that Mrs. Ferry still believed that she was beautiful, and she endeavoured to enhance this idea of beauty with the aid of every cosmetic that could possibly be used. Her rather dull complexion covered with a powder that was too light in shade; her lips made up with a lipstick of too dark a tint; her eyes edged with mascara which invariably ran: all these things combined to give her a most extraordinary appearance.

She was not, however, a laughable figure. There was something vaguely grim about Mrs. Ferry, although on occasions when she relaxed—and these were many—she still possessed an ability to dance neatly and lightly, supported by a pair of well-shaped legs on small feet invariably shod with the most expensive shoes.

Mrs. Ferry was the Persimmon Club, and the Persimmon Club was Mrs. Ferry. This resort of refreshment and joy, situated at the end of a narrow alley running off the street of the Two Fish, formed a natural cul-de-sac. You turned into it and there was no escape. You went into the Persimmon Club, and if you came out with your braces you were lucky. The attributes of the Persimmon Club were a certain light-heartedness evidenced by music—invariably played out of tune—which never ceased, and a smell on the ground floor which was quite indescribable. This odour improved as you mounted the stairs, and when you came to Mrs. Ferry's private office at the rear of the first floor, you were assailed by a languorous odour resulting from the spraying twice a day, by a Greek with one leg, of some peculiar perfumed liquid manufactured on the premises, which was held by some experts to be even worse than the smell on the ground floor.

There was also a basement reached by a flight of winding wooden stairs concealed by a bottle-rack behind the bar.

The alley in which the club was situate, known as the Place of the Seraphim, was distinguished by some picturesque Moorish architecture and two bordellos, both of which were controlled by Mrs. Ferry. Occasionally the inmates, resenting their lot, would give vent to unhappy shrieks and yells, of which no one in the neighbourhood took the slightest notice, and it is rumoured that on one occasion when a squad of native police under a French *sous-officier* had penetrated one night into the Place of the Seraphim, they retreated very quickly and in bad order, pursued by Mrs. Ferry with a shot-gun.

Few things happened in Suera—few things of importance. I mean—in which Angelica was not concerned. She was, as has been indicated, a woman of great organizing powers. Her perception was acute. She was, to say the least of it, *formidable* in many senses, and she had an amazing ability to be aware of events almost before the time of their happening. Seated in her office, with a Turkish fan in one hand and a half-filled brandy bottle within reach, she served her world with a quiet assurance which no rumours of wars, victories or defeats could shake.

Mrs. Ferry had seen many people come and go in Suera. She had seen successive chiefs of police appointed, endeavour to exercise their authority, and go. They had all learned to know Mrs. Ferry and to respect her. Even a chief of police realizes on which side his bread is buttered, and it must be admitted that when Mrs. Ferry buttered somebody's bread she laid it on thick. Meanness was not one of her characteristics.

Visitors to the Persimmon Club—hardy travellers who had heard of the place and wished to investigate—sometimes wondered about Mrs. Ferry, whose roving eye was inclined to look appraisingly at each male entrant. They wondered, but no one answered their questions. The thin dark individual with the black moustache and piercing eyes who operated the bar and answered to the name of Balbo, was not inclined to satisfy curiosity, and if the visitor asked questions, Balbo had a stock answer. He would say: "Mrs. Ferry ees a wonderful womans. I'm telling you! *I know!*" Balbo probably did know. He slept somewhere on the premises; worked all day in the club and seldom went out except for an occasional visit across the road to the nearest bordello to see his sister who worked there.

It was nearly midnight when Foden pushed aside the heavy, soiled curtain that hung across the inner entrance of the Persimmon Club, and stood leaning against the door-post absorbing the atmosphere. Opposite him, on the other side of the floor, Balbo presided at the bar, and on the left on a raised platform three half-caste so-called musicians produced a strange melody which they considered to be hot music. There were thirty or forty people in the place, drinking, talking, or sitting smoking and waiting. Most of the *habitués* of the Persimmon Club were waiting for something or somebody.

Foden stood looking at the girl who, a glass in her hand, stood leaning against the bar talking to Balbo. She had on a linen frock which was nearly clean; very high-heeled shoes. Her hair was dark and she had once been very attractive. Foden noticed that her figure was still good.

After a minute she turned her head. She saw Foden. She pushed herself away from the bar and walked slowly round the edge of the crowded floor. Foden watched her. There was something very graceful in her walk. She leaned against the side of the entrance opposite him. She said:

"Welcome to the Persimmon, m'sieu. I don' think we 'ave seen you before. We are at your service."

Foden grinned. He said: "I bet you are."

She smiled. "Would you like to buy me a dreenk?"

"Why not?" said Foden.

The girl walked back to the bar, and he went after her. She ordered some drinks; then she turned and stood leaning against the stained mahogany counter, looking at Foden. He put his hand inside his shirt and produced a fifty-dollar bill. He put it on the bar. He said to Balbo:

"I'll take the change in American money."

Balbo said: "Why not?" He served the drinks.

Foden drank his quickly; ordered another. He said to the girl: "Where do I find Mrs. Ferry?"

She said, with an impertinent look in her eye: "Perhaps you don'. Perhaps she won' want to see you. She don' see anybody, you know."

Foden said: "No? Well, she'll see me. You go and tell her that I'm here. The name's Foden."

The girl looked at him sideways. She said: "All right."

She went away.

Foden picked up his glass and stood, his back against the door, looking at the inmates of the Persimmon Club. He thought they were a lousy crowd. His eyes wandered from table to table looking at the faces that were bent close together in quiet conversation over the dirty table-cloths.

A hell of a place, he thought.

*

From downstairs came the sound of the thin girl singing a French love song. Her voice was high-pitched and inclined to crack on the top notes. This made the song sound rather more pathetic—although the pathos was probably lost on the customers.

Mrs. Ferry got up from her chair behind the desk; crossed the room; closed the door. She went back to her seat. As she passed Foden she gave him a quick sideways look.

Foden sat back in his chair. He was relaxed—poised. He wore a passably clean suit of white drill, a clean white shirt, the collar of which would not meet round his neck, and a pair of white tennis shoes. He was freshly washed and the natural waves of his fair hair glistened where the light from the lamp caught them.

Mrs. Ferry thought he looked pretty good. She picked up the bottle and poured out two drinks. She filled half the glasses with the brandy. She pushed one glass to Foden. She said:

"And you think you're going to get away with this?"

Foden said: "You tell me what's going to stop me."

She shrugged her shoulders. "I don't know anything that can stop you," she said. Her voice was low—almost caressing. "You look to me like what they call a go-getter. I should think if you made up your mind that you wanted something, you'd get it."

She smiled. Foden thought the colour of her lipstick was damned awful but that her teeth were very white and even.

He said: "For a man who's supposed to have the ability to get what he wants I haven't been doing so well, have I—not for the last nine months anyway?"

She said: "That wasn't your fault, was it? You just had a bad break. But I expect you did pretty well before the last nine months."

Foden said: "No. That was my own fault though. I had lots of chances but I didn't take 'em. In an odd sort of way I was happy."

"Yes," said Mrs. Ferry. "Doing what?"

Foden said: "Doing my own trade. I was second officer on one of the coasting boats. A hell of a good life if you know how to play it—interesting."

She nodded. "One of the coasting boats, hey?" she said. "Whose boat would that be?"

"The Two Star North Moroccan Line," said Foden. He picked a cigarette out of the box and lit it.

Mrs. Ferry began to laugh. Her immense bosom, perched on the edge of the desk, trembled heartily. "My God!" she said. "That set-up. Do you call that a Line—those two wheezy tubs?"

Foden said: "They might have been wheezy, but they used to do some business."

Mrs. Ferry smiled. "I bet they did," she said. "Business! You mean funny business. The sort of business that those two tub-thumpers used to do around Sfax and Sousse—Legion towns!"

Foden said: "What the hell's the matter with the Legion towns? I like *legionnaires*. They're rough but you know where they are."

Mrs. Ferry said: "My God, you do—especially when there's *not* a war on. Some business!" She looked at him wickedly. "I bet I could make three or four guesses as to what you were carrying in those two boats of yours. Which one were you in? Was it *Crystal* or *Evening Starlight*?"

Foden said: "I was in both of 'em. And what they carried was nobody's business except the owners."

She nodded. "You're telling me!" she said. "I used to know the owner pretty well—that is before somebody got rough with him one night in Sfax. You know what they did with him, don't you?"

Foden said in a voice that was a little bored: "I know."

Mrs. Ferry leaned back in her chair. She put her hands behind her hennaed head. She looked at Foden. She said:

"Give yourself another drink."

He said: "Thanks." He poured out the drink; began to sip it. He was watching her over the edge of the glass. After a moment he decided to drink the brandy. He took it in one gulp; put the glass down; poured out another drink. She leaned forward and pushed the cigarette box towards him. She said:

"My private guess is that you're a tough egg—a very tough egg."

"Yes?" said Foden. "So what? Just being tough doesn't get you anywhere. You've got to have brains."

"Ah!" said Mrs. Ferry. "So you've got those *too*?"

Foden drew tobacco smoke down into his lungs. He expelled it through pursed lips. He said:

"I've developed brains during the last nine or ten months."

"I see," said Mrs. Ferry. "So you're now a tough brainy guy? Well, if you want a proposition I've got one."

Foden said nothing. There was a pause; then Mrs. Ferry went on:

"I think Suera is a place that would suit you. There's room here for a man like you. There ought to be some nice pickings too."

"Yes?" said Foden. "And who would I be working for?"

"You'd be working for me," said Mrs. Ferry. "I'm not at all difficult to get on with providing I get my own way."

Foden said: "I don't like working for women."

"I think you're a fool," said Mrs. Ferry. "You could have a good time here. There's anything you want and lots of it. You can get away with anything in Suera if you know how—especially if you're a friend of mine."

Foden said: "That's what *you* think, and maybe that's right *now*. But maybe it won't be right in a little while. Take it from me there's going to be some cleaning-up on this coast."

Mrs. Ferry smiled. It was an odd smile. She said:

"Well, you might be right, but I wouldn't like to be the cleaner-upper. I don't think he'll have too good a time. Lots of people have tried to clean up Suera, for instance, and where have they got to—usually on one of the dumps at the back of the town or sometimes they find 'em in the river. And who cares? Life just goes on here and only a mug tries to throw a spanner in the works."

Foden said nothing. He looked bored. She said:

"You've made up your mind to go through with this? You think you can hold 'em up for what you want?"

Foden said: "I'm damned certain of it. I've got information and they've got to have it. All right. They had a chance of getting it for nothing and they wouldn't play. Now they're going to pay and pay plenty. What I've got is dynamite."

Mrs. Ferry said: "You know what you're doing, but personally I don't like dynamite. It's dangerous even for the people who've got it."

Foden said: "I'll chance that. The thing is what are you going to do? Are you going to do what I want or not? That's all I want to know."

Mrs. Ferry asked: "Supposing I say no—what are you going to do then?" She grinned. "Are you going to walk back to Marrakesh?"

"Like hell I am," said Foden. "If you're not going to play I'm going to stick around here until I get some means of getting out of here. I'm going through with this anyway."

She picked up a cigarette out of the box and lit it. Foden noticed that her finger-nails were long and tinted blood-red. He thought they looked like talons. She said:

"Well, if I decide to help, what do I get out of it?"

"You get a thousand dollars," said Foden. "That's all there is—just a thousand."

Mrs. Ferry said: "That's all right." She got up. "It's getting on," she said, "and I'm tired. We'll talk about this some more to-morrow. We'll take a look downstairs."

She began to walk towards the doorway. Foden followed her. She said as they went down the stairway:

"Make yourself at home. Anything you have is on the house. When you get tired, Balbo will show you where you can sleep. There's a room for you."

Foden said: "You're very generous."

"Like hell I am," said Mrs. Ferry.

Half-way down the stairs she stopped and turned, her hand on the banister rail. She said: "You can forget about that thousand dollars."

Foden said: "Can I? What does that mean?"

She said: "I'm for *you*. You've got something—I don't know what it is. Anyhow, I can fix you up all right, and we'll forget about the money." She gave him a smile intended to be arch.

Foden said: "That suits me." He grinned.

Downstairs, on the ground floor, Mrs. Ferry looked round with a professional eye. Business was just beginning to look up. A native policeman stuck his head round the corner of the doorway; saw Mrs. Ferry, gave her a wide smile that showed his big glistening teeth, and disappeared.

She said to Foden: "Go over to that table in the corner. I think I'm due for a little celebration—I don't know what for—but we'll have one."

Foden nodded. He walked round the edge of the crowded floor towards the table she indicated. Mrs. Ferry went over to the bar. Balbo stopped serving a customer at the far end and came over to her.

She said: "Send over a bottle of the old brandy, and some ciga-rettes. After we close go out and see you-know-who. Tell him I'll have something for him—probably early to-morrow morning."

Balbo said: "O.K., missus." He went back to his customer.

Mrs. Ferry, with a word here and there to members of her more select clientele, made her way through the atmosphere thick with cigarette smoke to the table where Foden awaited her.

The old clock in the Place des Fleurs struck four o'clock.

Mrs. Ferry, standing in the doorway of the room, the lamp in her hand, looked at Foden. He was lying full length on the patchwork quilt that covered the bed. His right leg hung down on the floor. His left arm lay on the bed in the complete relaxation of a drunken man. Across the pillow, his right arm hung down with the fingers just touching the floor. His mouth was open, but he was not snoring.

A hell of a man, said Mrs. Ferry to herself. She closed the door. She walked quietly along the boarded floor of the passageway to her office. Inside, she put the lamp on the table, blew it out; then she switched on the desk lamp; went back to the door, locked it. She returned to the desk, sat down, lit a cigarette. She smoked silently for a few minutes; then she emptied the remains of the brandy bottle into one of the glasses on the desk; drank it.

She reached down with a grunt; opened one of the desk drawers; took out some foolscap paper. She began to write. First of all she put the date; then she printed in black capitals:

"FODEN—GEORGE HERBERT—Aged about 35. Employed originally on the Moroccan coast by the Two Star North Moroccan Line (s.s. *Crystal* and s.s. *Evening Starlight*) mainly engaged in running women to Sfax and Sousse. He says . . ."

Mrs. Ferry's pen scratched across the foolscap paper. Her hand-writing was small, precise—almost beautiful. It was one of those incongruities for which Mrs. Ferry might have been noted had her minor qualities been sufficiently known. She wrote for half an hour. When she had finished she put the sheets into an envelope, licked it with a pointed tongue that was still pink in spite of the cigarettes and brandy, stuck it down carefully.

She went quietly down the stairs into the deserted club room. She walked unerringly in the pitch darkness. Behind the bar she opened the slit of the door and stood at the top of the basement steps. She called softly:

"Hey, Balbo."

Balbo came up the steps. He stood just below her—an oil lamp in his left hand, looking up at her. The light reflecting on his black face made it glisten.

He said: "Yes, missus . . . ?"

She gave him the envelope.

"Hurry," she said. She looked at her wrist-watch—once the property of a French woman tourist who had no further use for it. "You tell him he's just got time to get this into code and get it off. You tell him it's priority, see—*priority*." She repeated the word with emphasis. "He'll know what you mean."

"O.K., missus," said Balbo.

She took the lamp from him. Balbo, his bare feet making no sound on the wooden floor, crossed the room and opened the door. For an instant a patch of moonlight illuminated the tawdry entrance of the Persimmon Club, but Mrs. Ferry noticed it only vaguely.

The door closed. She stood for a minute; then went up the stairway towards her own room. Arrived there, she threw a look towards the door at the end of the passage where Foden slept.

She smiled. She said softly: "Well, sweetheart—you might get away with it. Who knows!" She sighed. She went to bed.

CHAPTER 4
GREELEY

I

THE clock in the hall of Quayle's flat struck midnight. Quayle heard it through the open bedroom door. He was stretched out on the bed. He wore a red and white spotted foulard dressing-gown over scarlet pyjamas. His hands were folded behind his head. He looked unblinkingly at the ceiling as if he were seeing pictures there. Beside him on the bed, typed out on yellow quarto flimsies, was the decoded report which Mrs. Ferry had been so self-sacrificing in securing.

Quayle read it through a dozen times. Now he was putting himself through a process which he used on occasions. He was visualizing the report. It had begun to rain. Almost subconsciously Quayle heard the raindrops beating against the window-pane. The pattering did not disturb him. His conscious mind was filled with Foden.

He concentrated on the Foden grievance. He tried to put himself into Foden's shoes; to think with the mentality of a man who had spent good years running up and down the Moroccan coast in the *Crystal* and the *Evening Starlight*, doing the odd things, meeting the odd people, doing the things that a Second Officer in a ship engaged on a dubious trade might do. Quayle thought he had got the picture all right.

According to Mrs. Ferry's report Foden had one good point—patriotism. According to Mrs. Ferry, Foden had not in the first place tried to *sell* his information to the Consular Service first in Casa Blanca, then to the agent in Morocco City, then again in Casa Blanca. He had wanted to give it. Foden had told Mrs. Ferry that these facts were on record; that they could be checked; that it would be found that what he had said was true.

And it was true. Quayle knew it was true. Quayle knew that Foden had, between the years 1936 and 1938, tried on no less than four occasions to get the British authorities to accept information which he had—information which concerned the activities of German espionage and counter-espionage organizations working along the Moroccan coast, preparing for something which was now obvious.

And nobody had believed him—a fact which seemed to have annoyed Foden greatly. So Foden had a grievance—and a justifiable one. The fact that his information was true, the fact that it had been checked on and found to be true, would not make the Foden grievance any the less. And now he had more information—bigger and better information—but this time he wanted money and a lot of it. Quayle realized that the picture was complete.

Quayle yawned. He got off the bed; went over to the mantelpiece; took a cigarette from the box, lit it. He stood, his hands on the mantelpiece, looking down into the fire. After a little while he went back to the bed; picked up the flimsies. He sat on the edge of the bed looking at the typescript on the thin yellow paper. In his mind's eye he could see Mrs. Ferry, a cigarette hanging out of the corner of her mouth, the inevitable brandy bottle on the edge of the littered desk, writing, in her neat hand, her original report.

Quayle grinned sardonically. He wondered if she was still using the same terrible make-up. . . .

For a few moments he allowed his mind to dwell on the peculiar characteristics of Mrs. Angelica Ferry. Then he read . . .

"Foden says that the Germans had been preparing in Morocco for a long time. He says they were fully aware of the fact that even if the conquest of France, aided by a highly organized fifth column, was going to be as easy as the German General Staff thought it would be, French North Africa was the dubious point in their calculations. They were not certain of what the Army would do. The Germans believed, Foden says, that the best types of French Army Officer were in the Moroccan forces. He thought that even if the Germans were successful in France they would have trouble. Events would seem to indicate that they were right. Foden says that every town along the coast was honeycombed with German Agents and that a highly organized intelligence system has existed since 1932.

"He says that some fifteen or sixteen months ago he got in bad with the man who owned the *Crystal* and the *Evening Starlight*. He says there was an argument about money. I don't believe this (*said Mrs. Ferry*) because Estalza, the owner of these two ships, was killed in a dive in Casa Blanca just over a year ago. The trouble was not over money but a woman, and I have an idea that it was Foden who fixed Estalza. I don't suggest he did it himself, but as you probably know it is not very difficult to get anyone knocked off here if you've got a little money.

"Foden says that as a result of the trouble with Estalza, and his death soon afterwards, the Germans got on to him. His idea is that Estalza was employed by one of the lesser German agents along the coast and that his ships had been used for running people into the country. Foden says that it is quite on the cards that Estalza had got to hear about Foden's visits to the British authorities and his attempts to put them wise as to what the situation really was. I think this may be true. It has been pretty hot out here for a long time—as regards the Germans I mean. They've got themselves dug in here. They know everything and they've got so many people working for them of all nationalities that it is going to take a hell of a time before this place is cleaned up and free from their influence.

"As a matter of fact I think things are worse here now than they ever have been, because the Vichy people—and take it from me there are lots of them—are working now not so much for the Germans but for themselves. They know if they don't get away with it there'll be a rope waiting for them somewhere. There are lots of places in this country where a de Gaullist would have as much chance as a celluloid rat in hell, whatever may be said to the contrary.

"So you will see that Foden's attitude is quite obvious and very understandable. As a result of all this business, he says the Germans got on to him some ten months ago. He was framed on some ridiculous charge and slung into one of the interior penal settlements. He says this place was a dump used by the German-Vichy crowd as a sort of a concentration camp, and he says that quite a lot of people who went in there did not come out again.

"He's a determined person, is Foden. He knows what he wants and he's backing himself to get it. He says his information is dynamite and the joke is that could be true. There's a great deal of organization and planning going on in a big way out here. You can't stop it. During the time that he's talking about, it would be a great deal worse. It might easily be that he's got something that matters.

"The trouble is he won't talk until he has money and a lot of it. He says the English authorities have taken him for a ride twice; that it was through them that he got put inside for ten months and had a hell of a time; that he's not standing for any more nonsense. He says he wants the money first and then he'll talk, and not before.

"Amongst other things he said . . ."

Quayle continued reading. The black typescript on the flimsy paper fascinated him. The words meant a lot. Quayle sighed. All sorts of things started with these yellow flimsies and their messages—all sorts of things—some of them not too bad—some of them not at all good—some of them definitely nasty. He wondered what the results of *this* packet would be.

He finished reading the report; then he carried the sheets of flimsy paper over to the fire and burned them. They made a nice little pile of black ash in the fender which surrounded the electric fire. He stubbed out his cigarette; walked into the kitchen, through the inner doorway into the flat beyond. In his office a young woman with blonde curls, dressed in a neat coat and skirt, was busy typing.

Quayle asked: "Where's Greeley?"

She stopped typing. She thought for a moment. She said:

"Greeley? He's not doing anything. He's at his own place in Swansea."

Quayle said: "I see. How long's he had?"

"He's been there for three weeks," she said without hesitation.

Quayle said: "That's quite long enough for him. Get into touch with him. Tell him to meet me to-morrow night as usual."

She said: "Very well, Mr. Quayle." She went on with her typing.

Quayle went back to his bedroom and lay on the bed. He tilted the electric lamp shade so that the light was off his face. His eyes closed. Half of his mind was asleep—the other half was, as usual, waiting for the telephone to ring.

II

Greeley, sitting at the wooden table, drank his second cup of tea and watched the half a dozen lorry drivers who made a quick supper before moving off. A hell of a life driving a lorry in war-time, thought Greeley. These men were good guys. It wasn't so bad on a moonlit night, but on a night like this when it was dark, you had to concentrate all the time. A nasty job, he thought. *He* wouldn't like to do it. He lit a cigarette; grinned slowly to himself as he wondered what any of the lorry drivers would have said had they been offered *his* job. Greeley thought philosophically that it was always the other man's job that was lousy. Personally he didn't mind his a bit. But then he didn't mind anything. He wondered what the new lay was going to be. He drew the cigarette smoke down into his lungs and thought about his small but well-kept home in Swansea, and his wife, who thought he was in a travelling munitions squad. Greeley grinned again. It was much better that way, he thought. What they didn't know couldn't hurt 'em, and the old girl had probably got enough to worry her.

Outside the wooden building, which stood on a patch of grassland set back from the cross-roads, the wind howled dismally. Greeley wondered why the hell Quayle had to make appointments in a dump like this miles away from anywhere. Then he qualified this idea with the thought that Quayle probably knew what he was doing. Greeley, like most people in Quayle's peculiar organization, knew just enough to do his job and no more.

Quayle knew his business all right. Greeley considered one or two of the jobs that had been pulled off during the last eighteen months. There'd been some narrow goes but never quite narrow enough. They'd always got away with it and they'd got away with it because of Quayle's flair for organization and his nose for danger. An odd guy Quayle, thought Greeley, a mixture—a mixture of toughness and caution. But he looked after his people. He did the best he could for them and if he "lost" one or two of them, Greeley had the idea that it worried him. He wondered what sort of a guy Quayle was underneath: whether he had any time to himself; whether *he* ever got three weeks' leave or whether he went on continuously, scheming, organizing, planning, without a break.

No sort of life that, thought Greeley. He wouldn't like to have Quayle's job. He'd rather be himself. He wondered why the hell Quayle did it. Maybe, he thought, Quayle *liked* it. Perhaps it fascinated him in the same way as Greeley's jobs fascinated him. There were some men whose constitution seemed to need the continuous strain of dangerous situations. It did something to them; in some weird, mysterious way they liked it. Greeley's grin broadened. Possibly, he thought, they were like the man who used to hit himself on the head with a hammer just because it felt so good when he stopped. He stubbed out his cigarette as Quayle came in.

Quayle went over to the counter. He was wearing an old stained fawn raincoat and a pair of flannel trousers. His boots were old. The soft hat that he wore on one side of his head was ancient and greasy. He looked like a superior sort of tramp—and not only because of his clothes, but because of his face. Quayle had the ability to look like anything he wanted to look like.

He bought a cup of tea and a cheese sandwich. He turned away from the counter and saw Greeley. He said in a surprised voice:

"Hello, Horace."

Greeley said: "Hello! Fancy seeing you!"

Quayle began to walk towards Greeley's table. He said as he sat down: "How's the missus?"

"She's all right," said Greeley.

The place was nearly empty. Outside four or five heavy lorries were being started up. One by one they rumbled off.

Quayle said: "This is it. There's a man called Foden coming over to this country from Morocco. He'll be here inside a day or two. You'll be told where the boat's docking. They'll let you know that to-morrow. When you leave here to-night, go back home. I'll have you telephoned about two o'clock to-morrow afternoon. Then you go down to the port."

Greeley said: "I get it."

"When this Foden lands," Quayle went on, "I want him picked up by accident. Foden's been kicking about Morocco for some time. He thinks he's got a lot of stuff to sell. He thinks he's got a big story. He wants a lot of money for it." He smiled.

So did Greeley. Greeley said: "They all seem to think that."

Quayle said: "I know. The point is if he has got a story, and it's as good as he seems to think it is, we might buy it off him. But I want this business handled carefully. When he lands he's going to run into you by accident and you've got to lead him along. You know . . . ?"

Greeley nodded. "I know," he said.

Quayle went on: "Do you remember a girl who did a job with you at Kingstown once—a girl with blonde hair—rather a good-looking one?"

Greeley said: "Do I? There was a one for you. I've often thought about her. I've often wondered . . ."

Quayle said quietly: "That doesn't matter. Her name's Zilla Stevenson. She'll be working with you. This is how it's being played. She's been up at the port for three weeks. She's made herself rather friendly with the dock superintendent. He talks quite a lot to her."

Greeley grinned. "Careless talk, hey?" he said. "I bet it is." His voice was a little bitter.

Quayle went on: "Foden will have to see him when he gets in, and Zilla Stevenson should be able to find out from the dock superintendent exactly when the boat docks and when Foden's coming ashore. I don't know how she's going to get it, but she will. When you get up there, give yourself a few hours to make yourself acquainted with the place and get the lie of the land. And you'd better go round and see Zilla Stevenson. Find out what the situation is. She'll give you the tip-off when Foden arrives. After that it's up to you."

Greeley said: "I've got it. Who do I hand him on to?"

"That depends," said Quayle. "Let him do the talking first of all, and if you think it's safe, tell him a little story about a woman you know who got five hundred quid for passing on some information that wasn't worth four pence. Maybe he'll fall for that one. If he does and opens up, we'll pass him on to Zilla Stevenson and let her handle him. I need not tell you to be careful."

"No, you needn't," said Greeley. "Up to the moment I've always kept my nose clean and I hope I'm going to. Is that all?"

Quayle said: "That's all."

Greeley asked: "Is this guy Foden a big fish or a little fish?"

Quayle said: "That's the point." He smiled amiably at Greeley. "We don't know. We want to know. He might be a very big fish. If Foden has the information that we hope he's got, he could be very useful to us. But not in his present frame of mind." He brought a tin Player's cigarette box out of his pocket; took out a cigarette and lit it.

"The trouble is," he went on, "that this Foden, who seems to be quite a decent sort of Englishman, tried to give our people some information out in Morocco and they weren't playing. He didn't like it. So now he's out for money."

"I get it," said Greeley. "He's after the big dough—practically blackmail. *Some* bleedin' Englishman!"

Quayle shrugged his shoulders. "He's a seafaring man," he said. "He was a second officer on one of the Moroccan coastal boats. They get tough, you know. But I think you and he might talk the same sort of language." Quayle smiled at Greeley.

Greeley said: "Yes, I'll talk the right language all right. Is that the lot?"

"That's the lot," said Quayle. "When will you be home?"

"I should be back by twelve noon to-morrow," said Greeley. "So if you get me after that . . ."

Quayle said: "The usual girl will phone you with all the necessary information between one and three to-morrow afternoon. Then you'd better get off right away. You ought to be at the port some time to-morrow evening. But when you get there you'll have to work fast."

Greeley said: "Who am I supposed to be?"

Quayle took a large envelope out of his pocket. He pushed it across the table. "Everything's inside," he said. "You're a munitions worker reporting on a special job at the main factory in the port. You'll find your name, special pass, identity card and everything inside."

Greeley asked: "Do I have a contact?"

"Yes," said Quayle. "But only if anything goes wrong. Otherwise no. If anything goes wrong and it looks as if you're going to lose Foden, you'd better go and see a man in the town. You'll find his name and address on a sheet of paper inside that envelope. He keeps a bookseller's shop."

Greeley said: "O.K."

Quayle got up. Two or three lorry drivers came in. One of them said:

"A bloody fine night this is! It's started to rain now."

Quayle said: "Well, good-night, Horace. Remember me to the missus."

Greeley said: "So long, old top. I'll be seein' you."

Quayle went out.

III

The public-house stood at the end of one of the long narrow streets leading away from the dockside. It stood back from the roadway with a semi-apologetic air, as if it knew it was old and not very clean.

Inside there was atmosphere. Greeley thought there was a basinful of atmosphere. The saloon bar had been formed by knocking down a wall and joining up two rooms of a converted house. The bar was long and semicircular in shape. There was a door at each end. The floor was of boards, with a sprinkling of sawdust, and some ship's kegs set along the wall opposite the bar, with a ship's anchor and other nautical effects, gave the place an old-time maritime air.

There was also a smell—a vague, acid, smell of beer and tobacco smoke—due to the fact that the saloon was low and the small windows were seldom opened.

Greeley sat placidly at the end of the bar, watching the barmaid. He thought her movements were deft. He admired the way in which her nimble fingers seized bottles and glasses, drew pints of beer, and generally carried out the orders of an obviously vital mind. Obviously a smart one, thought Greeley. She had a pleasant smile and a quick comeback for the wisecracks that the customers produced from time to time. Most of the men in the bar were seamen—crews of merchant ships of the Mercantile Marine, waiting for their ships to be turned round, or on leave. A tough bunch of boys, thought Greeley. He looked at one or two of them admiringly. They were good guys, he thought. They had a hell of a job—a tough job. For a moment he, who seldom thought seriously about himself, rather wished that they knew that his job was perhaps as tough and as dangerous sometimes as their own.

He was wearing a blue coat and trousers, with a maroon high-necked sweater. The neck of the sweater came up to his chin, accentuating his thin jaw-line. He had on a check cap slightly over one eye. He looked what he intended to look—a smart Cockney—one of the many men, members of travelling munitions squads, skilled in some special job, who went about the country from factory to factory. His name, according to the identification card and munitions pass in his pocket, was Horace Stevenson, who came from Bow, London, E., and was temporarily employed at the McCulloch Works.

He ordered a pint of beer and began to think about the instructions he had received that morning, together with an outline of the Foden story. Greeley thought constructively about Foden. He tried to get a mental picture of the man, and, through the facts at his disposal, to get an idea of Foden's mentality. It must not be thought that because Greeley was not particularly well-educated, that he had not the ability to think. He had and he knew it. He knew too that Quayle would never have put him on this job if he hadn't trusted him implicitly, because, for some reason which he could not at that moment put his finger on, he sensed that it was a big job, and a big job to Greeley meant a big job.

Greeley had been concerned in some of the toughest and cleverest operations conducted by Quayle—operations made necessary by the sinister necessities of war—operations in which the people who did the work got away with it or they didn't. If they got away with it, that was all right until next time. If they didn't get away with it, there was nobody to help them. It was no good squealing. They would be disowned—thrown overboard.

And that could be tough. That was the time when you had to show you had the ability to take it and *like* it. Greeley grinned to himself. Half the world didn't know how the other half lived, and three-quarters of the people in England didn't even realize the lengths that the Germans would go to in order to win the war—or the lengths that people like Quayle and the ones above him *had* to go to in order to stop 'em winning it. People thought that wars were fought and won on battlefields, on the sea and in the air. Well, they were; but they were fought in other places too—all sorts of odd places by all sorts of odd people who didn't have any uniform and who didn't win any medals. People who were on a good hiding to nothing.

Well . . . it had to be done. Greeley supposed that not one of them *had* to do it. Nobody *made* them. He often wondered how some of Quayle's operatives had got into the game—the people who looked as if they came out of the top drawer—people like Fells and Zilla Stevenson—people who had class. You would have imagined, thought Greeley, that a guy like Fells would have been in the Army holding down a big job. He looked that sort of guy. He looked like a soldier. . . .

But it was an amusing game if you liked it and if you didn't slip-up. If you did it was just too bad. You were on your own. You couldn't squeal. Nobody would believe you anyway. You just had to take it . . . and like it.

Greeley had known this to happen; had known one man go to prison for doing something which, on the *obvious* face of it, seemed to the Judge a very nasty piece of work; knowing that the said Judge, had he known the truth, the whole truth and nothing but the truth, would probably have wanted to recommend the prisoner for a decoration. Greeley had been in Court on the day that Serven was sentenced. He'd wondered throughout the trial if Serven would crack; would try to squeal or get out of it. Sitting in the crowded gallery, Greeley had watched Serven. Then his eyes, wandering along the row of faces, had picked out Quayle's. Quayle, looking like any prosperous business man, was sitting at the end of the public gallery with a benign smile on his face.

When Serven was sentenced he had thrown a quick look up at the gallery and Quayle's smile had deepened a little bit. Greeley had grinned inwardly. He had said to himself: "Nice work, chum! And how do you bleedin' well like that—three and a half years in quod for being a super Englishman! And I hope it keeps fine for you!" After which he had spat metaphorically and left the Court.

A cynical one, Greeley. Or was he? Perhaps under the cynicism was the character of a man whose sincerity, whose love of adventure, was that of a boy. Perhaps Greeley was a man who had never really grown out of boyhood, and if the jobs he did were a man's jobs, he was able to bring to them the mentality and atmospherics of the adventurous time of youth. His cynicism was in fact an armour adopted as a temporary defence against his own doubts. He put it on and took it off at will.

The door at the far end of the bar opened and the woman came in. Greeley whistled through his teeth. Yes, this was the same one. This was the girl at Kingstown. Jesus . . . what a girl! So *this* was Zilla Stevenson.

Greeley raised the tankard to his lips and drank his beer, looking over the rim of the tankard. That Kingstown job was eighteen months ago, and if anything she was prettier than ever. He used the word pretty in his own mind because lovely was a word that did not come easily to his tongue. But that is what he meant.

And she was not a blonde. Her hair was titian red, and Greeley realized that this was her real colouring. She had had her hair tinted up for that Kingstown business—peroxided. Greeley thought that he did not give a damn what colour her hair was—she'd certainly got something. He thought he had never in his whole lifetime seen a woman like Zilla. Face, figure and everything were perfect, and although the clothes she wore were rather smart and of cheap pattern, they could not disguise the grace of every movement. She stood leaning against the bar, ordering a gin and tonic, apparently unaware of the fact that the eyes of every man in the place were upon her.

She took her drink to one of the tables at the back of the bar. As she sat down her eyes swept along the bar until they came to Greeley. Greeley looked away but he knew she was looking at him. He put the tankard down on the bar with his right hand, felt in his pocket, produced a bent cigarette, straightened it out, lit it. He turned round casually and looked at her; then he finished his beer. He waited till the barmaid moved in his direction; ordered another half-pint. He drank it slowly.

He smoked his cigarette, drew the smoke down into his lungs, exhaling through his nostrils. He was wondering about Zilla Stevenson. Quayle was a bastard, thought Greeley. What the hell did he want to put a woman like this one on this job for? Putting her down here in this lousy hole just for the purpose of getting next to a dock superintendent, to get some information as to when a certain boat came in and when a certain man came off it. Damn it, you didn't want to use a woman like her for a job like that. Quayle had got other ones who could have done that. There was that girl who'd worked with them on the Surrey job. She'd have done—any ordinary sort of girl. But that Stevenson baby had got class. She was carrying it off all right. She looked the part right enough. But why use one like her for a lousy job like that? Because it *might* be a lousy job. She had to get the information and you've got to do all sorts of things to get information. Greeley wondered what the dock superintendent was like; then suddenly he asked himself why he was worrying. What the hell had this woman got to do with him anyway, beyond the fact that she was in on this Foden business until such time as she got the information to pass to Greeley, after which she would fade out. But would she? Maybe Quayle had some other idea. That was the devil of it.

You never knew what Quayle was doing. You could be as curious as you liked, but it wouldn't get you anywhere. Nobody ever asked Quayle any questions. Greeley grinned. The idea of somebody asking Quayle a *real* question amused him. Quayle's operatives were simply the means to an end, but only Quayle knew the end.

Greeley thought that perhaps that was just as well. Otherwise some of the boys and girls with sensitive nerves might not have slept so well at nights. What people didn't know couldn't hurt 'em.

Greeley began to think about his wife. He was fond of his wife. When they were married just before the war, Greeley had foreseen a long partnership with no side turnings. He grinned. Wars did funny things to you. He remembered the pang of parting when he'd volunteered for the Army. Then when he'd come back with a hole in one lung he seemed to have learned a lot more than she had. Then the circumstances had arisen which had brought him into touch with Quayle, and after that—well, he'd played it as best he could. A nice trusting woman, Mrs. Greeley, he thought—one of those women who had not much feminine curiosity in their nature; who accepted as truth the stones he told her, which was just as well for him perhaps.

Well, anyway, she got the pay envelope every week. The girl in Quayle's office saw to that. No matter where Greeley was or what he was doing, Mrs. Greeley always received a pay envelope, and the postmark was always the right one—the place it *ought* to have come from. Greeley, his nose buried in the tankard, wondered how the hell that girl of Quayle's wangled the postmark thing.

Quayle was a businesslike guy all right. Everything sorted out and classified and ready to hand when you wanted it. People for every sort of job. Satisfaction guaranteed and no slip-ups except when it couldn't be helped, and that wasn't often. You got your orders and you carried 'em out and you didn't ask questions. You were just told enough and no more. A good system that, because if anybody got on to you, well, you couldn't talk because you didn't know enough.

Greeley had guessed why Quayle used a number of operatives for a job when, on the face of it, just one or two seemed enough. The more people you used, the less each one of them had to know. They did their little bit, said their little piece and faded out.

Sometimes, if you were lucky, you knew a bit more than most. Greeley realized that *he* knew a bit more than most. That was because Quayle trusted him; because he, Greeley, had been through the mill and always come out right side up, because he could make up his mind quickly and because if a job had to have a nasty ending, well . . . that was O.K. with him.

But even he knew precious little. He thought of the number of people he had worked with during the last year. At least sixty—and most of them he would not see again. Here and there one might pop up suddenly—like this Zilla Stevenson was popping up—but that was the exception.

He ordered another half-pint, drank it slowly and continued to wonder how the Stevenson woman had got into the game.

IV

Greeley came out of the little house that stood in a road of little houses; began walking towards the docks. He did not ask the way. He knew it. He had spent two hours on a street plan of the neighbourhood because, like the other people who worked for Quayle, experience had taught him that the fewer people you met the better. Ten minutes' walking brought him to Marsh Street. He began to walk down the street. Odd numbers, he found, were on the left-hand side, and the darkness forced him to walk up the dirty steps leading to the front doors and peer at the numbers. Eventually he came to No. 17. He rang the bell. A buxom woman opened the door.

She said, looking at Greeley not unpleasantly: "Well?"

Greeley said, in a cheerful voice: "Good evening, Ma. I'm Horace Stevenson." He grinned amiably. "I believe you've got my sister living here," he said.

Her broad face broke into a smile. "So you're her brother, are you?" she said. "Well . . . well . . . well: . . . I'd never have thought that. Come in."

"Not so much of it," said Greeley pleasantly, stepping into the hallway. "Everybody's always makin' cracks because my sister's so much better-lookin' than I am. Why shouldn't she be? If she'd had to put up with what I have had to go through, she'd look a damn' sight worse than I look."

"You should worry!" said the woman. "She told me you might be around some time to-night. I suppose you're keen to meet her intended?"

Greeley thought: Like hell! So that's how she was playing it. The dock superintendent would be the "intended."

He said: "Well, that's the way it goes. What's this guy like?"

"He's a nice man," said the woman. "A nice feller. I like him. He's got a good job too—down at the docks, you know."

"I know," said Greeley.

She said: "Well, I've got to get on with my work. Her room's the first on the right off the first landing." She smiled. "I bet she'll be glad to see you," she said. "Life isn't much fun for a girl these days in a town like this where it's so dark you can't see your nose in front of you." She disappeared down the passage.

Greeley went up the stairs. At the first landing he knocked on the door. Somebody said: "Come in."

He went in. He stood just inside the doorway, closing the door behind him, his cigarette stuck to the left-hand side of his mouth, his check cap over one eye.

The room was surprisingly large; not badly furnished. In the corner by the window Zilla Stevenson was sitting on the bed. She was smoking a cigarette. Greeley thought she had a hell of a pair of legs and ankles. The thought flashed through his mind that he could fall for legs like those. He made a mental note to keep his mind on the business in hand.

He took off his cap. He said, in a cheerful voice that did not match his cynical grin: "Well, how's the little sister?"

"Not too bad," said Zilla Stevenson. Her voice was very low, very soft—a cultured voice. Greeley realized that she was no longer playing her part. She was being herself. She said:

"I don't think we've got very long. I'm expecting the boy friend round."

Greeley said: "You don't say. Some guys have all the luck. Has it been tough gettin' next to this docks fellow?"

"Oh, no," she said, "it hasn't been tough. I've seen to that. He's easy. He thinks he's going to marry me."

Greeley said: "Poor swine! And he's a talker, hey?"

"No," she said. "He doesn't talk very much normally, but he talks to *me*. He trusts me, you see."

"I see," said Greeley. "Well—it's careless talk in a good cause even if he don't know it. What's the racket?" He moved his cigarette to the other side of his mouth, rolling it with his tongue. His cap was under his left arm, his hands in his pockets. He leant against the shut door. He said:

"You remember the last time you and I played something together? It was at Kingstown. You remember that job?"

She said, in a cool voice: "I could if I wanted to, but I've always found it better to forget things, haven't you?"

He nodded. "I've always been able to forget things pretty easily before," he said. "I don't want to flatter you, but it wouldn't be easy to forget a girl like you."

She said: "Thanks." She smiled at him.

"Another thing," said Greeley, "I ought to say thank you to you. If you hadn't shot that bastard just when he was getting through the window, it would have been all up with me. I suppose you realize that?"

She nodded.

Greeley said: "You've got a hell of a nerve."

She thought for a moment; then she said: "So have you. I've heard about you."

Greeley grinned. "You don't mean to tell me the boss has been issuin' me with any medals behind my back, do you?"

She said: "I don't know about that, but he thinks a lot of you. He must. You wouldn't be handling this job if he didn't."

Greeley said: "That's what I thought. This thing smells pretty big. I don't know why, but it does."

She said: "Yes! I think it does."

Greeley thought she was mysterious. He liked looking at her. She had allure—that was the word—allure. And by God—she was beautiful. Quayle had been wise to put her on this job. Getting information out of a dock superintendent would be chicken-feed to her. This one could get blood out of a stone. Greeley sighed inwardly. Life was lousy! He'd like to talk to this woman, and couldn't. They'd probably never have the chance.

He said: "Well, how does it go?"

"It goes like this," she said. "The boat's in. It docked at five o'clock this morning. Foden had to see the port officer about landing, and papers, and where he'd come from—the usual sort of normal questioning. That's kept him busy most of the afternoon. He's living at Vazeley Street—No. 22. My boy friend put him on to that. He's paid a week's rent in advance."

Greeley said: "I see. How do I pick him up?"

She said: "Opposite Vazeley Street is a pub—a rather nice sort of place. It's very popular. It's called the Hunting Horn. Well, there's nowhere to go at night, is there? And he's got to go somewhere. It's my guess he'll go there."

Greeley said: "Any cinemas here?"

She said: "By what I've heard of Foden he's not likely to want to go to the pictures." She smiled. Greeley noticed her perfect teeth. "A man with a record like Foden's doesn't want to go to the pictures," she said. "He's *done* it all."

Greeley nodded. He said: "Yes. It looks as if it'll be the Hunting Horn."

She said: "I suppose you've got it all worked out?"

"Yes," said Greeley. "If he falls for the line I'm going to hand out, then he'll want to get up to London to meet you. I'm goin' to play it goddam carefully. But I think it's goin' to sound O.K. If he falls I'll give you the tip and you get out good and quick."

She nodded. "Yes," she said. "And what about you?"

"Directly I know he's goin' to London after you, I'm getting out myself," said Greeley. "The idea is that the Works here transfer me back to London for some special job. I think the boss wants me around while you're handling the boy in the big city."

She said: "Perhaps I'll be glad of that." She smiled suddenly. "Perhaps Mr. Foden may be a little tough for a girl like me."

Greeley said: "I wouldn't be surprised. Quayle's going to work on this boyo, and evidently he doesn't think it'll be easy."

"No," she said. "I don't think it'll be easy. I think it'll be a lot more difficult than even you think."

Greeley said: "Maybe." He inhaled cigarette smoke. "Maybe you know more than I do?"

She looked at him. He could see that her eyes were very blue.

She said: "Perhaps I do."

There was a step on the landing outside. Greeley moved away from the door as it opened. A big man with a peak cap and a blue double-breasted jacket came into the room. His face was bronzed and there was a one-day's growth of beard on his chin. Greeley thought: The dock superintendent! This is going to be interesting!

The man closed the door behind him and stood looking from Zilla Stevenson to Greeley. He looked nasty. His eyes were bright. Greeley thought they looked at him almost menacingly. He thought, too, this one's been a sailor. He's tough, suspicious and jealous. For some reason which he could not quite explain to himself he felt very antagonistic. He leaned up against the wall smoking his cigarette, looking as insolent as he could when he wanted to.

The man said to Zilla: "What the hell's going on here? Who is this?"

She put her hand to her hair. She said casually: "What's eating you? I don't like the sound of that."

He said: "Maybe you don't. I'm simply asking you who this guy is. What the hell's going on around here? You didn't think I was coming back so early, did you? I wonder—"

She swung her feet onto the bed and lay back. Greeley thought her face and head made a perfect picture against the pillow. She said casually:

"You wonder if I'm running another boy friend behind your back. Is that it? You know, if you feel like that about a girl, you oughtn't to talk to her about marriage. It means you don't trust her, see?"

Greeley grinned inside. She was playing the superintendent, he thought. Having got what she wanted from him she wasn't going to stand any old buck. She could have put the situation right immediately by saying who Greeley was supposed to be. She just wouldn't do it. She was throwing the ball to Greeley to see what he would do. He liked that. It created a sort of cynically humorous bond between himself and the woman.

He said, rather offensively: "So you think you're going to marry her, do you? Why don't you try and behave yourself a bit better instead of shootin˘off that big mouth of yours like that?"

The superintendent looked at Zilla. He said: "Look, I'm not standing for this."

She put her hands behind her head and stretched. Greeley thought she looked quite luscious.

He said: "Well, what are you going to do about it, big mouth?"

The man's face went brick-red in colour. He turned quickly on Greeley. He said over his shoulder to the woman:

"I'll talk to you in a minute. Just now I'm going to fix this bastard. I'll teach him a lesson. Do you think I'm the sort of cuss who has fellers chasing this girl? I'll make an example out of this rat."

He took a quick step towards Greeley, swung an immense fist. Greeley didn't even trouble to take the cigarette out of his mouth. He moved like a flash. He caught the punch on his left hand but he did not return it. He made two quick cuts with his right hand held extended and brought down with a chopping motion first on the superintendent's right forearm and then on the upper muscle. The edge of Greeley's hand was as hard as iron. The two blows, perfectly timed, placed in the exact position as only a *Judo* expert could place them, almost paralyzed the brawny arm. Instantaneously, Greeley stepped in. He swung his left hand in a downward cut on to the solar plexus behind the blue double-breasted coat. Zilla's boy friend gasped for air and subsided on the floor. He was effectively winded.

Greeley unstuck the cigarette stub from his lip. He threw it into the fire. He took a packet of Player's cigarettes from his coat pocket; lit one with a dilapidated lighter.

Zilla swung her legs down from the bed. She sat there for a few seconds looking from her boy friend to Greeley and back again. Greeley thought there was definite amusement in her eyes. She got up. She went over to the washhand stand; poured some water over a sponge; went over to the now heavily breathing figure. She knelt down just behind the man; took his head on her lap; began to bathe his forehead with the sponge.

She looked up at Greeley. She was smiling. For a moment one eyelid flickered in a comprehensive wink; then she leaned over the head in her lap. She said:

"Willie dear . . . you're such a silly fellow, aren't you? You always come to the wrong conclusions. Horace here is my brother. Only, like you, he's a bit short-tempered sometimes. He got annoyed, see? You ought to think a bit before you start talking, oughtn't you, Willie dear?"

Willie dear scowled at Horace. He said, breathing heavily: "Well, why the bloody hell didn't somebody tell me?"

Greeley smiled amiably. He said cynically: "It's always the same with fellers who want to get hitched up with my sister. They always suspect everybody." He paused for a moment to draw on his cigarette. He waved his hand airily. He said: "Anyway, Willie, I can understand that. If I was stuck on her I'd be suspicious myself. There are damned few women look like she does. You know, she's got something."

Willie said: "So have you. I'd like to know where you learned that stuff you tried on me. That wasn't fighting, you know."

Greeley said: "No—maybe not. It's a sort of Japanese battlecraft. It's good too. I reckon if you'd hit me once you'd have knocked me through the wall."

Zilla Stevenson said in a soothing voice: "You two ought to shake hands and make friends. After all, you're going to be brothers-in-law, aren't you?"

Greeley said: "Yes. Still, fellers can always be good friends after a scrap. I'll come round and see you at the docks—maybe to-morrow. We'll have a drink. I want to talk to you about Zilla." He looked sternly at the dock superintendent. "I always take an interest in the guys who want to marry my sister," he said. "Maybe one of these fine days one of 'em's going to pull it off."

Willie said in a pained voice: "So there have been other ones, hey?"

Greeley opened the door. "You're tellin' me," he said. "Seven, to my knowledge. But none of 'em seemed to make the grade. She's a very particular piece, you know. But maybe you've found that out. Maybe that's why you're so bleedin' bad-tempered. Good-night, Zilla."

He went down the stairs. The landlady was standing round the angle of the stairway on the ground floor listening.

"Don't you worry, Ma," said Greeley. "It's all right. My sister's intended tripped up and fell over. Nearly knocked himself out. What did you think it was—a bomb?"

He opened the front door and walked into the dark street, whistling quietly to himself.

CHAPTER 5

Zilla

I

It was dark. Zilla stood on the corner where two mean streets met. The brown blanket coat she wore merged with the background of the wall behind her. Only her face and her beige silk stockings could be seen. There was a drizzle of rain—a steady regular drizzle—swept by an occasional gust of wind. By now her woollen blanket coat was soaked. Her ungloved hands, one of which held a damp cigarette, were wet.

After a while, she threw the cigarette into the gutter; put her hands into the side pockets of her coat; leaned against the wall. She was relaxed. Her attitude was so casual that the process of standing on street corners in rainstorms might have been one which was normal, if not even pleasurable, to her. Her face, which had now taken on the look of pathetic wistfulness which had so fascinated Greeley during the Kingstown business, was turned towards the opposite corner. Her clear blue eyes gazed steadfastly into the darkness beyond the circle of dim blued light cast by the street lamp.

Greeley came across the road towards her. He was smiling. He stood in front of her looking at her with frank admiration.

He said: "Hello, Gorgeous. I'm glad to see you looking so happy. When I got your telegram I wondered what the hell had happened. Is anything wrong?"

She looked at him. She smiled; shook her head.

She said: "No, there's nothing wrong."

"No?" said Greeley. "This is interestin'. You don't mean to say that you made this date with me in the rain just because you wanted to see my beautiful face?"

She shook her head. "You're quite right," she said. "I didn't. But there's no reason why I mightn't have wanted to do that, is there? Why shouldn't I want to talk to you?"

Greeley said: "What is this?" His voice was more than interested.

She said: "You're strange, aren't you, Greeley. You've got an idea that there's no possible reason why a woman like me might be interested in a man like you."

Greeley said, in a flat sort of voice: "If there is a reason I'd be damned glad to hear it. What have *I* got that would interest you?"

She did not speak for a moment. She seemed to be considering something; then she said: "I suppose you think because you don't look like a film star, because you're not good-looking, because you don't speak with a B.B.C. announcer accent, that a woman might not be interested in you. You're funny. You're very funny, aren't you, Greeley? You think nothing of all the really important things about yourself. You're a fearfully superior person possessed of an odd inferiority complex. You ought to get rid of it. Believe it or not, you're a very interesting person."

Greeley grinned. "You'll make me blush in a minute," he said. "But even if what you say is true, it would be a damn' sight better if I *did* look like a film star; if I did talk with a blinkin' accent that you could cut with a knife. . . ."

She interrupted. "Why?" she asked.

Greeley said: "Take a look around you. We're in the third year of this bleedin' war, an' do you see virtue coming into its own? Lots of the boys who look like film stars an' speak with pretty accents are still duckin' the Services—one way or another—the west-end's full of 'em—but nobody seems to mind. There's supposed to be a total comb-out in this country, isn't there? All right . . . you don't find the guy who drops his aitches missin' the comb. They get him all right. It's the guy who looks good and speaks prettily who gets himself a nice uniform, goes on doin' the job he was doin' before there *was* a war an' kids himself he's servin' his country—at least he kids his friends."

She said: "Those people don't matter. You know they don't matter. So do they. And before they're through they'll pay the bill—one way or another. In any event all that doesn't alter the fact that *I* think you're a very interesting person."

"All right," said Greeley. "I got a bleedin' raindrop runnin' down my nose and I'm half drowned, but I'm quite prepared to stand here up against this lousy wall hearin' why I'm interestin'. That's the thing—you tell me why."

She said: "One night Mr. Quayle was in an expansive mood. He talked quite a lot about you. You've done some terrific things, haven't you?"

Greeley said: "Hooey! I haven't done any more than anybody else has done. Anybody else on this job, I mean. I've just lasted, that's all."

"That's just it," she said. "You've lasted—God knows why—you've taken *some* chances."

Greeley grinned. His cap was soaked. He took it off, shook it so that the raindrops ran off the peak. He put it on again. He said:

"Well, you can fall under a bus, can't you? A lot of people do. I've just been lucky. I haven't fallen under the bus yet. Maybe I will one day."

She said: "I believe you're a fatalist."

"Fatalist my fanny," said Greeley. "I take what comes. I'm a philosopher. If your name's written on something, you get it. If it isn't, you don't."

She asked: "Are you married?"

Greeley nodded. "Yes," he said, "I'm married. I got a nice wife. She believes in me. She thinks I'm what you call a good husband. She thinks I'm on one of those travelling munitions squads. A good girl—Nellie—not very exciting, but good."

She said: "That's the trouble, isn't it? Her not being very exciting. You've *got* to have excitement, haven't you?"

"Why not?" said Greeley. "Some people like going to the pictures, don't they?"

She nodded. She smiled slowly. She said: "Yes, some people like going to the pictures. You prefer this. . . ."

Greeley asked: "Look, what is all this leadin' up to?" He produced a box of Player's cigarettes; gave her one; flicked open his lighter. Her face was close to his as he lit her cigarette. He put the lighter away and drew a deep breath of tobacco smoke. He repeated: "What's all this leadin' up to? You're getting me in a state of mind where I could believe that you had a bit of a lean on me."

She said: "The joke is, Greeley, I'm beginning to believe that I have."

Greeley said: "You're suffering from what they call a fit of temporary insanity. A woman who *looks* like you look, *is* what you are and *knows* what you know, could make any man she wanted to."

She said: "Yes? I made a man like that once—a man I wanted to make—my husband. He's dead now. Since then I've been rather more interested in what I can do to men rather than in what they can do to me."

"I get it," said Greeley sarcastically. "I can spin you round my little finger, can't I?"

She said: "The trouble with you, Greeley, is—you're cynical. Your cynicism, of course, is quite insincere. You use it as a sort of self-protection."

He said: "Any time I have to protect myself against you I'll take poison. Do your worst, Sweetheart. All I ask is, do we have to stand here in this bleedin' rain? I'm half drowned already."

She said: "I never mind rain."

"No," said Greeley, "it's good for the complexion, isn't it? But believe me, yours doesn't need any beauty treatment." There was a pause. He went on: "Look, nobody could accuse me of being curious, but why the hell does Quayle want to use *you* on a job like this? What's the matter with him? He's got half a dozen women could have done this. Why does he have to use somebody like you? Hasn't he got any really *intelligent* work to be done?"

She said: "Don't be too fast, Greeley. This job is intelligent enough. You don't have to be sorry for me."

He said: "Well, what you've had to do up to the moment isn't very intelligent, is it?"

She moved. She turned a little towards him. She said:

"I haven't started yet. I shall start when you turn Foden over to me."

Greeley grinned. He said: "I'm beginning to wish I was this guy Foden. He must have something."

She said: "I think he has got something—possibly more than he knows."

"I see," said Greeley. "So that's it! Maybe he knows a damn' sight more than he thinks he knows. Maybe he's supplying one of those missing pieces that Quayle keeps fittin' into those jigsaws he's always workin' on. I get it, but I still don't see why he had to use you."

She said: "I do. He's got a good reason. Foden comes from Morocco. I know quite a bit about Morocco. When Foden's talking—if he *does* talk—I'll not only be able to hear what he's saying, I'll be able to visualize places. That's important."

Greeley said: "So you know Morocco. You've been there? That's a place I've always wanted to go to."

"It's an amusing place," said Zilla Stevenson. "My husband was there for a long time. He died there."

"Ah!" said Greeley. "So that's why you know Morocco."

"That's the reason," she said. "He knew it even better than I did." She laughed softly. "He had every reason to know it," she said.

Greeley said: "What was his job?"

"He was an engineer," she said, "sometimes. The rest of the time he was doing exactly the same thing as you and I are doing."

"You don't say," said Greeley. "Well, it just shows you. It shows you how small the world is, doesn't it?" He threw his cigarette stub away.

She said: "I sent you that telegram because I wanted you to know about Foden. He's moved. He's taken a room at the Hunting Horn. That's going to make it a lot easier for you."

"You're tellin' me," said Greeley. "That means I can practically get him any time?"

She said: "Yes, I shouldn't waste any time if I were you. I've got an idea there's every reason for us to hurry."

Greeley nodded. "You mean, before Foden gets impatient and starts shooting his mouth all over the place tryin' to get this big money he's after?"

"That's right," she said. She brought her hand out of her pocket; looked at her wrist-watch. "It's twenty minutes to nine," she said, "and there's no time like the present."

"I get it," said Greeley. "All good things have to come to an end. I'll get after him now. Well, good-night, Beautiful."

"Good-night," she said. "One of these days we'll have a real talk, somewhere where it isn't raining."

Greeley said nothing. He walked away into the darkness.

II

Foden and Greeley sat at a small table set away from the counter in the saloon bar of the Hunting Horn. Outside, the rain pattered dismally and each time someone came into the bar—pushing aside the black-out curtain in the process—a cold draught swept across the room.

Greeley said: "This weather ain't going to do you much good—being used to a hot climate, I mean. It don't do me any good for that matter. I get rheumatics like hell."

Foden did not answer. He drew on his cigarette.

Looking sideways, Greeley could see the thin bronzed profile, the mobile mouth and the steady eyes that from time to time wandered round the bar. A hell of a fellow this Foden, Greeley thought—as sharp as a terrier and tough. You'd only make one mistake with him—just one.

He went on: "All the same, I think you were a mug to come back over here. This country's bloody awful at the moment. Black-out everywhere, and you go to work like the devil, and if you make some dough you can't spend it." He sighed. "I'd like to be in Morocco," he said. "There's romance and adventure there."

Foden looked at him. He said: "Don't you believe it, Stevenson. Morocco's just like anywhere else. It's not a bad place if you know the ropes." He grinned. "I knew 'em all right," he said. He drew on his cigarette. "Maybe you're right about England. This place is dark enough and gloomy enough. But perhaps I shan't do so badly here."

"You'll do all right," said Greeley. "You look like the sort of fellow who'd do all right anywhere. Let's have another drink." He picked up the glasses; carried them to the bar; ordered fresh drinks; brought them back. He sat down again.

He said: "It's all right here if you know your way about. It's all right if you can get in with the right sort of people. But there's always a streak of luck, if you know what I mean, though *I've* never had it. I just go on doing the same sort of jobs—travelling around doing my own special job in munitions factories. Every bleedin' place I go to is practically the same as the last one, and I keep on doing the same sort of things." He grinned ruefully. "When I was a kid," he continued, "I was mad keen on adventure. So what do I get? I get this. Whereas that sister of mine, who never wanted to do anything except punch a typewriter in an office—look at her!" Greeley paused for a moment.

"Still," he went on, "maybe it wasn't only luck with her. Maybe it's because she's so damn' good-lookin'."

Foden asked casually: "What happened to her?" He was thinking that he was not particularly interested in Greeley's sister.

Greeley said: "What happened to her? What didn't happen to her? It just shows you how funny life is. She gets a week's leave from the office she was working in, see? O.K. She decides to go off to the country, and in the train she gets talkin' to some old geezer. Well, I got to admit that Zilla is a pretty cute number. There's a sailor in the carriage, see?—a bit cockeyed—and this other fellow keeps on asking a lot of questions. Zilla don't like it, but she don't say anything. When she gets to the place she's goin' to, the old boy gets out and Zilla, sort of curious, I suppose, went after him, and made a note of the house he went to. Then she called in at the police station and told the police about it."

"Did she?" said Foden. "What happened then?"

"Oh, I don't know," said Greeley. "But she did pretty well out of it. She was sent for to London and asked a lot of questions about what the old boy had talked about and what he wanted to get out of the sailor. And one thing Zilla has got—she's got a hell of a memory. She could remember anything that happened last July if she wanted to—one of those good-lookin' girls who by some sort of accident have got some brains as well. The next thing is that these people that sent for her gave her a job, see? The old boy was a spy or something—a Jerry tryin' to get information. I ask you! Five hundred quid for that, and a job."

Greeley paused to light a fresh cigarette. He was thinking: What a hell of a tale! Five hundred for that—I don't think! But he wasn't taking a chance. Foden had been away too long to know what did or did not happen in cases like that.

Foden said: "So they gave her a good job?"

"That's right," said Greeley. "A hell of a job! I don't know what she gets, but she's always dressed up to the nines and she's always got money. But is she close?" Greeley laughed softly. "Believe it or not," he said, "I sent her a wire yesterday. I told her I was properly in the cart; that if I didn't have twenty-five quid I'd probably find myself in the clink. An' I'll take you six to four she does sweet Fanny Adams about it. Some sister!"

Foden said: "Was that true—what you said about going into the clink if you didn't get twenty-five pounds?"

"No," said Greeley, "it wasn't. That's just a tale I told her. I owe twenty-five quid to a bookmaker and he's makin' things a bit tough for me. Anyway, I can always use twenty-five."

Foden said: "Well, she might come through. You never know. I suppose she works in London?"

"Yes," said Greeley. "Mind you, she gets about a bit. I've met her two or three places in the country when I've been goin' around. But she's never got time for me. She seems to get time off too—pretty well any time she wants it."

There was a silence; then Foden picked up the empty glasses; walked to the bar. He came back with them re-filled.

He said: "Perhaps I could put you on to twenty-five pounds."

Greeley said: "For cryin' out loud! What for?"

Foden said: "Look, I expect you can keep your mouth shut, can't you?"

Greeley said: "You bet. Especially if there's twenty-five quid knockin' about. What's the trouble?"

"There isn't any trouble," said Foden. "But I want a little advice, see? And I think maybe your sister could give it to me."

Greeley raised his eyebrows. "Say, what is this?" he said. "I don't get it. Are you pullin' my leg?"

Foden said: "No, I'm not pulling your leg. Didn't you tell me just now that your sister got five hundred pounds for cashing in some information—something she'd picked up from some German agent in a railway train—and a job?"

"Yes, that's right," said Greeley. "But what the hell's that got to do with me gettin' twenty-five pounds and keepin' my mouth shut?"

Foden said: "Suppose for the sake of argument *I* had some information—only something a damned sight bigger than anything your sister ever had. Well, I'd be in a bit of a jam, wouldn't I?"

Greeley said: "Why? How would you be in a jam?"

Foden said: "Look, I'm a sailor, see? I'm not up to all the tricks of these wise birds over here. If I went in to somebody with my cap in my hand and told them what I know, they'd be as wise as I am, wouldn't they? But if I don't tell 'em, but I let 'em know I've got something; if I just give 'em an idea what it's about, I could do a little negotiating, couldn't I? Understand?"

"I get it," said Greeley. "You think you've got something really big and you want to make certain you're going to get some dough for it?"

Foden smiled. "That's roughly the idea," he said.

Greeley thought for a moment. He said: "Well, maybe Zilla could give you a tip, but I doubt it. She has to be in with some of these guys who're lookin' for stuff like that. I don't know what her job is and I don't suppose it's very important. I reckon they thought that she was a bit fly over that first business. She's probably a secretary or typist to one of these big shots. But she's a hard case." He grinned at Foden. "Although . . ."

"Although what?" asked Foden. He picked up his glass and drained it. It was his fifth double whisky. Greeley thought, here was a man who could go on drinking but nothing would ever happen to him. One of those people who were always sober no matter what they drank. He grinned at Foden.

"Zilla might fall for a guy like you," he said. "She always had a lean on big tough guys like you. Maybe she'd give you a tip or two just for the fun of it. Although I'd lay six to four she'd want some money. If I know anything of Zilla she certainly would." He finished his drink. "But what the hell!" he said. "It's no soap anyway. We probably couldn't get hold of her. I've told you what she's like."

Foden said: "You said she was in London. Do you know her address?"

Greeley shook his head. "No," he said. "I sent that telegram to some club she belongs to. I was hoping that they'd have her address and send it round to her. I never really thought she'd take much notice of it. Just a sort of chance. You know."

Foden said: "I know. What about a drink?"

Greeley said: "Why not?" He started to get up but Foden put out his hand.

"That's all right, Stevenson," he said. "These drinks are on me."

He went to the bar. When he came back, Greeley said:

"You seen any of the cinema shows around here? That's all there is to do in this cockeyed place. I thought maybe I'd toddle along and see a film."

Foden said: "No. I'm not very interested in pictures."

Greeley began to drink his whisky. It was very strong. Foden had made it a treble one, he thought. Maybe he was falling for the line. Greeley began to talk about places he'd been to in England—things he'd seen. He rambled on aimlessly, talking in the manner of a man who likes to talk. Foden listened perfunctorily. After a bit he said:

"You listen to me. If you can fix up for me to see your sister—to have a little talk with her—I'll give you that twenty-five pounds you want. How do you like that?"

Greeley said: "I like it a hell of a lot. I'll do my best. But whether she's going to play or not is another matter."

Foden said: "Well, you can only do your best, can't you? You try and fix it."

Greeley said: "Look, I'll tell you what I'll do. You let me have an advance of ten quid off that twenty-five and I'll get a day off and slip-up to London and see what I can fix. How's that for an idea?"

Foden said: "No." He grinned sideways at Greeley. "That's *too* good an idea," he said. "I tell you what I'll do. You can have a five-pound note and the balance when you fix it."

Greeley said: "That's a bet. I'd like to see Zilla anyway." He drained his glass. "I think we'll have one more for the road," he said. "Then I'll get back. If I get myself stuck on a nightshift to-night maybe I can get the day off to-morrow. There's nothing like doin' a thing when it's hot." He went to the bar; returned with the fresh drinks. He sat down.

He said: "Is life goddam funny, or is it! Here am I lookin' around for twenty-five quid and I fall into this bar to-night and meet you, and with a bit of luck I'm goin' to get it. It's wonderful how things happen."

Foden said: "Yes. That's a fact. Most big things happen by accident." He smiled.

"That's right," said Greeley. "Life itself is a sort of accident, isn't it? You never really know what's waitin' round the corner. But the breaks don't come even. Some fellers get a helluva time an' some fellers get a lousy deal. And nobody knows why. A guy like you gets adventure—you been in Morocco—you've seen things." He sighed. "I wish I'd been to Morocco," he said. "If I had I reckon I'd have *something* to think about."

Foden nodded. He said: "That's right. Morocco is the sort of place where things happen." He felt in the inside pocket of his jacket. "I'll show you something, Stevenson," he said. "Look . . . I'm *trusting* you. This'll show you the *sort* of information I've got." He took a photograph—postcard size—out of his pocket and handed it to Greeley.

Greeley took it. It showed a small group of five men in shorts and shirts, standing under some palm trees. The five men looked as if they'd had a very tough time. One of them was Foden.

"That was taken in the concentration camp I was in," said Foden. "One of those God-awful places run by the Vichy crowd for the Germans. They stuck me inside because the Huns knew that I'd tried to give information to the British. I'd hate to tell you the sort of time I had in that goddam place. One thing I do know is that I was damn' lucky to get out of it. Most of the people there just used to disappear. They went—and no one ever knew where they went."

Greeley nodded. "I suppose they used to knock 'em off," he said. "They knew too much . . . hey?"

"That's it," said Foden. "But I got out and I'm still here and I know more than the whole lot of 'em put together." He took the photograph back from Greeley; returned it to his pocket. "And if I get away with this," he said. "If I can fix things through your sister so that I get what I want, you needn't worry. I'll look after you all right."

Greeley picked up his glass. He said: "Well, here's to it."

They put the two empty glasses back on the table.

Foden said: "You could stand one more, couldn't you?"

"You'd be surprised," said Greeley. "I've never had enough whisky in my life."

Foden said: "All right. We'll have one for the road." He went to the bar.

Greeley looked at his back. He said to himself: You're hooked, sucker. You're hooked!

III

The waiter brought the coffee; put it down on the table. Zilla noticed that his hands were very white; that the veins stood out on them; that they trembled. She thought it could not be very interesting to be a waiter—not unless you took an interest in the people you served. This waiter obviously took no interest. He was old and very tired. She wondered what he had to look forward to; then wondered cynically what *she* had to look forward to anyway. After all, there was not a great deal of difference between people. Everybody was waiting for something. And usually it did *not* arrive.

The waiter went away. Quayle offered her a cigarette. She saw that there was some engraving inside the gold cigarette case. She thought that someone had given the case to Quayle. It must have cost a great deal of money that case, but then probably *somebody* had been grateful.

She watched Quayle under her eyelids as he lit his cigarette. His fingers were very deft. He snapped the flame of his lighter on and off with definite precise gestures. She thought: He thinks like that. Everything's in a watertight compartment. Everything's filed and indexed and numbered. He just presses a button in his brain and he gets what he wants.

She said: "It's nice being back in London. That last place was awful. Shall I be here for long?"

Quayle said: "Why not?" He drew the Turkish cigarette smoke into his lungs.

She thought: I wonder why he never answers a question directly. I suppose he doesn't want to. She felt a little angry with Quayle—as angry as it was possible to feel with him.

He said: "Well . . . Zilla, you'll want to know about the next step, won't you?"

She said: "Yes, I suppose that's why I'm here."

Quayle said: "You wouldn't be angry with me, would you? You know, really it isn't any good being angry with me. I'm in pretty well the same position as you are. I have to do things whether I like them or not." He smiled, a little grimly, she thought. "That means to say," he said, "that you people just have to take life as it comes, consoling yourselves with the thought that there's a war on but that it can't last for ever."

She said: "I know. That's the trouble. I think it'll be worse when it's over."

Quayle nodded. He said: "You think things will be even more boring then?"

She said: "Yes. That's what I think."

Quayle flicked the ash off his cigarette with a neat gesture. She began to pour out the coffee.

He said: "Foden's hooked all right. Greeley was through on the telephone last night. The situation's perfect for you to step into. Foden will probably come up to London to-morrow. His idea is that he can use you as a sort of intermediary between himself and whoever he thinks he's going to get a great deal of money from. Greeley's planted the idea in his head that you're a bit of a gold-digger and that, because you once showed your astuteness over getting a German agent whom you met in a railway train arrested, you've got a job as secretary working for somebody connected with one of the Service Intelligence Departments. That's what Foden will think."

Zilla said: "I see. And what do *I* think?"

Quayle said: "You think this: You'll be a tough young woman of course, with your eye on the main chance—rather well-dressed in a smart sort of way but not too smart. You'll have learned quite a lot about clothes. But the thing is that you'll be rather attracted by Foden. You understand? In spite of yourself—in spite of the fact that you're a tough young woman with an eye on the main chance—you'll be attracted by him. That could easily happen, because it's always the so-called tough young woman—those who're inclined to be gold-diggers—who fall for a man like Foden in spite of themselves. Foden's got brains. He's tough. He's good-looking. He's been all over the place. In his way he's a romantic figure. You understand?"

She nodded. "I've got that," she said. "So in spite of myself I'm rather attracted. I hope you're not going to ask me to sleep with this paragon?"

Quayle said quite seriously: "No, I shan't have to ask you to do that." He smiled at her. "I never have yet, have I?" he said. "Although you know perfectly well if it were necessary I should."

She said, a little bitterly: "If you considered something necessary you'd ask *anything* of *anybody*. You've only got one redeeming feature."

"Yes?" said Quayle. He looked quite disinterested.

"Your only redeeming feature is," Zilla went on, "that you're rather more tough on yourself than you are on any of us."

Quayle said: "Thank you for nothing. You're getting a bit nervy these days, aren't you? When this job's over you'll have to have a little leave."

"That's very kind of you," she said. "And I'd like some leave when this job's over. Then I could come up all nice and fresh and smiling for the next one, couldn't I?"

Quayle nodded. "That's right, my dear," he said. He went on: "Quite obviously Foden will want to use you as a means of getting into touch with someone in authority to whom he can sell this information. You see, his trouble is this: He thinks his information is pretty big stuff and it might easily be that. But he's in a difficult position because whatever information he has is such that he can't divulge *any* of it without giving the whole thing away. Therefore he feels he's got to make certain about getting the sum of money which he considers adequate before he talks at all. That's not an easy situation for him, is it?"

"Not particularly," said Zilla. "But if he thinks I'm falling for him—"

"Exactly," said Quayle. "If he thinks you're attracted to him, he'll begin to consider you as a person in whom he might possibly confide—more especially if the suggestion comes from you that you would be prepared to take a rakeoff in this business. Foden might easily consider you as a partner. That's common sense, isn't it?"

She said: "Yes, that's common sense all right." There was a pause; then she said: "There's one thing I don't understand about this business."

"Is there?" said Quayle. He sounded quite sympathetic.

She said: "If Foden has information—if the information's good—if we want it—if it's really necessary for the war—why don't we give him the money and get the information? Why all this funny business?" She laughed a little, suddenly.

Quayle asked: "What are you laughing at?"

She said: "I feel like the silly young woman at the party who keeps asking intimate questions and says after each one: 'I hope that's not an indiscreet question.'"

Quayle said: "I never mind people asking me questions—whether they're indiscreet or not."

"I know," said Zilla a little acidly, "because you never answer them unless you want to."

"That's right," said Quayle. "But I don't mind half answering this one. Consider the situation: Supposing for the sake of argument I was prepared to do a straight deal with Foden. Supposing we were to say we would pay him a thousand pounds for the information he's got—not knowing exactly what that information is—you see the difficulties that would arise?"

She said: "I can't say I do."

"No," said Quayle. "That's because you haven't had as much experience as I have in buying information." He stubbed out his cigarette; lit a fresh one.

He went on: "Experience has taught me that it's a very bad thing to *buy* information. Let's take this case as an example. Supposing for the sake of argument I offered Foden a thousand pounds for his information. First of all he'd want the money first, wouldn't he? When he'd got the money he'd realize that he'd done a very easy deal and would begin to think he could have got two—or possibly three—thousand pounds if he'd asked for it. Realizing that, what would he do? He would take his thousand, tell us just as little as possible, and then two or three weeks afterwards remember some very salient facts that he'd omitted and suggest that we pay him another thousand or so.

"That," said Quayle, with a little smile, "would be human nature, wouldn't it? Especially," he went on, "when you consider that, according to reports, Foden has on two occasions tried to *give* our authorities in Morocco information for nothing, see?"

Zilla nodded. She said: "I see. I was foolish to ask the question. I might have known that you'd have every possible angle covered on this business."

Quayle said: "I hope I have. That's my job. Do you think you understand yours now?"

She said: "Yes, I understand. Briefly, I'm going to be a little attracted by Foden. I'm going to do my best to make him think that he could trust me. I'm going to suggest that if I got some money out of this I might be able to play this thing the way he wants it. I think," she went on, "it would be rather a good idea if I were to suggest that I was fed up with my present job, that I wanted to get away somewhere—to South Africa for instance. That I could get away; go to a job there that's waiting for me; but that I want some money first."

Quayle said: "I think that would be an excellent way to play it. I don't think you can go very far wrong working on those lines. Now as to details: As I told you Foden will probably come up to town to-morrow. He's not the sort of man who will waste any time. He'll have got your address from Greeley. He'll probably telephone through to you; tell you he's a friend of Greeley's; try to make an appointment. That's all right. Your attitude is that you're very keen on finding out what your brother—Greeley—wants that twenty-five pounds for. You're doing a little snooping, see? So you'll meet Foden. He'll probably try to make a hit with you by informing you that *he* will give Greeley that twenty-five pounds. He'll think that'll go well with you. As a matter of fact, you'll like that. That'll start the ball rolling. After that, it's going to be up to you."

Zilla nodded. She said: "After that it'll be up to me." She smiled, a little ruefully.

Quayle finished his coffee. He said: "I don't have to tell you, Zilla, that you always do a good job. You know that. I don't know what I'd do without you."

She said: "You'd find somebody else, wouldn't you? I expect you've got lots of them—all sorts and shapes and colours of women—all ages and types—all lined up. You press a button. They step forward and do their little act. I wonder what you'd do if one of them ever let you down." She laughed. She added wickedly: "Or is that an indiscreet question?"

Quayle said: "I *know* what I'd do."

She said: "Yes, so do I."

He smiled at her. He said: "I wonder if you do."

"I could make a damn' good guess," said Zilla. She picked up her handbag.

Quayle said: "You be getting along. When Foden gets a little warm ring me up."

She said: "All right. But if I get into this thing a little too deep I expect you to get me out."

Quayle said: "You've been in deep before, haven't you? Have I ever failed to get you out?"

She said: "No, I'll say that for you." She paused; then she said suddenly: "You're an odd person, aren't you? You must have a hell of a time. I don't think you have any real life at all. Isn't there something else you want to do besides this—something you believe in?"

Quayle said, in a semi-humorous voice: "I'm one of those besotted idiots who still believe in their country. That sounds rather like something out of a play, doesn't it? But it's true. You and I, Zilla, are doing a job that *has* to be done whether we like it or not. The fact that it's a pretty awful sort of job shouldn't matter. It *doesn't* matter anyway so far as I'm concerned."

She said: "I know. I'm an idiot, aren't I? I think I need that leave. Well, directly I've hooked your big fish for you I'll come and ask for it."

He said: "You'll get it all right. You're a good girl, Zilla. So long."

She got up; walked along the restaurant balcony, down the stairs. Quayle watched her. A damn good girl, Zilla, he thought—cool, steady, reliable—a first-class operative.

He thought about her for a moment; stopped when he realized that he was becoming a little sentimental. He could not afford to be sentimental.

CHAPTER 6
TANGIER

I

FELLS poured himself out a second cup of tea, put the *Bystander* on the table beside the tea-things, went to the window and looked out.

It was half-past four. Soon it would be dark. A wind was blowing. Fells thought it would probably be a nasty night. He drew the black-out curtains, switched on the electric fire, went back to his chair. He picked up an illustrated paper, began to turn over the pages, reading the captions under the pictures. The pictures were graphic. They showed the landings of the Americans in Tunisia, pictures of the Eighth Army and the First Army.

Fells lit a cigarette. Every time he looked at a picture which showed soldiers in action his heart beat a little faster. Waves of regret surged through him. He should have been there, he thought. He saw himself with his battery taking part in these operations; being what he had always intended to be—a soldier—a soldier whose years of training reached their climax on the battlefield.

Instead of which . . . Well, Quayle had been right. You could only blot your copybook once. You were only allowed to blot it once, and after that you went on paying the bill. He looked round the little sitting-room. A poor ending to all the dreams he had dreamed when he was a subaltern officer. He began to think. His mind went searching back through the years to his first meeting with Quayle—when Quayle had offered him the alternative which he had been glad to accept. Fells knew now that he had been right to accept. In any event the years had not been wasted. He thought about the work he had done with Quayle—the first years of preparatory training during the time he had been supposed to be in prison; then his official release from prison; then the meeting with the charming man who said he was a Swiss, but who afterwards turned out to be very much of a German— and an important German at that. Fells smiled to himself. Quayle had been right again. Quayle had said that the Germans would pick him up; that they would go after any British officer who had been broken and sentenced to a term of imprisonment. Well . . . they had. And Fells, carefully instructed by Quayle, had fallen for their line. He had been to France, to Germany, to Austria; had done all sorts of odd jobs; learned all sorts of things for his German masters, receiving adequate payment but reporting all the time to Quayle. He thought perhaps it had been lucky for him he had been in England when the war broke out; wondered if Schlieken and the other German Army Intelligence people who had been running him were annoyed or otherwise at that fact. Perhaps they had intended him to remain in England. Perhaps Schlieken would still want something done. . . .

Life was odd, thought Fells. It did no good to think about it. If you had blotted your copybook, thinking about life was not a profitable proposition. That was a process reserved to people whose records were clear, who had not been sentenced to be cashiered from His Majesty's Service, who had not been sentenced to terms of imprisonment for selling information to a foreign power.

The telephone rang. Fells looked at the instrument which stood on the small writing-desk in the corner of the room. He wondered who it would be. Quayle, he thought. Quayle would have a job. Fells had done nothing now for weeks. He wondered what the job would be. He crossed the room; picked up the receiver.

It was Tangier.

Fells smiled. He was experiencing the thrill that always came to him when he heard Tangier's voice on the telephone. He could visualize her at the other end of the line; visualize her smile, her eyes, the kindliness she exuded and which was a part of her.

She said softly: "Is that you?"

He said: "Yes. It's me. How are you, Tangier?"

She said: "I'm very well. I want an explanation from you. You haven't been near me for weeks. You haven't even telephoned. Why are you behaving like this?"

Fells said: "Well, when I'm fond of people—when I like them as much as I like you—I don't want to bore them. I'd hate you to get sick of me."

She laughed. She said: "How do I get sick of you? I've seen you about three times in the last five months. Besides, one *has* friends because one wants to talk to them."

Fells said: "I like talking to you—even on the telephone. It's rather a treat to talk to you."

She said: "You say the nicest things. But then I think you're rather a nice man."

Fells grinned. He looked rather like a schoolboy who is given a prize and stands nervously snuffling, unable to find words to express his thanks. He said nothing.

She asked: "What are you doing?"

He said: "I've been having tea and looking at illustrated magazines."

Tangier said: "I know. You've been looking at pictures of soldiers, haven't you?"

Fells said: "Yes." His voice was a little surprised. "How did you know that?"

She said: "On the rare occasions when you've been here I notice you always make a bee-line for any illustrated magazine that's about the place. You like looking at pictures of soldiers, don't you?"

Fells said: "Well, supposing I do?"

She said: "Why don't you come round and look at some pictures of soldiers with me? Why don't you come round and drink a cocktail and talk to me? Or don't you want to?"

Fells said: "I'd like that awfully. When shall I come?"

Tangier said: "You come now. I want to talk to you."

Fells hung up the receiver. He was still smiling. He went on smiling until he remembered; then the smile disappeared. Somewhere in his mind a miniature gramophone was playing a record of Quayle's voice and the words were distinct: "When you come out, you won't have a background and a man who has no background has no friends.

How can he? Not because people wouldn't want to know you, but you wouldn't want to know *them*—just in case they found out."

Fells sighed. He went out into the dark hallway, put on his overcoat and hat. He was thinking that he must not see Tangier very much more. She might find out; then she'd think him an outsider. Nice women like Tangier didn't want to know cashiered ex-officers— men who had done terms of imprisonment. No nice woman would. Perhaps, thought Fells, this would be the last time he would see her. He must make the most of it.

As he walked along the street, he made up his mind. This must be the last time he saw Tangier. He must be definite on this point once and for all. And not only because he was knowing her under false pretences, but because of Quayle.

Quayle would have something to say about Tangier—if he knew about her. Quayle had definite ideas about his operatives becoming mixed up with women. Women wanted to know too much. If they were friendly with a man they wanted to know about him; what his job was; what sort of person he was. Quite naturally they were curious about their friends.

Fells possessed the instinctive loyalty of his type. He worked for Quayle and must therefore sacrifice everything to the job. Also he was grateful to Quayle. Quayle had trusted him. Or had he?

He began to wonder about Quayle. As to whether Quayle *really* trusted him—or anyone else for that matter. You never knew what Quayle was thinking or what he was planning. He saw a long way ahead. He used people rather like pawns in a game of chess—little pieces of carved wood that were moved about the table and sometimes got knocked off. . . .

Knocked off . . . that was Greeley's expression. Quite one or two of the pawns had been "knocked off" . . . Greeley had said once that if the war went on long enough they'd all be knocked off, but it would not matter. There'd be someone else to step on to the blank square on the chessboard.

Greeley was right. The great thing was not to think. Thinking, said Greeley, got you nowhere.

The thing was to take life as it came.

II

Greeley sat in the two-shilling seats in the cinema. He was adequately thrilled by the romance which unfolded itself before him on the screen. Greeley liked the cinema. As he would have said, it took him out of himself. Also he was fond of adventure. The fact that his own life was very much more adventurous than anything he might ever see on a film never occurred to him. What he did was a *job*. What the film actress did was *adventure*. And he liked Greer Garson. He thought she was a honey. He liked the way she looked and moved and spoke. He liked the tremulous attitude of her mouth when she was about to kiss somebody.

He thought there was a definite resemblance between Greer Garson and Zilla. They both moved in the same graceful manner. They both possessed the same type of allure. Yes . . . that was the word . . . allure. Greeley began to think about allure and all the women he had encountered in his life who possessed it. Allure, he thought, was having something that made men go for you in a very big way. It was something apart from looks, or figure, although women who had it usually had looks and figure too. But it was something on its own. Women who had allure were usually hard to get, he concluded.

You would have thought, ruminated Greeley, that Zilla would have found it good and easy to make a first-class marriage, to find a man who was in the money, who could look after her, give her what she wanted, make her independent of everything and everybody. Instead of which she was spending her time kicking around in the Quayle circus. Well . . . maybe she liked it. There was no accounting for tastes.

He began to think about Quayle. He could not understand Quayle putting a woman as good as Zilla Stevenson was on this Foden job. It wasn't worthy of her. Greeley felt quite nasty about it. He felt sure that Quayle had put Zilla on the job because she had charm and appeal. That woman, thought Greeley, could charm a bird off a tree. But maybe he could see through Quayle's game. Zilla was going to charm that information out of Foden. That way Quayle was going to get it without paying for it.

He removed the cigarette stub that was stuck as usual to the left-hand corner of his lip. He dropped it on the carpet; lit a fresh one. Of course, he thought, he could see Quayle's point of view all right.

Foden knew something and he wanted paying for it. He wanted big money. During his experience as an operative in the Quayle organization Greeley had come across people who had information to sell before. And they were always damned difficult to handle. They all thought that the stuff they had was invaluable, and they usually had another funny idea too. They had an idea that Governments had hundreds of thousands of pounds to pay out to all sorts of odd people who thought they knew something that mattered, and thought that the information they had about the enemy was simply terrific. Usually they were quite wrong. Usually it wasn't terrific at all. Greeley thought that this wouldn't be the case with Foden, however.

Foden had something all right. Greeley was sure of that, but Foden was a tough egg. He was going to play his cards properly. He had got something to sell and he was going to get plenty for it. He was clever all right and he *knew* he was clever. Greeley began to grin. *So was Quayle.* Quayle was a damned sight more clever than Foden was. Greeley began to remember odd little things about Quayle.

He was a smart one all right, and Greeley could see just how he was going to play it. Zilla Stevenson was to be put next to Foden, and Foden would fall like a sack of coke for her. Zilla would make out— continuing on the line that he, Greeley, had put into Foden's head down at the port—that she was working for somebody connected with one of the Service Intelligence Departments. Foden would probably want to know just how much money he could get for what he had to sell and he would try to find out from Zilla. In the process Zilla would probably get enough from him for Quayle to get an idea of what it was all about.

Well, there it was. What the hell! Greeley began to ask himself why he was thinking so much about Zilla Stevenson, and what she did or did not do in connection with Foden. Then, quite suddenly, he realized that he'd fallen for her. He sat looking at the flickering screen in front of him, his cigarette hanging precariously from the corner of his mouth. He said to himself: "Well, I'll be sugared! So I've fallen in love, have I? Well, I'll be *damned*!"

The thought not only amazed him but it also amused him. He sat there grinning in the darkness, considering the implications of falling for somebody—of being stuck on a woman so that it really mattered. So he was in love! Hear him laugh.

Love was a hell of a business. It knocked a man sideways if he was silly enough to let it get hold of him. It was rather like drinking too much. You lost your sense of proportion and, worse than that, you began to talk. Love released something in men that made them juvenile. They wanted to strut about the place. When a man really fell for a woman she'd got him where she wanted him. She could play tunes on him. Love was a serious proposition that wise men sidetracked if they could.

After a while he took out his dilapidated lighter and relit his cigarette. Life was damned funny, he thought. Life was damned funny and there was nothing you could do about it. One of two things happened. Either you played it along or it played you along. It wasn't very much good struggling against it. It was just one of those things. Just occasionally a woman like Zilla floated into your life quite suddenly. And something happened to you.

He remembered his first meeting with her at Kingstown—the meeting in a soft Irish mist. He remembered the funny little public-house, and he remembered that marvellous snapshot of Zilla's that had saved his life. Then she'd gone. Some years had rolled by and she'd floated in again on this Foden job. He wondered what she'd been doing in the meantime. He wondered what other jobs she'd been doing. He wondered how many other people she had used her charm on in order to extract information. He wondered about a lot of things.

He began to think about Mrs. Greeley. This line of thought disturbed him. He sighed, lit another cigarette and concentrated on Miss Garson.

That was the thing to do—to concentrate on Miss Garson. That was the safe sort of love. You could fall for a woman on the screen and you could go along and pay your two bob every time the right film came to the local cinema, and you could see her and think about her. If you wanted to, you could write her a letter and, if you sent the stamps, maybe she'd send you a signed photograph. You could imagine yourself in situations with her; you could make up all sorts of things about her. All you wanted was imagination and two bob—or even less if you didn't mind the cheaper seats.

That was the safe sort of love. Playing it that way, you knew just where you were, and any time you got tired of the baby you could get up and go out.

And the worst thing that could happen to you was that somebody might tread on your toe in the darkness.

Not very far away was the hum of the traffic in Leicester Square. Foden, sitting on the high stool in the saloon bar, ate a sandwich and drank a whisky and soda. Near him two American soldiers talked about Morocco. He lit a cigarette and listened to what they were saying. It amused him.

He began to think of Zilla Stevenson. He wondered what she would be like. According to her brother Horace she was a good-looking girl and she had brains. Foden grinned a little. He liked good-looking girls—especially when they had brains.

His experience of women had shown him that a woman with a certain amount of intelligence was an easier proposition than one who was dumb. Words and technique were wasted on the dumb type. It was like talking to a brick wall. But if a woman was intelligent you could watch closely and see how things were going.

Up to the moment everything had been smooth and very lucky. Making a contact with Mrs. Ferry (Foden's grin broadened when he thought of Mrs. Ferry) through the unfortunate Aked had been a bit of luck. He thought about Aked. He came to the conclusion he had been wise to deal with that situation in the way he had.

And running into the fool Horace Stevenson had been lucky. It was just one of those things which had broken at the right spot and at the right moment, because even if the Stevenson woman wasn't as useful as she might be, perhaps through her he could reach somebody else—get nearer to what he wanted.

Foden, who had been supplied with some clothes coupons by the dock people at the port, looked very presentable. He was wearing a dark-blue suit with a faint stripe, a light-blue shirt and collar, a dark-blue tie. A slate-grey felt hat slightly on one side of his head accentuated the slimness of his face, the angle of his jaw-line. He looked like a tough, hard-living colonial, or might have been a tough soldier in plain clothes. He looked at his wrist-watch. It was half-past six. This, he imagined, would be the best time to telephone the Stevenson woman. He thought about what he would say to her. The best line would be that he was a friend of her brother Horace; that Horace had put him on to her; that Horace had suggested that his, Foden's, business might interest her. Foden thought that quite casually he would let Zilla know that Horace was in a bit of a jam. That would intrigue her. She'd want to know what it was, but he wouldn't tell her—not until she had agreed to meet him. He ordered another whisky and soda. She'd meet him all right, and when she did, well, it was up to him.

When the whisky and soda came, he drank it quickly. He put his cigarette back into his mouth, got off the stool, walked out of the bar. Across the road was a tube station. Foden went into the entrance. He looked about him for a telephone box.

III

Zilla Stevenson sat in front of the dressing-table in her first-floor flat in a little street off Lower Regent Street. She looked at herself in the triple mirror; concluded that she looked quite attractive. She was dressed to kill. She had worked out in her own mind the sort of woman who would appeal to Foden. Foden was tough and a sailor and he had brains. So he would want a woman to be intelligent, well-dressed, good-looking. She smiled at herself in the mirror. Definitely, she thought, she was intelligent, well-dressed and good-looking.

She made a little *moue*. It was an awful pity that one had to develop allure merely for the purpose of men like Foden; men in whom one was not interested; men on whom one was to have a certain effect, in order to make them think along certain lines—do certain things.

She got up. She crossed the room; went to the mantelpiece; helped herself to a cigarette. She lit it; turned away and looked at her full-length reflection in the pier glass in the corner of the room. She was wearing a black coat and skirt—very cleverly cut. The skirt was perhaps a little too tight at the hips and the cut of the coat accentuated Zilla's superb figure. This effect was deliberate and planned for Foden's benefit.

In her wardrobe were many coats and skirts—many frocks— most of them provided on the generous expense account supplied by Quayle. She smiled wryly. Even if Quayle didn't overpay his operatives, he certainly took trouble to ensure that they were well supplied with adequate "make-up" and "props" for the jobs they had to do. She thought that her own wardrobe must have cost at least five or six hundred. But it was a pity, she thought, that such excellent clothes should be wasted and merely used as properties in an act. She thought it would be very nice to dress oneself carefully and well because one was going out to meet someone who mattered—instead of some pig-headed sailor with a bee in his bonnet about selling information.

She drew on her cigarette; gazed at her reflection analytically and finally approvingly.

She wore black court shoes of glacé kid with heels that were high enough to show her well-turned instep and ankle to the best advantage; sheer beige silk stockings. Beneath the superbly cut coat was a chiffon blouse in a very soft shade of duck-egg blue with a ruffle about the throat that accentuated the lovely colour of her skin. She wore a smart little tailor-made hat with a tiny curled ostrich feather matching her blouse caught on one side of it. Beneath the hat, her expertly coiffured titian red hair formed an exquisite framework for her face. She hoped Mr. Foden would be duly impressed.

She went back to the dressing-table and sat down. She tapped the ash from the cigarette into the onyx ashtray. She said to herself:

You're an awfully good-looking woman, Zilla. You've got a good figure. You're still young. You're attractive. You know how to dress. Men look at you. You've taken a lot of trouble with yourself. What for? For some damned ridiculous sailor—some man who thinks he's got information to sell. For some man who wants to drive a hard bargain—and you, my dear, are to use such gifts as you possess, and any you can develop, in order to see that the bargain isn't too hard. She laughed. What a waste! Or was it?

She began to think about Greeley. Why, she asked herself, did she think about Greeley? What was there about this odd, rather common man that made the picture of him spring uninvited to her mind. She could find no answer. It was all the more extraordinary because since her husband had died there had been no man who mattered in her life. Perhaps, she thought, there was some point of similarity between Greeley and her husband, whom she had adored so utterly.

But certainly not in appearance or education or outlook—only in a certain characteristic of casual courage, of not caring, of being above fear. She liked Greeley and, because since her husband she had liked no man, she thought she *more* than liked Greeley. Perhaps, she thought, she was even a little fond of him—just because of that thing. And that was the greatest thing—courage. No man could have true courage, which is neither a physical nor a moral thing, but a mixture of both, without having something good—something very good—in his make-up. She pondered on this.

Zilla realized that she admired Greeley. Once or twice Quayle had amused himself by giving her small sidelights on some of Greeley's experiences—not enough to tell her anything that mattered, but enough to show her what sort of man he was.

Nothing would ever frighten Greeley. She sighed. She thought: Because of this, because Greeley had this thing which her husband had, she thought about him. It was for this reason that his odd, rather humorous-looking image came to her mind. It was for this reason that she felt close to him. She began to smile. She thought: You're becoming an introvert, my dear. You're beginning to indulge in self-analysis—the first sign of an inferiority complex.

She held her face between her hands, stared at herself in the glass. She thought: If I continued doing this for long enough I suppose I could hypnotize myself. She thought it would be wonderful to be able to hypnotize oneself—to take oneself away from life—to find some pleasant place in the recesses of the mind in which to rest.

She thought back through the years. She saw herself as a bride. She remembered her honeymoon in Paris; then the years that had come afterwards; then the time when she had discovered that beneath the *façade* of being an engineer her husband had another job— that he worked for Quayle. She remembered the travelling and the ships—the liners and the dingy cargo boats; the cold and the heat. She remembered Morocco. Suddenly, she began to cry. She covered her face with her hands. She sobbed bitterly.

The telephone on the little table in the corner of the room began to ring. Zilla got up and walked towards it. Two large tears were running down her cheeks. She sat for a moment in front of the telephone regaining control; then she picked up the instrument.

She said casually: "Yes? Who is that?"

A voice came to her—a strong, cheerful and attractive voice which told her that the speaker's name was Foden.

IV

When Fells came in, Tangier was sitting at her desk in the far corner of the room. She looked at him over her shoulder. She smiled, and there came to Fells that peculiar feeling of happiness and well-being that he invariably experienced when he saw her.

She was wearing a coral wool frock and there were small coral leather buckles on her shoes.

There was no one else in the world like Tangier, Fells thought—no one who radiated the same kind of happiness—of quiet poise. To him she represented something for which he had been looking most of his life—a woman who was experienced, beautiful, good.

She got up and came towards him, her hand held out.

"How are you, Hubert? Sit down and help yourself to a cigarette." She went to the sideboard. "Believe it or not," she said, "I can give you a whisky and soda, which I think is what a man needs at this time of an evening."

Fells said: "Thanks." He did not want to talk; he was quite prepared to sit there and to be happy. Simultaneously, he realized that it was impossible for him to sit there and be happy. Something had to be done about Tangier, and in his life Fells had found that most of the things that *had* to be done were unpleasant things. It would be nice, he thought, if just occasionally—just for once—something *had* to be done that was a nice thing.

She came towards him with the glass in her hand. She said:

"You owe me an explanation. You haven't been to see me for a long time. You haven't even tried to get in touch with me on the telephone. Why?" She stood close to him, the glass of whisky and soda held out towards him, smiling.

He took the glass from her. He said: "Well . . . I've been busy. I've had a lot to do. It isn't because I haven't wanted to see you."

She sat down on the arm of a nearby chair. She said: "So you wanted to see me, Hubert? But you haven't tried. I believe that people always do the things they want to. Your explanation isn't good enough. You've been in London, haven't you?"

He said: "Yes, I've been in London."

She said: "Well, when you're in London you've got to see me. I insist. That's what my friends are for."

Fells drank some of the whisky and soda. He said:

"You know, Tangier, I've got to talk to you. I've *got* to. Perhaps I'm not being fair to you."

She said: "I wonder what you mean by that, and I wonder why you have to be so mysterious. Do you feel you don't know me well enough to talk to me?"

He shook his head. He said: "It isn't that. I feel I know you very well."

"That's just it," said Tangier placidly. "You do know me very well. I suppose we've met about half a dozen times altogether. Yet we feel we know each other well. That's because we're really and truly friends. But you're not satisfied with the situation. You feel you've got to tell me something?" She smiled. "Well, that means you've told me a lot already."

Fells said: "Really! What have I told you?"

She said: "You've got some idea that there's something I shouldn't like, haven't you? But you're much too nice to go on knowing me and not tell me about it. If that's so you'd better get it off your chest, because in any event it won't matter."

Fells said: "I wish I could believe that." He finished the whisky and soda, got up, carried the glass back to the sideboard. He turned and stood leaning against it, looking at her.

He said: "D'you remember when we first met? D'you remember how it was we met? I don't."

She said: "We met at a party. I saw you there and I made up my mind I wanted to know you. So I got my host to introduce us. Then we talked and we liked each other. That's all."

Fells said: "Yes."

There was a pause; then she said placidly: "Hubert, what's the matter?"

Fells said: "Well, here it comes. This is the end of it. When you telephoned me this afternoon I was very glad. I was glad to hear your voice. It does something to me. The sound of your voice and the sight of you brings me as near to happiness as I think I shall ever get. I'd be quite content with that," Fells went on, "but I can't even have that. I haven't the right."

Tangier said: "That's awful nonsense, Hubert. In any event, that *must* be nonsense."

He shook his head. "No, it isn't," he said. "It's the truth. You see, you don't know very much about me. If you did, you probably wouldn't want to know me."

She smiled mysteriously. She said: "Hubert, how do you know what I know or don't know about you? In fact, I know an awful lot about you. One has only to look at you to know practically all there is to know about you. You're a very nice man."

Fells said: "I'm glad you think so. But you're wrong; I'm not. Supposing I were to tell you—"

She laughed. She laughed very softly—a delightful musical laugh that interrupted Fells more effectively than any words could have done.

"Supposing you were to tell me that you'd had an awfully troublesome period in your life," said Tangier: "that some rather nasty woman or someone had got you into a jam that you couldn't very easily get out of; that as a result of all this business you were cashiered from the Army and sentenced to a term of imprisonment. Well . . . ?"

Fells said: "My God! How did you know?"

"I've known for quite a time," said Tangier. "Someone who saw you at that party evidently recognized you. They told me about you. I was very curious. I looked up the newspaper files. A little thought soon told me that you must be the same person."

Fells said: "I see. And you were prepared to go on knowing me."

"More than that," said Tangier. "I was prepared to go on liking you." She went on: "You know, whatever people may say or whatever people may think, I happen to know that you are *not* that type of man. There's an explanation for all this somewhere, one which doesn't matter—at least not so far as I'm concerned."

Fells said: "Of course this is quite wonderful—your knowing and not caring. But it still doesn't help."

"Doesn't it?" said Tangier. She put her hands behind her head and lay back in the chair looking at him provocatively. The cigarette held between her lips sent out a little spiral of smoke. Fells watched it. He was thinking: Isn't life amazing? One never knows what's waiting round the corner.

He said: "It still doesn't help. The world doesn't consist of just you and me, Tangier. There are lots of other people. They might not be half as forgiving—half as nice—in their minds as you are."

She said: "Candidly, Hubert, the rest of the world doesn't matter. Things are moving much too quickly these days for people to worry about other people's pasts, and I don't suppose that one in ten thousand people would even remember what you looked like in those days. Anyhow, it doesn't make any difference to me, and it mustn't make any difference to you."

He said: "It must make a difference to me. I'm not going to take advantage of your generosity. I had my fling and I've got to pay the price."

She said: "Honestly, Hubert, I don't think you've ever had a fling in your life, and in any event so far as I am concerned I'm not going to allow you to sacrifice yourself for some odd idea you have. There are some people who feel they must go on paying indefinitely. You're one of those people. But I don't see why you should. Even if *you* do, I don't see why you should make *me*."

Fells said: "I don't quite understand what you mean by that. I don't see how my life touches yours, Tangier. I'm not going to allow it to."

She laughed. She said: "It isn't a matter of what you're going to allow or what I'm going to allow. It's a question of facts, Hubert. You're in love with me, aren't you?"

He thought for a moment; then he said: "I don't know how you know that, but of course I am. I've always been in love with you. I always shall be."

"Precisely," said Tangier in a matter-of-fact tone. "Now let me tell *you* something. I'm very much in love with you. I have been since the first time I saw you, and whilst it may be very nice for you to want to immolate yourself on the altar of your own conscience, I don't see why I should be included in the process."

Fells said: "You're a most bewildering and amazing person, aren't you? Do you realize what I was cashiered for doing? Do you realize what I was sentenced to prison for?"

Tangier gave a deliberate little yawn. She said: "My dear man, I know all about it and I think nothing of it. All those things happened in quite a different world to the one that you and I are walking in to-day. In any event I've made up my mind that I'm not going to allow it to matter. In other words, I'm going to pursue you relentlessly until I get my way."

Fells laughed. He realized suddenly that it was the first time he'd heard himself laugh for years. He felt extraordinarily happy—excited. He said:

"Tangier, tell me, to what ends are you going to pursue me? What's at the back of that attractive head of yours?"

She said: "My dear Hubert, by fair means or foul I'm going to marry you—I hope. I believe you'd like to marry me and I think it would be a very good thing for both of us. Besides which," she said, "I'm thirty-seven years of age and may not get another chance." She laughed. She got up. She came close to him. She said softly:

"Are you going to turn me down, Hubert?"

Fells brought himself back to earth with a jerk. He said: "It's not as easy as you think, Tangier. Even if all the things you say are true, it still wouldn't be easy. Anyhow, not while this war's on."

She said: "I don't know about that. Everything is possible if one wants it enough." She moved away from him; picked up his glass. She said: "I'm going to give you another drink. You look as if you need it. Then I think you might take me to a movie and then we might come back here and eat. We won't talk about this any more to-day. We'll just put it in the back of our minds and brood over it. It's my business to find a way out of this situation—to find a way in which I'll get what I want. I'm going to do it. So it's no good your trying to put obstructions in my path. But we won't talk about it any more now, because talking doesn't do an awful lot of good sometimes. Do you see?"

Fells said: "I see."

She mixed the drink; came back to him with it. She put it on the sideboard beside him. She said:

"Well, do you feel happier about things?"

Fells said: "Yes. But then I always feel happy when I'm near you."

She made a little grimace. She said: "That's nothing. You wait a bit. Life's going to be quite amusing, and probably sooner than you think. Do you see?"

Fells said: "Yes . . . I see."

He stood looking at her.

CHAPTER 7
THE SPANNER IN THE WORKS

I

FODEN tilted back his chair. He was feeling vaguely amused and happy. He was certain that things were coming his way; that everything was going to be as he wanted it to be. For some reason which he could not quite understand, he felt an extraordinary sense of power. The atmosphere of the Club to which Zilla Stevenson had brought him was pleasing. It was a change after the sort of place he was used to. As a club it was neither distinguished nor pleasing to the eye, but there was at least some sort of atmosphere. The music made by the small band placed in one corner of the tiny dance floor was soft and not disagreeable. Life, thought Foden, could be a great deal worse.

He said: "I suppose you know a lot of places like this?"

She looked at him and nodded her head. She said: "Yes, I do. There's not very much to do in the evening and I get taken out a lot. I'm lucky I suppose."

Foden said: "I heard from Horace this morning. He was coming up to London to-day. He gave me an address and telephone number. I shall be seeing him to-morrow." He went on: "You know, it's difficult to realize that you're his sister."

Zilla tossed her head. "That's what a lot of people tell me," she said. "And sometimes I don't feel like his sister. Horace has been a fool all his life. He's quite content to go on doing the same job day after day—week after week. He's never tried to better himself. He doesn't want to get anywhere. He's always doing odd things—underhand things." Her voice was hard.

"Such as what?" queried Foden.

"This business about the twenty-five pounds," said Zilla—"sending me a wire trying to put the wind up me; making out that it was a matter of life or death. I bet it was!" She laughed sarcastically. "Probably a bookmaker's account," she said.

Foden grinned. He signalled to the aged waiter; ordered more drinks. He said:

"You don't know how right you are. It *was* a bookmaker's account. You evidently know Horace."

"I know Horace all right," said Zilla. "The trouble is he doesn't know me. He only *thinks* he does. Mind you, I'm his sister, and so I'm sorry when he gets into a jam, but it's usually his own fault."

Foden said: "You know, Zilla, there are some people who get into jams, and there are some people who don't—or if they do they know how to get out of them. You and I belong to the second class. We're the sort of people who always fall on our feet because we've got brains. Horace isn't. Horace is what is commonly known as a mug."

He lit a cigarette. He said expansively: "Anyway, I don't mind about Horace and I'm going to give him the twenty-five pounds to square things up with the bookmaker, because whatever *you* may think of him he's done me a very good turn."

She said: "Well, I'm glad he's done somebody a good turn. I suppose I'd be curious if I asked what it was."

Foden said: "Well, I've met you through him, haven't I?"

She said: "Yes, I suppose you have." She smiled at him suddenly. She said: "It's funny you being friends with a man like Horace. You're not his type, are you?"

Foden said: "No, I'm not. Perhaps that's why I like him. Maybe I feel a bit sorry for him."

Zilla thought to herself I bet you do. She looked at Foden out of the corner of her eyes. A very tough, attractive man, she thought, with a great deal of personality and brains—a man who knew what he wanted and would take the most direct way to get it—a man who would be dangerous where women were concerned.

She said pleasantly: "I think you're a card. I think you're rather nice, but I must say all this business is a bit mysterious, isn't it? Your wanting to meet me and Horace being so keen to fix up that we met, and getting my telephone number. I thought there was something in it for him."

She stubbed out her cigarette. "I suppose that's why you're giving him the twenty-five pounds?" she asked.

"That's right," said Foden. He put his elbows on the table. He said: "Look, Zilla—and you don't mind me calling you Zilla, do you—because I think you and I are going to be friends?"

She said quickly: "That's funny you saying that, because directly I saw you I had a sort of odd feeling about you. I felt I'd known you for quite a while. *I* felt we were going to be friends, and that *is* funny, because usually I don't go for men—not the ones I meet sort of casually."

Foden said: "Of course you don't. You don't have to. A woman who looks like you look, who wears her clothes like you do, doesn't have to go for any sort of man." He grinned at her. "You're a tough egg, Zilla," he said. "Under all that allure of yours you're as hard as nails. But you've got brains. Horace was right about you."

She said a little petulantly: "Oh, I see. So Horace has been talking about me, has he? That's very nice of him, I'm sure."

Foden said: "Don't worry about poor old Horace. He talked about you because I asked him about you. He mentioned you in the first place quite casually. He thinks a lot of you. But I asked him questions about you because I wanted to know the sort of person that you were."

"Oh, did you?" said Zilla. She looked at him archly. "May I ask what for?" she said.

Foden said: "Listen. In course of conversation with Horace it came out that you were pretty smart on one occasion; that you got some German agent wiped up; that you got five hundred pounds for it—"

She interrupted acidly: "It's very nice of Horace to go discussing my private affairs, I'm sure—"

Foden said: "Take it easy, Zilla. You listen to what I'm going to say."

She said: "All right, I'm listening." She picked up her glass of crème-de-menthe. She hated crème-de-menthe but she was drinking it because it was the sort of drink that the Zilla she was being at the moment *would* drink.

Foden said: "I was very interested because I've got some information—some very big information. I want to sell it, but I'm not going to be taken for a ride. You see, I've had some experience of trying to give information to the authorities, and it got me just nowhere. The stuff I wanted to give 'em, free gratis and for nothing, they didn't even want to listen to. So this time I'm going to sell it and I'm going to get my own terms."

Zilla said: "Well, that's talking, isn't it? You must have some pretty big stuff to sell."

"I *have* got some pretty big stuff to sell," said Foden. "I've been kicking about Morocco for years. I've spent nine months inside a Vichy internment camp. You'd be surprised at what I know, but I'm going to sell it, and—" he smiled at her—"I want you to help me."

She said: "Well, that's all very well. But I don't see how I can. What can I do that you can't?"

"Listen," said Foden, "Horace told me that when you gave that information about that agent you met in the train they sent for you and talked to you. Then they gave you five hundred pounds. Horace sort of suggested that you had a job working for these people—Intelligence people or something like that. He suggested that you might be secretary to somebody who mattered."

She said hesitantly: "Well . . . I suppose that's true in a way. I'm secretary to a man, and I suppose you'd consider him a pretty big shot, but I'm *only* a secretary. I don't know anything about his business. I don't know what he does." She laughed. "He doesn't talk to girls in the outer office," she said.

Foden said: "That doesn't matter. You could find out things if you wanted to. You could talk to him. You could tell him that you'd met somebody who'd got some pretty good information. You could see what his reaction was, couldn't you?"

Zilla said: "That all sounds very nice, but the first thing he'd say is what is it. You can take it from me they don't pay out money for nothing in this country, and there's one thing I do know—there are hundreds of hare-brained people rushing about thinking that they've got information about the Germans. I know that. We deal with a lot of the stuff in my office, and it even makes me laugh."

"That's all right," said Foden. "But my information is not like that. *My* information matters. But before I give it, I've got to have a lot of money."

Zilla said: "Well, you've got your nerve all right. Can I have a cigarette?"

Foden said: "Of course." He brought out his cigarettes; gave her one; lit it for her. She noticed that the hand that held the lighter was brown and strong and sinewy. She looked into his eyes through the flame of the lighter. She smiled.

"You're a one," she said. "You've not only got your nerve, but you've got something else too. I ought to tell you to go to hell, but as a matter of fact I rather like you."

Foden grinned. He said: "Strangely enough women usually do. They like me because they understand me; because I never try to make fools of them. Women have a lot more brains than men think."

She puffed out cigarette smoke; looked at him sideways.

"I bet you know a lot about women," she said. "And I bet you've known a lot of women and they've been a damn' sight kinder to you than they ought to have been. You remind me of a dance number I used to be fond of—'*He's Love 'Em and Leave 'Em Joe.*' You're like that. You're the type that takes what it wants or what's going and gets out while the going is good."

Foden smiled at her. He thought she knows something, this one. She's got brains all right, but underneath she's like the rest of 'em. But she'd be damned amusing. . . .

He said: "You were saying that you ought to tell me to go to hell?"

"That's what I ought to do," said Zilla.

"But you're not going to?" asked Foden.

She said: "No. I'd do anything I could to help you for two reasons—first of all because I rather like you, and secondly," she looked at him seriously—"possibly there might be something in it for me." She smiled—a delightful odd little smile.

Foden put his large brown hand over her small white one. He said: "Look, Zilla, don't you worry about that. There'd be something in it for you all right, and more than something, I promise you. Do you want some money badly?"

She nodded. "I want some money, and I want some money that looks like real money," she said. "I'm fed up with this country; I want to get out of it. I want to go to South Africa where there's warmth and sunshine—where it's not so damned miserable as it is here. I could get myself a good job in South Africa, but I want some money. When I do a thing I like to do it in style."

Foden said: "I know. I can tell that by your clothes." He paused for a moment; then he said: "You can take it from me that if we played this job the right way there'd be quite enough money for you to go to South Africa or anywhere else you wanted to."

She drew on her cigarette. She blew out the tobacco smoke through pursed lips. She said:

"That's what you think. But you don't know how tough these people are. Naturally they're tough. They've got to be. And they've always got you where they want you."

"Have they?" said Foden. "Why?"

Zilla laughed. "Work it out for yourself," she said. "You go along with your information and you've got to tell them what it is before they'll tell you what they're going to do about it. When they've got it they can make their own terms, can't they? And if you don't like it, you know what you can do. Besides which," she said, "there's another way they've always got you."

"Oh, is there?" said Foden. "And what's the other way?" He was thinking that Zilla was being *very* useful.

"They've always got you under one of the Defence of the Realm regulations," said Zilla—"withholding information. You'd be surprised at what they can do."

Foden said: "I see. Are you trying to tell me that this is hopeless?"

She shook her head. She said: "I'm not trying to tell you anything. I'm telling you that it's going to be a very hard job."

Foden said: "No, it isn't. You listen to me. You said just now that I'd have to give them the information first. Well, I wouldn't. I'll tell you why. The information I've got is rather peculiar. It's divided into four parts. Each part—if you understand me—is dependent on the part before it. All I have to do is to tell 'em part one. That tells 'em that I know parts two, three and four, and they don't know. All right. If they want to know they've got to pay."

She said: "I see. It's like that, is it?"

"That's right," said Foden, "it's like that. And another thing," he went on, "they're not going to bluff me with threats. You've got to realize, Zilla, that on two separate occasions, years ago, I went to the British authorities in Morocco and gave them information for nothing. They said thank you very much and showed me the door. They did nothing about it. On both those occasions I was proved to be a hundred per cent right. Well, now the stuff I've got is dynamite and they're going to listen. Do you know *why* they're going to listen?"

Zilla said: "No. You tell me why they're going to listen."

Foden said: "Because they've got to. It's a matter of life or death for them. They'll know that."

She said: "I see. You're pretty sure of yourself, aren't you?"

Foden said: "I'm dead sure of myself. All I want is to be put next to somebody who matters. But it must be somebody's who's important. I know these junior officials. If you tell them the whole story and it looks as if it matters they mess you about while they see how they can make it work to their advantage and if you don't tell them anything much they turn you down. You give me fifteen minutes with somebody who matters—some man who's big enough to know what I'm talking about, and he's going to pay me exactly what I want, and he's going to like doing it."

Zilla said: "Well . . . if it's like that . . ."

Foden said: "So you've got an idea?"

She said: "Yes. My own boss is a pretty big shot in his way, but he's tough and he's a hard nut. He'd have to be convinced."

Foden said: "It won't take me long to convince him."

There was silence. Zilla, her chin resting on one hand, her elbow on the table-top, looked at the wall on the other side of the Club. She appeared to be thinking deeply. After a while she said:

"What do you think you're going to get for this information?"

Foden said: "I don't think—I know. I want five thousand pounds. I want to start a business in Morocco. If I had five thousand pounds I could start it. So that's the price. And I'm going to get it."

"I see," said Zilla. "And what do I get?"

He said: "You put me next to the right man and you get five hundred."

She thought for a moment; then she said: "All right. It's a deal. But there's only one way that this can be done."

Foden said: "Yes? What's the way?"

She said: "What you'll have to do is to tell me enough about this thing to prove to my boss that you've got some real information. You'll have to tell me that first part you spoke about. All right. Then I'll make an opportunity of speaking to him and I'll tell him that through Horace I've met a man who's told me so-and-so. Well, that ought to interest him, oughtn't it?"

Foden said: "Don't worry. It'll interest him all right. Directly you tell him the little bit I'm going to tell you, he'll want to ring the fire alarm he'll be so excited."

"All right," said Zilla. "Well, then the next thing is he'll want to see you, won't he? He'll want to ask you all sorts of questions about yourself. He'll want to know who and when and what you are."

"Don't you worry about that," said Foden. "He can ask what he likes, but before I do any more talking I want the money."

Zilla said: "Yes?" She looked at him—her red lips parted in a smile that showed her brilliant, regular teeth. She said: "The joke is I believe you're going to get it." She laughed. "Do you know," she said, "I believe I'm going to get that trip to South Africa."

Foden said: "I know you are. Only perhaps you'll change your mind about South Africa."

She said: "What do you mean by that?"

He said: "You never know, you might want to go to Morocco."
He laughed at her.

Zilla said: "You've got your nerve, haven't you? You hate yourself!" Her smile disappeared. She said: "We've got to talk this over. We've got to be serious about this. When are you going to tell me this first part—the stuff I ought to know—the stuff I'm going to pass on to him?"

Foden said: "I'll meet you any time you want. I'm at your service."

Zilla said: "Well, I'll see what things look like to-morrow. I've got an idea he's going to be in town for two or three days. You'd better ring me up to-morrow evening—somewhere about nine o'clock. If he's going to be in town the day after, you'd better let me know what that information is and I'll talk to him."

Foden said: "That's all right. But I don't think I'd better telephone you. I wouldn't like to talk about this stuff over the telephone. I'd better come and see you."

"All right," said Zilla. "You come and see me to-morrow night at nine o'clock. I'll be in by then."

Foden said: "I'll be there." He looked into her eyes. He said coolly: "I'd like to see you on your own. You've got something, Zilla."

She said: "Look, this is business, isn't it, and I don't believe in mixing business with pleasure."

Foden said: "Don't you?" He squeezed her hand. "You will, my dear, before you're through, believe me."

Zilla said nothing. She left her hand in his.

Foden signalled the waiter. He ordered some more drinks.

Zilla said: "I'll have to be getting along soon. I've got to be at the office early to-morrow."

"All right," said Foden. "When we've had our drinks we'll go. But I don't think we're going to do any good by wasting any time. I don't see why we should wait till to-morrow."

She looked at him. She said: "I don't get you."

Foden smiled at her. She felt the pressure of his fingers on her hand. He said:

"The best thing is for me to talk to you to-night. When we leave here. . . . I'll take you back to your place and put you wise to the stuff you ought to know. Then you can see your boss to-morrow and talk to him. Then you can fix things up right away. I don't believe in wasting time."

She said: "So it seems." She was thinking this is going to be tough. This man is going to want handling.

Foden squeezed her hand again. He said: "That's quite a good idea, isn't it?"

"You wouldn't have anything else on your mind, would you?" asked Zilla. She looked at him out of the corner of her eye. "You wouldn't think that I was as easy to make as all that! But perhaps you're not as intelligent as I thought you were."

Foden laughed. He said: "Feeling a little bit frightened of the big bad wolf?"

"It would take more than you to frighten me," said Zilla. "But if you want to do that we'll do it. You can come back with me and have some coffee and give me this information. Then I'll get to work to-morrow. I'll see the chief about it, and after that it's up to you. But don't think that you can get away with any funny business round at my flat." She laughed. "I've got medals for *ju jitsu*," she said.

He smiled at her.

"Don't worry, honey," he said softly. "I'll behave. You'll be surprised."

Zilla laughed. "That's what they all say," she said softly. She moved a little closer to him.

II

Foden came out of the narrow turning and stood on the corner, looking down Lower Regent Street towards Pall Mall. He leaned up against the wall. After a little while he crossed the road; walked up towards Jermyn Street, looking about him. He was looking for a telephone box.

He turned into Jermyn Street. Fifty yards down, in the courtway that leads up to Piccadilly, he found a phone box. He went inside, fumbled in his pocket for two pennies. On his forehead were three or four little beads of sweat. He put the pennies on the edge of the box; brought out a notebook from his pocket; looked up the number; put the pennies in the box. As he did so the dial of his wrist-watch showed him that it was ten-thirty.

He waited, listening to the ringing noise at the other end. After a minute Greeley's voice said: "Hello."

Foden said: "Is that you, Horace? This is Foden." His voice was flat. It sounded peculiar even to himself.

Greeley said: "I see. Well, how are you? What's the matter?"

Foden said: "It's not so good, Horace. You'd better prepare yourself for a shock."

Greeley said: "All right. I'm prepared for it. What's happened?"

Foden said: "Zilla's shot herself."

Greeley said: "What the hell do you mean?"

Foden said impatiently: "I'm telling you what I mean. I had a date with her this evening, and she's shot herself. God knows why! I don't."

Greeley said: "I see." There was a pause; then he went on: "All right. So Zilla's shot herself. Where is she—round at the flat?"

"Yes," said Foden. "I've just left there. I came to the nearest call box and telephoned you. I didn't know what the hell to do."

Greeley said: "Look, let's get this straight. Take it easy Don't get excited. There's nothing to get excited about. Did you find her like that when you got there?"

Foden's voice was quiet now. He said: "I'm not getting excited. I'm just trying to tell you what happened. I had a date with Zilla to-night to talk about that business. Well, everything was all right. We met at a place we'd arranged on the telephone and had dinner. Then she took me along to a club where we had a few drinks. She was absolutely O.K. Right on the top of her form. Laughing and cheery and all that. Then we got down to talking business and she said she'd have a word with her boss to-morrow. Then we went back to her place so that I could give her an outline of what I'd got; so that he would know I wasn't talking nonsense. Have you got that?"

"I've got it," said Greeley.

"All right," Foden went on. "Well . . . we left the Club and went to her flat. When we got there I asked her for a cigarette—I hadn't any—and when she looked she found that she hadn't any either. I said I'd go and get some if she could tell me where. She told me—a little tea shop near Panton Street that's open up till midnight. She told me to leave the door on the latch so that I needn't ring when I came back. Have you got all that?"

"I've got it," said Greeley.

"I went and got the cigarettes," said Foden, "and I went back. I suppose I was away about twelve minutes—certainly not more than fourteen or fifteen minutes. I went inside. Well . . . as you probably know, there's a hallway to the flat and the sitting-room's on the other side. I went in. Zilla was lying on the hearthrug in front of the electric fire. She was dead. She'd got a pistol in her hand—an automatic. There was blood all over the place. God knows what had happened—I don't. I've never been so near having the jitters in my life."

Greeley said: "I see. Well, it's no good having the jitters, is it? When you came away did you close the door? Did you put the latch up so that it locked?"

"Yes," said Foden. "When I was coming out of the flat I pulled the catch down so that the door would lock. I thought it would be the sensible thing to do. I wanted to get some time to think; to talk to somebody about it. This isn't so good."

Greeley said quietly: "You're telling me!"

Foden said: "What could have made her do a thing like that?"

Greeley said casually: "What's the good of asking me? Things like that happen. Perhaps she didn't commit suicide. *Somebody* may have seen you talking to Zilla at that club to-night. Somebody might know that you two had something big on. See what I mean? Someone's trying to throw a spanner in the works, and they've started off by getting her."

"I see," said Foden. "The idea being that now they've got her they might easily get me. You think there's somebody who thinks I know too much?"

"Why not?" said Greeley. "Things like that happen, don't they? There's a war on."

Foden was getting his nerve back. He said: "Well, where do I go from here? What do I do? I'm a stranger round here, you know. Do I go to the police or what?"

Greeley said: "No. You don't want to do a thing like that. This is the sort of thing they might want kept quiet. Listen, you take a tip from me and you keep under cover. Maybe somebody thought it worth while to get Zilla because they connected her with you. Well, you never know your luck. They might try and get you. The best thing for you to do is to go home and keep your head shut. Stay under cover. I'll get in touch with you. Are you staying at the place you said?"

"Yes," said Foden. "In Victoria."

"All right," said Greeley. "You go home and smoke cigarettes. If I were you I wouldn't go out. I'll probably come and see you sometime to-morrow. I'd better look after this thing the best I can."

Foden asked: "What are you going to do?"

Greeley said: "What the hell can I do? If I go to the police I might be doing the wrong thing. As I said before maybe this is the sort of thing they don't want a noise about. All I can do is to go and see the guy that Zilla was working for. I know where the office is. I'll have to get in touch with him somehow. I'll have to tell him about it. I'm going to pass the buck to him."

Foden said: "This isn't so good, is it? It spoils everything. The devil of it is that Zilla and I practically had everything arranged. She'd agreed to go into this thing with me. She was going to talk to her boss. I was going to meet him."

"That's all very well," said Greeley. "But that's all past, isn't it? What we got to think about is the future and what's to be done. Well . . ." He sighed. "Poor old Zilla. She always used to laugh at me. She thought I was a bit of a mug. Anyway, I'm still alive and that's more than she is."

Foden said: "Look, don't you think you're getting the wrong sort of idea here?"

Greeley said: "How?"

"This idea about somebody having killed Zilla. I tell you she killed herself. She was lying there with a gun in her hand. It was sticking out a foot she'd killed herself. I know when somebody's been shot and when they've done it themselves. I've seen dead people before, you know."

Greeley said: "Yes. That's funny, isn't it? What was she like during the evening? How did she behave?"

Foden said: "She was a hundred per cent. We had a good evening. She took me to a club. We had some drinks. We were getting on like a house on fire. We talked this thing over. She told me she'd want some money out of it; that she wanted to go to South Africa. I tell you she was as keen as I was."

Greeley said: "That's funny, isn't it—very funny? Well . . . what's the good of our talking about it like this? It's not going to get us any place. You do what I told you. You stick around until I see you to-morrow. Then I'll tell you what to do."

Foden said: "All right, Horace. I'll do what you say. You're a great guy. I'm sorry. I can't tell you how sorry I am."

"Well," said Greeley. "I always believe that it's no good crying over spilt milk. She was my sister of course, but then we were never very pally. You know, I always thought there was something a bit odd and funny about Zilla. I always had an idea she was playing around with some strange guys. Though what the hell she wants to shoot herself for I don't know. Still, what do *I* know? *I* don't know anything about her. She might even have had a good reason for doing that. Something might have happened to-night while you were getting the cigarettes. You never know."

Foden said: "No. That's true enough."

Greeley said: "Well, good-night. Stick around. I'll see you to-morrow, pal."

Foden said: "All right."

He hung up the receiver. He came out of the call box into Jermyn Street. He began to walk towards St. James Street on his way to Victoria.

Greeley put the receiver back on its hook. He stood for a minute looking at the telephone. Then he felt in his pocket for a cigarette. He lit it. He stood in front of the fire, his hands in his trouser pockets, the cigarette stuck to the left-hand corner of his mouth, looking at the carpet. He stood there for a long time, his brain revolving round a dozen ideas—a dozen implications. He said to himself: Well, what do you know about that? He was curious—very curious. He was more curious than perturbed. He had been attracted to Zilla. He'd fallen for her in a big way. If she'd gone on living, one day, in some fortunate circumstances, he might have tried to do something about it. But she was gone—finished. That was the end of that episode.

Greeley, whose mind was tough and hard, realized without making any ado about it that it was no good thinking of Zilla in terms of the flesh. There were other and more important things connected with her that must be done. He switched his mind on to Foden. What the hell, thought Greeley. Here was a fine set-up for Foden. In certain circumstances, he was sorry for Foden—those circumstances being that what Foden had told him had happened was the truth. It's pretty tough, thought Greeley, to have a date with a girl like Zilla; to think you're going to do a nice little bit of business and have a little flirtation in the process; to go out and when you get back to find she's dead. You find she's lying on the hearthrug not looking at all pretty. If that had happened he was sorry for Foden.

And supposing it had not happened—supposing there was some other explanation. He shrugged his shoulders. Then he went to the telephone, dialled a number.

After a minute the girl in Quayle's office—the one who sent Mrs. Greeley the pay envelope—said: "Hello."

Greeley said: "Hello, this is Greeley. Is Mr. Quayle in?"

She said: "Yes. Shall I put you through on this line or do you want a private line? He's in his flat."

"You give me a private line," said Greeley, "and see that it's cut out."

"Very well, Mr. Greeley," she said.

Greeley waited. There was a click. A few seconds afterwards Quayle's voice said: "Yes?"

Greeley said: "Hello, this isn't very good, I'm afraid."

Quayle said: "No? How bad is it?"

Greeley said: "Zilla Stevenson. Foden's been through to me from a call box. He had a date with Zilla to-night at her flat. He went out to get some cigarettes. He says he was only gone about fourteen or fifteen minutes and when he got back he found things weren't so good. He found that they were rather bad."

"I see," said Quayle.

"He said they were as bad as they could be," Greeley went on. "He thinks she did it herself."

Quayle asked: "What happened to Foden?" His voice was almost disinterested.

Greeley said: "I've told him to lie low. He's gone home. I said that the best thing I could do was to try to get into touch with Zilla's boss—the man she was secretary to. I said I knew where the office was and I might be able to contact him."

Quayle asked: "Had Foden any suggestions to make?"

"Only one," said Greeley. "He got an idea that perhaps he ought to go to the police. I killed that. I said no. I said that possibly somebody had been out to get Zilla; that it might be a thing which ought not to be handled openly at the moment. He believed that."

Quayle said: "I see."

Greeley went on: "I think there's the hell of a mess there—something that ought to be cleaned up."

Quayle said: "I see. Did Foden lock the door when he came out?"

"That's what he says," said Greeley.

There was a pause; then Quayle said: "Listen, you get round there. See that you're able to fix the door when you get there. I think there's been a case of illness in those flats. You get it?"

"I get it," said Greeley. "You mean like we did that thing at Lee?"

"That's right," said Quayle. "Just like we did that thing. There'll be an ambulance and a nursing sister there in about half an hour. That ought to give you time to do what you want to do, oughtn't it?"

"That'd be about right," said Greeley.

"All right," said Quayle. "It's ten-fifty now. The ambulance will be round there at eleven-fifteen. There's no need to make any secret about it—just a very bad case of illness. The nursing sister will know what it is, and possibly a doctor will come round too."

"All right," said Greeley. "I've got it." He hung up the receiver. His cigarette had gone out. He removed it from his lip; lit another one.

He went to the dilapidated wardrobe and took out his coat. He stood in front of the small mirror; put on his coat, pulling down his shirt sleeves. He said to himself: Jeez! Life is a hell of a game! He smiled sadly at himself in the mirror; then he picked up his cap and went out.

III

At eleven o'clock the blonde girl who worked in Quayle's office came to see Fells. When the landlady let her in, she asked for him and waited in the hallway. When Fells came down the stairs she said:

"Good evening. I've got a message for you."

She held out the envelope towards Fells. The envelope was a bright pink. It told Fells a lot. Whenever Quayle sent a message in a pink envelope it meant that for reasons best known to himself he could not use a telephone and that the situation was dynamite.

Fells took the envelope. He asked: "Is there any answer?" He noticed vaguely that the blonde girl was very good-looking.

She said: "No. There's no answer. Good-night." She opened the door and went out.

Fells went up to his room. He slit open the envelope. The message was in code. Fells thought to himself: What a careful fellow Quayle is. He never takes a chance and he's quite right. Even if the blonde girl had lost the message en route or if something had happened to her, the contents of the pink envelope would not have meant anything to anyone who found it.

Fells took the sheet of quarto paper under the lamp and decoded the message, writing in the blank space under the typing. It read:

"A woman operative 'Z' has had an accident. Her address is No. 3 Thurles Court—just off Millard Street, Lower Regent Street. There is no caretaker in the house and her flat is on the first floor. There is no other flat on that floor. On receipt of this message go to Ferrins Garage, Great Smith Street, and ask for Vane. He will know who you are. He will have an ambulance, a nursing sister and an attendant's uniform for you. Vane will drive the ambulance. Both he and the nursing sister work for me. If by any chance there should be any query you are an ambulance attendant by the name of Green removing a special case for observation at the Middlesex Hospital. When you have collected the patient from the flat, return with the ambulance to the garage. Vane and the nursing sister will look after what has to be done. Then go back to your own place and await a call from me any time during the next two or three days."

Fells read the instructions through twice; then he snapped on his lighter; burned the sheet of paper and the envelope. He looked at his watch; lit a cigarette.

He wondered who the woman operative "Z" was. He wondered what had happened to her. He had a pretty good idea. It was not the first time during the last three years that Fells had picked up an ambulance, worn an attendant's uniform and removed a "patient." It had happened on three previous occasions and usually the story was the same. Somebody had "caught up" with the operative. And that was all. Fells did not know what happened to the bodies. He had never been curious about that. He had contented himself with wondering if one day or one night someone else would accompany an ambulance to pick *him* up.

Fells put on his hat and went out. It was turning cold. He walked swiftly down Victoria Street towards Great Smith Street. The garage was in a narrow turning off the main street. Fells found a bell; rang it. A middle-aged man with grey hair opened the door. He said:

"Good evening. Are you Fells?"

Fells nodded.

The man said: "My name's Vane. Come in."

Fells went into the garage. It was quite a big place. In the middle of the floor was a conventional County Council ambulance with the engine running. Fells noticed that Vane was wearing a driver's uniform.

Vane said: "There's a uniform coat and cap inside the ambulance. You'd better put them on and sit up with me in front."

Fells went back to the back of the ambulance and opened the door. The inside of the ambulance was lighted, and seated on one side on a stretcher rack was a pleasant looking woman of about forty. She wore a nursing sister's uniform.

She said: "Good evening."

Fells said: "Good evening."

Vane said: "Well, let's get going."

He went to the front of the garage and began to turn the wheel that opened the folding doors. Fells got up into the seat on the cab. When Vane had opened the doors he came back; got into the driver's seat. He drove slowly out of the garage.

Greeley, with a quick look up and down the street, turned into Thurles Court. He slipped through the black-out curtains and stood in the darkened hallway listening. He could hear nothing. There was a blued-out electric globe down the passage and by its light he could see the lift and the staircase.

Greeley went up the dark curving stairs. At the top of the short flight he flicked on his electric torch. The passageway ran left and right at the top of the staircase, but he could see the door down the right-hand branch. He moved towards it.

He tried the door. It was locked. He put his hand in his trouser pocket and produced a small bunch of keys. After a little while he opened the door. He stepped into the hallway, found the electric light switch, snapped it on. He closed the entrance door behind him. He thought it was odd that he should find the flat in darkness. He wondered why Foden had taken the trouble to turn the light off before he left.

Greeley put his torch in his jacket pocket. On the other side of the hall was a door, half open. He walked across the hallway; put his hand round the edge of the door, switched on the light. He found himself in a sitting-room.

It was a nice room. The furniture was good and carefully selected. There were pretty chintz curtains over the black-out curtains. The ornaments were in good taste. A nice room, thought Greeley—the sort of room that Zilla would have liked.

He looked at her. She was lying on the thick rug in front of the fireplace in which the electric fire, turned low, was still burning. As Foden had said she was not at all a pretty sight.

Greeley stood, relaxed, his cap over one eye, his hands hanging straight down by his sides, looking at what remained of Zilla. One leg was a little drawn up and Greeley noticed the superb line of the calf and ankle—the neatness of the shoe. Zilla was lying on her right side, her left arm and hand hanging a little grotesquely behind her, the white palm and fingers spread in an almost supplicating gesture. The soft lace frill protruding beneath the cuff of her jacket hung in graceful folds over the long white fingers with their tinted finger-nails. The top part of her right arm was beneath her, but the forearm protruded towards the fire and, clasped in the fingers of it, was an automatic pistol. Greeley thought it would be a .35 or .38 calibre. He looked at the hand that held the pistol carefully. Its position and the grip on the butt of the gun—with the first finger still curled round the trigger—was absolutely natural.

He thought to himself nobody stuck that gun in her hand. She was holding the gun all right. It looked as if Foden was telling the truth. It looked as if she had shot herself.

He wondered why the hell she should have wanted to do that. Almost simultaneously he thought why should she *not* have wanted to do that? What did he know about her? There might have been all sorts of circumstances, tragedies, dramas, in the life of Zilla Stevenson of which he and possibly all the other people who knew her as superficially as he did were unaware.

Greeley thought it was a case of suicide all right. Quite obviously the barrel of the pistol had been held next the head. It must have been because very little of Zilla Stevenson's beautiful face and head remained. Greeley, who had seen all sorts of unpleasant sights, thought that there was something doubly unpleasant about violent death when it happened to a woman. A woman, he thought, was a beautiful thing. She should not meet her end quickly, suddenly, and brutally like this.

He looked at his wrist-watch. Soon the ambulance would be here. There was a lot to be done. Greeley took off his coat and cap. He began to think about the conversation he had had with Zilla on the street corner at the port that night. It had seemed a nice night to him. It had held some sort of promise for him. Greeley, who was inclined to take life as it came, had almost believed after that conversation that there might be a suggestion of romance for him at some time in the future. Well, that was all over. But he would have liked to have known why it was necessary for this to have happened. He would have liked to have known the story.

On the other side of the fireplace, almost in the corner of the room, was a door. Greeley walked round the body, opened the door, looked in. It was a bedroom. The electric light was switched on and Quayle was standing in front of the low dressing-table with its big triple mirrors looking at something. His soft hat was on his head. He was wearing rubber gloves. He seemed very interested.

He said to Greeley: "Come here, Greeley. Does that mean anything to you?"

Greeley took the picture that Quayle held towards him. It was the photograph that Foden had showed him at the port—the photograph of the group including Foden beneath the palm trees in Morocco. He said:

"I've seen this before. Foden showed it to me. He's in the photograph. It was taken when he was in some Vichy internment camp in Morocco. I wonder how it got here."

Quayle shrugged his shoulders. He said: "I found it behind the dressing-table."

Greeley said: "That's damned funny, isn't it? Does it make any sense to you?"

Quayle did not reply. He put out his hand and took the picture from Greeley. He put it into the breast pocket of his coat. He said:

"We'd better get busy." He turned towards the bed. Greeley saw that on the quilted pink coverlet of the bed was a large attaché case that was open. Inside were broad bandages, cotton wool, pads.

Quayle said: "We'll have a couple of blankets off the bed. We've got to make it look like a case of sickness. Fells will be here in a few minutes with the ambulance. They'll bring the stretcher up. We've got to work fast."

Greeley said: "Yes." He thought of Zilla lying on the rug in the other room. He said: "Well, it's going to be a nice job, isn't it?"

Quayle said: "Exactly. So the sooner it's done the sooner we shan't have to think about it."

He picked up the attaché case. They went into the sitting-room.

CHAPTER 8
CONVERSATION OF LOVE

I

TANGIER finished writing a letter. She put the pen into its tray; sat looking at it vaguely for a few seconds. Then she got up. She went to the telephone on the far side of the room; took the transmitter off the hook; stood hesitating for a moment; put it back again. She went to the sideboard, took a cigarette from the silver box, lit it. She began to walk up and down the room. She was telling herself that she was a fool; that there are times when all rules must be broken; that there were certain natural laws that must be carried out; that the most important natural law was that of love. It was ordained in the beginning, she thought, that men and women should love one another; that nothing should stop that process.

She went back to the telephone, but this time she did not hesitate. She dialled the number and waited. The voice of the blonde girl in Quayle's office came to her ears.

Tangier said: "Hello. Is Mr. Quayle there? If he is I want to speak to him. This is Miss Lawless."

The blonde girl said: "Hello, Miss Lawless. It's nice hearing your voice again. It must be a year since I've spoken to you. Hold on, I'll put you through."

There was a pause; then Quayle's voice said: "Hello, Tangier. Fancy you ringing up. You haven't rung up to tell me that you want to do some more work, have you?" His voice was pleasant.

Tangier said: "No, I haven't. But tell me, Peter, suppose I did want to work for you again, would there be a job for me?"

Quayle said: "No, there wouldn't. You're the one person who is *not* going to work for me. What is it you want, Tangier?"

She asked: "Are you terribly busy?"

Quayle said: "Yes, I've got a lot on, but I'm not too busy to talk to you."

Tangier said: "Well, I want you to give me lunch, Peter. I want to talk to you, and I want to talk to you to-day."

He said: "I see. All this sounds very serious." His voice was humorous.

She said: "It *is* serious for me."

"If it's serious for you," said Quayle, "then I must make my time-table fit. Suppose you meet me at the Ritz at one o'clock? How would that do?"

"That would be marvellous," said Tangier.

Quayle put down the receiver. He got up and began to walk up and down the room. He walked restlessly, with a certain impatience—like a tiger in a cage.

After a little while he walked through the kitchen of the flat into the office on the other side. He said to the blonde girl:

"I shall be out from one till half-past two. This afternoon I want to talk to Greeley. Get him. He'd better see me at the office in Lyle Street at four o'clock. Then get on to Fells. I want to see him too. I want to see him to-morrow—sometime in the evening—about seven I should think. He'd better come here. Have you got all that?"

She said: "I've got it, Mr. Quayle."

He stopped at the doorway. He said over his shoulder: "You wouldn't make a mistake, would you?"

She said acidly: "Mr. Quayle. Have you ever known me to make a mistake?"

He grinned at her. He said: "No, I never have. But I live in hopes!"

Quayle was waiting in the foyer of the Ritz when Tangier came. He thought she looked quite delightful; that her taste in clothes was on a par with her fastidious mind. She was wearing a frock of navy blue angora wool, and over it a three-quarter coat of white clipped lamb lined with the same material as the frock; beige silk stockings, navy-blue glacé kid court shoes and a navy-blue felt hat. As she came towards him Quayle thought that she was worried about something.

He wondered what it could be. She was not the sort of person who worried unnecessarily. Her mind was too well-balanced. Tangier would face the most unpleasant set of circumstances with equanimity; would probably succeed in putting everything to rights in her own quiet, decisive, almost placid manner before the situation got out of hand. Unless of course it was a situation that could not be dealt with by normal methods; unless it was a situation of somebody else's making—something that she could not handle by herself.

He shook hands with her. He said: "You look wonderful, Tangier. But then you always did—just as if you'd stepped out of a bandbox. You present to the parched male the rarefied atmosphere of complete and utter femininity."

Tangier laughed. She said: "Do I really? Well, I think that's marvellous. Incidentally, I don't think I've ever heard you say anything quite so nice to me before."

"I have a lot of time for saying nice things to women, haven't I?" asked Quayle sarcastically. "But one of these days, when this war's all over, when I can relax, I'm going to think up a lot of nice things to say to you. Supposing I told you that I was very fond of you, Tangier; that I've an idea in my head that I've always been rather fond of you, but that I've never had time to tell you, and in any event if I'd had the time it wouldn't be any good telling you a thing like that in these days."

She said quickly: "You're not trying to make love to me by any chance, Peter, are you?"

He said: "I don't know. When I saw you come in just now I felt quite odd for a moment—almost human."

She said: "I'm glad about that."

They went into the restaurant. When they had finished their luncheon and the waiter had brought the coffee, Quayle asked:

"Why did you say before lunch that you were glad that I was feeling human?"

Tangier looked at him. Her eyes were large and very blue. They were very lovely, sincere eyes, he thought.

She said: "I'm awfully keen on you being human to-day, Peter— not that I think that you aren't human. You are, basically. But I don't think you get very much chance of being human—not with a job like you've got."

Quayle said: "What do you know about my job?"

"Not very much," said Tangier. "But I can guess."

Quayle smiled. He said: "Well, anyway, we didn't come here to talk about my job. We came here to enjoy each other's company for a little while, I hope."

She said: "Peter, I'd better be quite straight with you from the start. I came here to talk about your job—well, about something that's part of your job."

Quayle's expression altered. It was as if his face had suddenly frozen a little.

He said: "Yes? Go on, Tangier."

She said: "I rang you up to-day because I want to talk to you about Hubert Fells."

Quayle said: "I see. What do you want to say about Fells?"

"Only this," she said. "He and I are in love with each other."

Quayle said: "My God! That's not so good, is it?"

"Why not?" asked Tangier. "Is there anything wrong with it?"

"Nothing at all," said Quayle, "providing there are possibilities of something happening as a result of your being in love with each other—which possibilities at the moment seem very remote."

She said: "Does that matter? It doesn't affect the fact."

Quayle said: "No, it doesn't affect the fact. Tell me something, Tangier, how much have you seen of Fells?"

"Very little," she said. "You remember that a long time ago you asked me to get him asked to a cocktail party? You wanted me to have a look at him. You wanted me to keep an eye on him. You remember you thought he was going through rather a bad time. He was doing important work. You wanted my opinion as to whether he could be trusted to do even more important work."

"That's right," said Quayle. "I wanted to know how much he was drinking, how he was behaving, who his friends were. I wanted to know all about him."

Tangier nodded. "You were doing one of your periodical checks," she said. She smiled at him. "It must be terrible to be you, Peter; to have to check on the people who are working for you from time to time just to see they are not slipping, just to see their nerve is still holding."

Quayle said: "I only check on *some* of my people. Most of them I don't have to. But Fells was a unique case. Anyhow—" he shrugged his shoulders. "Fells is all right. He's thoroughly reliable, thoroughly trustworthy. I know that now. I was worried because—well, he's rather a strange and lonely sort of man."

She said: "I know. He hasn't got *anything*, you see, Peter."

"You're quite wrong," said Quayle cheerfully. "He's got his job with me, and that's important. Fells is just as much a soldier as if he were fighting in the front line in the Western desert." He leaned a little nearer towards her. "Have you ever thought," he went on, "about some of the other people who are working for me? Some of the people who aren't lucky enough to be working on this side of the Channel—the people who are working in France, and even in Germany. What about *them*? They're having a hell of a time, aren't they? One slip-up and—"

He looked at the table-cloth. "Have you ever wondered what happens to one of my people who get taken by the enemy abroad?"

She said: "No, I never have. I don't think I want to."

Quayle said: "You're quite right not to want to. Up to the moment Fells has been lucky. In point of fact he's been more than lucky."

Tangier said: "I know. That's true, but as you have said this war isn't going on for ever, Peter. One day it's going to be over. One day Hubert is going to be free."

Quayle took his cigarette case from his pocket. He gave her a cigarette; took one himself; lit them both. His movements were deliberate.

She said: "Something not very nice is coming in a minute." Quayle smiled. He asked: "Why do you say that?"

"Whenever you are slow and deliberate in your movements as you were just now about giving me a cigarette," said Tangier, "I know you're giving yourself time to think."

Quayle said: "Well, my dear, I don't have to give myself a lot of time to think about what I'm going to say to you now, and because it's rather important you might listen to it carefully. I've always trusted you more than any other woman I've known. You know more about me and my work than any other person. You've done jobs for me—usually keeping an eye on operatives—seeing how they're shaping. And you came across Fells in that process. Well, I'll be quite candid with you. I'm jealous of Fells. I'm jealous of him because you're in love with him."

Tangier said: "I never thought—"

"Quite," said Quayle. "You never thought. You never thought that I might possibly be rather keen on you myself. Well, that's all right. Somehow I've the idea that I shall never have very much time to indulge in the softer sides of life. I've got an idea that I'll have my nose to the grindstone until I drop. But I wish to God you could have fallen for somebody else except Fells."

Tangier's eyes were wide. She said: "Why? What is there strange in my falling in love with a man like Hubert Fells? He's a most attractive man. He's a first-class person. He just made a silly mistake once—a mistake which you, for your own ends, managed to turn into something that looked a great deal worse than it actually was." She put her hand on his.

"Don't mistake me, Peter," she said. "You've been awfully kind to Hubert. Your action in handling things the way you did was a good one. It was the only possible thing to do. As a result of it, as you say, he's had a job. He's retained his self-respect. Even if he hasn't been able to follow his own profession as a soldier, he's been able to fight the enemy in a different way and to take lots of risks in doing it. I'm always going to be glad that you were able to give him a chance. But when this war's over there's no reason why he shouldn't live the life of an ordinary man."

Quayle drew on his cigarette. He said: "The trouble with you women is you don't know anything about men. You only think you do. I suppose you've told Fells that you're keen on him?"

Tangier nodded. She said: "Yes, I've told him."

"All right," said Quayle. "Well, he's probably rather stunned with the shock. He was probably delighted, like an over-grown schoolboy who suddenly realizes that something he thought was entirely out of his reach is not so very far away after all. That's all right. But he hasn't had a chance to think."

"And what is, going to happen when he has had a chance to think?" she asked.

Quayle said: "Fells is an intelligent, sensible man. He's going to realize that there are still quite a lot of people knocking about who know him, and anyway, even if there were only one or two people who knew him and knew his story, he's going to think it would be a pretty low-down trick to marry you. He knows people would talk. He knows it would come to your ears. He can guess what the results would be. It's all very well for Fells to be a person with no background and no friends, but even he will realize that it wouldn't be very nice for you as his wife. You'll find he's going to back out. In any event," said Quayle grimly, "he's *got* to back out."

Tangier said: "I don't like the way you said that, Peter. Why has he *got* to back out?"

Quayle said: "I think you forget, Tangier, that Fells is working for me."

She said: "I don't forget that, Peter. I'm remembering it all the time. You don't think I'd come between Fells and his job, do you?"

"No," said Quayle. "I don't think that—not wittingly. You wouldn't wittingly come between him and his job, but a woman in love does all sorts of stupid things and thinks about them afterwards."

When Tangier spoke there was a little anger in her voice. She said: "You know, Peter, you haven't the power to control our lives."

"Haven't I?" said Quayle. He smiled at her. "Don't be angry with me, Tangier," he said. "But you know what I mean. You know you're much too good an Englishwoman to upset my applecart at any time, and Fells happens to be an important passenger in my applecart. You wouldn't do that."

She said: "Of course I wouldn't, Peter. Nobody's proposing to upset your old applecart. Haven't I always been loyal to you myself when I've worked for you, and I'd have gone on working for you if you hadn't laid me off. Incidentally, I've often wondered why you did."

"Believe it or not," said Quayle, "I make the same laws for myself as I do for other people. I laid you off when I realized I was beginning to be a little too fond of you. But aren't we rather talking in circles?"

She said: "No, we're not. We're not talking in circles at all. We're arriving at a decision."

"I see," said Quayle. "The decision being?"

"The decision being that I'm telling you that I'm going to marry Hubert Fells directly this war is over and directly he can legitimately stop working for you. Is there anything wrong with that?"

Quayle said: "No, there's not a lot wrong with it, except that I'm afraid that it's not going to work."

Tangier said: "I'm an awful nuisance to you, aren't I—with my ideas about love and marriage and odd things like that—flinging them at you at a time like this when you're probably harried and worried sick about all the things you've got to do and think about? And I'm very fond of you, Peter. I'd hate to be the person who throws the spanner in the works."

Quayle laughed. He said: "That's good! You're not really throwing a spanner in the works, Tangier. This is merely a feather in the works. The biggest spanner that I've ever had thrown in the works was thrown last night." His voice was grim.

Tangier asked: "Something *really* bad?"

"Something *really* bad," said Quayle. "*That* sort of spanner."

Tangier said: "I'm so sorry, Peter—so terrible sorry."

Quayle signalled the waiter. He ordered more coffee.

He said: "Tangier, I've always been pretty straight with you, haven't I?"

She said: "You've always been absolutely straight with me, Peter."

"All right," said Quayle. "I'm going to be straight with you now. If you'd come to me two days ago and told me all this, I'd probably have been rather pleased in an odd sort of way. I shouldn't have been pleased about myself, naturally." He smiled wryly. "I shouldn't have been pleased to find out that I wasn't the big thing in your life, but I should have been glad for you, and I should have been glad for Fells, because I'm rather fond of him. In his odd way he's really a very great fellow. In any event I should have been the first person—when this war was over, when Fells might have had a chance to pick up his life again—to say go ahead with it, and bless you, my children. But not now."

Tangier's voice was low. She said: "I see . . . because something has happened?"

"That's right," said Quayle, "because something has happened. Fells' future is very uncertain—much too uncertain to think in terms of love or marriage at *any* time—that is if he's *able* to think after the war."

Tangier asked: "What do you mean by that?"

"I'm not quite certain," said Quayle. "But I'm warning you, Tangier, that I don't think Fells is going to be with us for very long. I've got a job for him. There's no one else can do it. He's got to do it. He's going to be the star performer. You know"—he smiled sarcastically—"how the picture papers used to talk about somebody being groomed for stardom. Well, I've been grooming Fells for stardom for a long time, just in case the situation ever arose in which it became necessary for him to play a leading part. Well, the time has come."

Tangier said: "And what am I supposed to say, Peter? That I accept that; that I'll forget all about him?"

"There's no reason why you should forget about him," said Quayle. "But you've got to accept that because I say it—I mean it and it's a fact."

Tangier said nothing. She looked across the restaurant. Quayle could see that her eyes were clouded. She asked miserably: "What's going to happen to him, Peter?"

Quayle said: "I don't know. I wish to God I did. But I don't. But I know what you'll do if you're fond of him. I know what you'll do if you're in love with him. I know exactly what you'll do if you're the woman who wanted to marry Fells." His voice softened. He said: "You know, Tangier, I've never given you bad advice, have I?"

She said: "No, you've never done that. I think more of your opinion—of your judgment—than any man I know." She smiled. "I've never known you to make a mistake," she said.

Quayle said: "I'm not making one now. The thing for you to do is not to see Fells any more; to get out of London and stay out of London. If you're here he might think too much about you. His mind might not work in the way that it ought to work. In other words you'd be doing him a very bad turn by being here."

"Do you mean that?" asked Tangier.

"I mean just that," said Quayle.

She said: "Very well, Peter. If you say that's the right thing for me to do, I'm going to do it. I'll leave London to-day."

"Good girl," said Quayle. "And don't write any pathetic letters either. If you must say something to him, drop him a line saying that you're going off; that you hope to meet one day and that when you do meet you hope he'll have done his job. By the time he gets it," said Quayle grimly, "he'll probably guess what you mean."

Tangier said: "You know, Peter, he doesn't know that I know you. He doesn't know that I've worked for you. He doesn't know that you put me in originally to keep an eye on him."

Quayle said: "Don't worry. I'll explain all that. I'll make things as easy as I can."

Tangier began to put on her gloves. She said: "Do you think there's a chance for him? Do you think there's a fifty per cent chance?"

"There's a chance for everybody," said Quayle. "But if he gets out of the job he's going into he'll be the luckiest man I've ever met in my life. That's how it is."

Tangier nodded. "I see," she said. "That's how it is. A very bad spot, Peter?"

"Right," said Quayle. "A very bad spot. And all you have to do is to keep your chin up and grin. For a woman of your capabilities that should be easy." His voice was almost casual.

She said: "Well, I share one virtue with you, Peter."

He grinned. For a moment he looked almost boyish.

He said: "I didn't know I had any virtues."

"You've got a lot of virtues," said Tangier, "but one particular one. You never give up. Neither do I. I still believe that what I'm dreaming of is possible."

Quayle said: "Go on believing that. That's not going to hurt anybody. When you write your farewell note to Fells you might tell him he can go on believing it too. It won't hurt him." He laughed. "I'll promise the pair of you this much," he said. "I don't quite know what's going to happen, but I've got a pretty good idea, and if Fells gets out of this thing—the thing that I think's coming to him—I'll hand him to you on a plate—because he'll deserve it!"

II

It was five minutes to four when Greeley turned into Lyle Street. He walked slowly along the right-hand side, looking up at the windows on the other side of the street. Soon he saw what he was looking for. On the opposite side of the street, printed on some first-floor windows were the words "Birmingham and District Hardware Company." Greeley grinned as he crossed the road. He wondered how many "branch offices" of this description Quayle employed and under what strange titles they operated.

He went into the building. It was an old-fashioned house converted to offices. He went up the curving wooden stairs to the first floor, knocked at a door marked "Enquiries," and entered. Inside the doorway was a counter and on the other side of it at a desk a middle-aged man was busily engaged in making entries in a ledger.

Greeley said: "My name's Horace Greeley. I've an appointment here at four o'clock. Is this the right place?"

The middle-aged man nodded. He said: "Mr. Quayle's waiting for you inside. Go right through, will you?"

Greeley lifted the flap of the counter; walked across the office, pushed open the door on the other side. The room before him was small and well-furnished, and a fire was burning in the grate. Quayle was sitting behind a desk on the far side of the room smoking a cigarette.

He said: "Hello, Greeley. Come in."

Greeley said: "Good afternoon. It's been a nice day, hasn't it?"

Quayle said: "Quite a nice day. A little cold, that's all." He picked up an inter-communicating telephone off the desk; said to the man outside: "I don't want to be disturbed." He put back the transmitter. He turned to Greeley. He said: "This is a fine kettle of fish, isn't it?"

Greeley said: "I suppose you mean about Zilla Stevenson?"

Quayle nodded. He pushed a box of cigarettes towards Greeley. He said: "Have a cigarette and sit down."

Greeley sat down in the leather armchair by the side of the fire. He was feeling rather pleased with himself. He felt he was being important. This was the first time that he'd ever been alone in an office with Quayle. A hundred times before he had encountered him only in the odd places selected for their meetings. Greeley felt that he was getting on.

Quayle took a cigarette from the box and lit it. He smoked silently for a few minutes; then he said: "Have you any ideas about this business?"

Greeley shrugged his shoulders. "Only what I've told you," he said. "I must say it stinks a bit. But she certainly looked as if she'd shot herself, didn't she?"

Quayle said: "I doubt it." He got up, began to walk up and down the room. He went on: "This is a bad business about Zilla Stevenson. It makes things very inconvenient. It's put us in a bad spot."

Greeley nodded. "I know," he said. "Somebody's thrown a spanner in the works."

Quayle said: "You don't know how right you are." He thought it rather odd that Greeley should use the expression that Tangier had used earlier in the day. He smiled grimly. There was a difference in the *size* of the spanners—that was all!

He said: "Someone certainly has thrown a spanner in the works." He stopped pacing, sat on the edge of the desk, looked quizzically at Greeley. He said: "You're an odd bird, Greeley, but you're a very reliable one. You've got a good nerve and you've never let me down." He smiled. "I sometimes think you enjoy working for me."

Greeley grinned. He said: "Well, I always did like a bit of excitement."

Quayle frowned. "Personally, I wish we had a little less excitement."

Greeley said: "You wait till this bleedin' war's over, Mr. Quayle. It'll be so peaceful that a lot of us won't even know what we're doing. We shall feel lost."

"I expect you're right," said Quayle. "We shall—those of us who are still here."

Greeley said: "Yes, I forgot about that bit. Well, the others won't be able to mind, will they?"

Quayle said: "The trouble from now on is that we've got to be opportunists. I mean by that that it's no longer possible to work along definite laid down lines as we were doing before. Zilla Stevenson's death upsets a whole lot of things. Now we've got to take chances."

Greeley drew on his cigarette. He thought something's coming in a minute. I wonder what it's going to be.

Quayle went on: "The first thing is Foden. I don't want Foden to feel alarmed or rattled too much about Zilla Stevenson being dead. I expect he's worrying about it a great deal—very naturally. He feels possibly that he'll be implicated in some way. It was clever of you to suggest that Zilla Stevenson's boss might have wanted the whole thing kept quiet; might be big enough to keep it quiet for reasons of policy. That was a good idea of yours."

Greeley said: "It seemed common-sense to me. I know this guy Foden is important to you. I didn't see any use in putting the wind up him. I know you want to get something out of him."

"Right," said Quayle. "I do want to get something out of him. So the first thing is to re-assure him. You'd better go and see him sometime this evening. The line you take is this—that nobody knows about Zilla Stevenson's death yet; that she's still locked up there in the flat; that she had no maid and that anyway that situation will be dealt with. Then you tell him that you've been able to see her boss; that you thought the best thing to do was to tell him the whole story as you knew it—the story being what?"

Greeley said: "That's easy. That I met Foden down at the port; that I palled up with him; that I listened to him talk and I thought there might be a little money in it for me; that he was decent to me. He let me have a fiver on account of twenty-five quid."

"Right," said Quayle.

"That's the line," Greeley went on. "I put him next to Zilla because I knew she'd got five hundred for giving some information before and I got the idea in my head that she'd got herself a job working for some-body connected with one of the Service Intelligence Departments. All right. I fix up for him to meet her and then this thing happened; that I didn't know what to do about it, but I thought the best thing was to lie low until I'd seen her boss."

"Right," said Quayle. "And you've seen her boss. You understand? You went round to the office where she worked—an office in Pall Mall. I'll give you the address before you leave. And you saw her boss. Her boss is a man who is working in connection with one of the Army Intelligence Departments. His name's Quayle."

"I see," said Greeley. "You?"

"Right," said Quayle. "Me. You saw this Quayle and he thought you'd handled the job very cleverly. He was specially pleased with you because you kept the thing away from the police. He told you that neither you nor Foden were to worry about the Zilla Stevenson thing; that he thought he had an idea about that; that there'd been somebody after Zilla for some time; that they'd caught up with her. Quayle is going to look after the removal of the body. No one will be making any inquiries about your sister's disappearance. But Quayle is very keen to meet Foden. You've got to make Foden understand that Quayle was very interested when he heard that Foden came from Morocco; that he'd been there for some time. Do you understand that?"

"I've got it," said Greeley.

Quayle went on: "You want to be careful to play this carefully. You want to give the idea to Foden that you think that there's quite some money in this and that as you've helped him right through this business you want to get your share. In other words come to some sort of financial arrangement with him. Don't tell him where he's going to meet this Quayle until he's agreed to pay you something. Play it as Horace Stevenson—a travelling munitions worker who's too fond of backing horses—*would* play it. Realize that this is terribly important."

"I'll be careful," said Greeley. "Don't you worry about me, Mr. Quayle."

Quayle smiled. "I don't, Greeley," he said. "All right then. Give Foden Quayle's address." He went behind the desk, took a piece of paper, wrote it down, brought it to Greeley. "There it is," he said. "Make an appointment for him to come along to the Pall Mall office and see me at three o'clock to-morrow afternoon. But be very careful to make another appointment to meet him later in the evening after he's seen me—the idea being that you want to know what's happened about the money. You want to make certain that you get your cut. Do you know if Foden's got any money?"

"I don't know," said Greeley. "I should think he'd got a bit."

"You're probably right," said Quayle. "He'll have enough but not too much. He probably needs some money anyway. Well, I'll see he gets something on account. By the time I have finished with him," said Quayle, "he'll believe that he's getting away with it. He'll have given me some sort of indication of the information he's got to sell. He'll realize that I'm interested. When he sees you later in the evening you'd better suggest a little celebration. You've got to make him fall for that idea. In any event he's not supposed to know anybody in London, so he will fall for it all right. About nine o'clock you get him to a little upstairs club called the Silver Boot, off Albemarle Street. There'll be a woman in the bar there—a very good-looking woman. Her name is Mayola Green. She'll recognize you. She'll come over to you and talk to you. She'll remind you that you met her once with your sister; that she's a friend of your sister's. She'll ask about Zilla and you'll tell her that Zilla's away on sick leave. You understand?"

"I've got it," said Greeley.

"It's more than possible," Quayle went on, "that Foden is going to be rather interested in that woman." He smiled. "She has a great deal of appeal," he said. "She's the sort of woman that a man like Foden will probably fall for. If possible she will take you both back to her flat in the vicinity. When you arrive there she'll probably find an opportunity to give Foden a 'Mickey Finn,' and then you get over to his place in Victoria and go over his room. Go over it with a fine tooth comb. Of course you'll go over him first."

Greeley said: "Yes, that sounds all right. But what's this Foden guy going to think when he comes round after the Mickey? He's going to be a bit suspicious, isn't he?"

Quayle laughed. "I don't think so," he said, "not the way that Mayola will do it. They're never suspicious with Mayola."

"All right," said Greeley. "Well, when I go over his place what am I looking for?"

"You're looking for anything that doesn't fit in with the story you've heard from Foden—anything at all."

Greeley said: "Well, that doesn't tell me very much, but if you'd wanted to tell me any more you would have. I suppose you wouldn't like me to ask you a question, Mr. Quayle?"

Quayle said: "There's no reason why you shouldn't ask a question, Greeley. I don't have to answer."

Greeley said: "No, but I'd like to ask this: Is there something screwy about this Foden bird?"

Quayle said: "Don't you worry your head with that."

Greeley said: "I'm not. I just thought it might help me a bit if I knew a little more about him, because apparently you know more than I do."

Quayle said: "You're wrong about that, Greeley. The thing for you to do is to do what you're told. If you know too much about anything it's inclined to alter your point of view. You begin to think about all sorts of things that it's not necessary for you to think about. Believe me I've told you as much as it's good for you to know."

"All right," said Greeley. "Well, what's the next move?"

"Don't spend too long in Foden's place," said Quayle—"not more than an hour. You can get in touch with me at the usual place on the telephone late to-morrow night. Let me know what's happened. Then possibly I'll be able to give you some further instructions."

"O.K.," said Greeley. "Is that all, Mr. Quayle?"

He got up. Quayle went to the window. He stood there for a few moments looking out; then he turned. He said:

"There's only one thing, Greeley. You've done quite a bit of work one way and another with Mr. Fells, haven't you?"

Greeley grinned. "I've done a hell of a lot of work with Mr. Fells. What him and I haven't done together is just nobody's business."

"Quite," said Quayle. "You get on with him pretty well, don't you?"

Greeley said: "I'm very fond of Mr. Fells. If ever there was a gentleman he's one. I like him. He's quiet and he's as brave as a lion."

Quayle said: "I know. Well, that being so I'm certain you're going to play this thing very carefully, because owing to this spanner in the works I'm afraid Mr. Fells is going to be in rather a spot."

Greeley said: "I see. So it's like that, is it?"

Quayle nodded. "It's like that," he said. "He hasn't got much of a chance of getting out of this, but there's a slight chance. One never knows. So let's take all the trouble that we can to see that he *does* get a chance."

Greeley said: "O.K., Mr. Quayle. I'll remember that."

"Right," said Quayle. "I'll be seeing you."

Greeley picked up his hat. He went to the door. He said: "Good afternoon, Mr. Quayle."

Quayle said: "Good afternoon, Greeley."

Greeley closed the door quietly behind him; nodded to the middle-aged man in the outer office; went down the wooden stairs. At the bottom he paused to light a cigarette.

He was wondering about Zilla Stevenson.

CHAPTER 9
THE DEAL

I

AN EAST wind was blowing. Foden, whose blood—thinned by years in the heat—had not accustomed itself to the English climate, shivered a little and turned up the collar of his recently purchased overcoat. The cold, however, did not annoy him. He walked down Pall Mall with an assurance, his hat at its accustomed angle, his lean handsome face and jaunty air winning more than a few glances from feminine eyes.

He turned in through the imposing doorway of a large block of offices. A commissionaire, seated at a table in the hall, looked at him inquiringly.

Foden said: "My name's Foden. I've an appointment with a Mr. Quayle."

The commissionaire consulted the list on his desk. He said: "Oh, yes, sir. You might fill in this pass form, will you? You'll need it to get out of the building."

Foden filled in the pass. The commissionaire rang a bell and a messenger appeared. Foden followed the man along the corridor to the lift. They went up two floors, down the passage. The messenger knocked on a door; opened it. He said:

"Mr. Quayle's waiting for you, sir."

Foden went in. The room was large—expensively furnished. The desk at which Quayle was sitting was ornate and matched the splendour of the room.

Quayle got up. He came round the desk with hand outstretched. He was smiling. He gave the impression of being a wise, benevolent and understanding man. The sort of man who would win a big job for himself in a department dealing with matters where tact and knowledge of human nature were of primary importance. They shook hands.

Foden thought to himself this is pretty good. I think this is going to be easy. He's going to play this the nice way first of all. He's going to try and make friends. If he gets what he wants without trouble, well and good, but he could be nasty and tough enough under that good-natured exterior if he wanted to.

Quayle said: "Take your coat off, Mr. Foden, and sit by the fire. It's a cold day and I expect you're feeling our English weather."

Foden said: "I am, I'm afraid. I haven't got used to it yet. Anyway I don't like it. I like the heat."

Quayle said: "You mean you like Morocco?"

Foden grinned. "That's it," he said. "I like Morocco. Morocco suits me. This place"—he jerked his head towards the window—"is a dead and alive hole in war-time. If I were here for long I'd die of boredom."

Quayle brought a box of cigarettes from the desk. Foden took one. Quayle snapped on his lighter. He said:

"Candidly, Mr. Foden, I don't think you're the type that would like to live in war-time England for very long. We English are a cabbage-like nation. We attune our point of view to the weather. We're inclined sometimes to be dull-witted."

Foden grinned again. He said: "I wouldn't go so far as to say that."

Quayle went back to his desk. He sat down in the big chair. He looked very benevolent—almost jovial. He said:

"You wouldn't *say* a thing like that, but I expect you think it, and I don't know that I blame you—not after the deal I understand you got from our people in Morocco."

"So you know all about that," said Foden. He drew on his cigarette appreciatively. It was a good cigarette—the sort he liked.

"Yes," said Quayle. "I heard about that from Horace Stevenson. A bright, intelligent fellow that—a characteristic cockney with all the astuteness of his type. Every time I think of him I thank Heaven that he had enough common-sense to stop you going to the police and reporting that unfortunate business about his sister. However, we don't want to talk about that at this moment. But I wanted you to know that I think our people in Morocco were foolish to treat you so cavalierly."

Foden said: "Perhaps you're right there. But that's all over. I'm a man who's always inclined to let bygones be bygones."

"That's as may be," said Quayle. "But it doesn't alter the fact that you must have been annoyed." He got up; came round the desk; pushed a leather armchair to the other side of the fire; sat down facing Foden. He said:

"Let me tell you what's in my mind, Mr. Foden, so that you and I may understand each other perfectly. I don't think you had a square deal from our people in Morocco. After all, Consulates and Agents should be intelligent. You went to those people as a patriotic man to give information which was—as we know now—important. They didn't treat you very seriously. In point of fact I believe that one of them was inclined to be rather rude to you."

Foden shrugged his shoulders.

"Well, I want you to get all that right out of your mind," Quayle went on. "I want you to realize that I'm *very* interested in what you've got to say; that I'm not inclined to do anything that's going to annoy you in the slightest degree. You understand that?"

"I understand perfectly," said Foden. "And I'm very relieved that Stevenson did the right thing in telling me not to go to the police about that unfortunate girl. It was a nasty business. I've been worried about it."

"Naturally," said Quayle. "But I don't want you to worry about it. Quite candidly, I'm not fearfully surprised about it."

Foden raised his eyebrows. He said: "No?"

"No," said Quayle. "You see, Miss Stevenson's done one or two odd jobs for me—jobs which were outside her normal business as my secretary. She was keen on them. I think she found a certain romance in imagining herself as a sort of semi-secret service agent." Quayle smiled—a sad little smile. "In point of fact I think she talked too much, and there are quite a lot of people in this country who might have had reason for thinking she would be better out of the way.

"The lucky thing about the whole business was," he went on, "that her brother Horace Stevenson, had enough sense to take the trouble to find out where I was and got in touch with me, without getting unduly excited and going to the police."

Foden said: "That was lucky. Most men would have done just that."

"I know," said Quayle. "But if there's one thing that we in this Department *don't* want to do it is to draw too much attention to ourselves. As far as the Zilla Stevenson business is concerned, you can remove it entirely from your mind. Officially, she's been given a month's leave to go to Scotland. Well, she'll be taken ill there and she'll die. As far as you're concerned you needn't worry about it. Now shall we talk about more interesting business?"

Foden said: "I'm at your service, Mr. Quayle."

Quayle got up. He went to the wall opposite his desk, pulled down a cord, switched on a wall-light. Foden saw that Quayle had pulled down—in the same manner as one pulls down a blind—a large scale map of Morocco. The wall-light illuminated it perfectly.

Quayle came back to the fire. He stood with his back to it, looking at Foden. He said:

"Stevenson told me that his sister had an idea that you have some very important information to give me; the idea that you weren't very pleased with the deal that you had from the British authorities before; that you wanted paying for it, and well paying for it. Well, that's all right with me, Mr. Foden. If *you've* got the information, *we've* got the money. But we've got to know that you *have* got the information."

Foden said: "That's fair enough, Mr. Quayle, but you've heard the proverb 'Once bitten twice shy.' I'll tell you what I propose to do. I propose to tell you just enough about what I know to show you that I know what I'm talking about. After that, we'll come to terms about money if you don't mind. Then I'll give you the rest of it. How's that?"

Quayle said: "That's all right. You go ahead."

Foden said: "I was working for sometime with the Two Star North Moroccan Line in the *Crystal* and the *Evening Starlight*. Those two ships were owned by a man called Estalza. I've got an idea that it was Estalza who was responsible for having me put away."

Quayle raised his eyebrows. "Really?" he said. "What happened?"

Foden grinned. "Nothing very much," he said. "But my idea is that after I'd been to the authorities for the second time with my bits of news, Estalza got wise to me." Foden drew on his cigarette. "I believe Estalza was working for the Germans," he said. "I believe he'd been working for them for years. Although I didn't know that at the time. But I guessed it a year ago when they wiped me up and chucked me into that filthy Vichy internment camp." He sighed. "It wasn't so good there, I'm telling you, Mr. Quayle," he said.

Quayle said: "I bet it wasn't. This is interesting."

Foden smiled. He said: "You'd be surprised. The thing was," he went on, "they never intended me to get out of that camp. I was for it. I was going to be rubbed out. Fortunately, I had a bit of luck. I made a break and got away. Well, with what I knew before I went in there, and what I found out while I was there, I know plenty."

Quayle nodded. He said: "You've got some general idea as to what the Germans proposed to do there?"

Foden grinned. "Don't kid yourself, Mr. Quayle. When you talk about '*proposed*' as if it was all over. Just because you've pulled off this landing in Tunisia—just because the Americans and the British are there—you think everything's in the bag. Don't you kid yourself you've finished with the Germans in that part of the world. It isn't what they *proposed* to do; it's what the people they've left behind propose to do *now*."

Quayle said: "I see." His face was serious. "So there's still some sort of organization there?"

"There's a lot of organization there," said Foden. "For four or five years before this war the Germans were organizing Intelligence sections, working from hide-outs spread all over the country. I wouldn't mind betting some of the allied armies have been right over them with being any the wiser. Those people are absolutely *big* personnel. They're out to make all the mischief they can, and they'll do it."

Quayle said: "I see. The usual business—sabotage, espionage, murder, assassination?"

"All those things," said Foden. "They've got enough organization out there to start trouble any time they want to, and when I say trouble I don't mean the sort of trouble the Army can deal with. I mean underground stuff. That's sometimes much more dangerous."

He threw his cigarette stub into the fire; got up, walked to the desk, helped himself to another one. He said:

"I hope you don't mind my helping myself, Mr. Quayle."

Quayle said: "No, I like you to. But go on. I'm interested."

"I'll interest you a great deal more," said Foden. "The British had a man working for them in Morocco called Gervase Herbert. He had an accident last year, didn't he?"

Quayle said, "Yes, that's right."

"All right," said Foden. "Well, he didn't have an accident. He just found out something that I knew. He found out the situation of three or four of the German organized groups. Two of 'em were situated in the foothills about ten miles outside Casa Blanca—in well concealed hide-outs—with everything that opened and shut. Herbert walked into it by accident. So they got him and they finished him. Right?"

"That's right," said Quayle. "Do you by any chance know the location of those organized groups—the exact location—Mr. Foden?"

Foden said: "Come over here and I'll show you." He went over to the map; indicated two points. He looked at Quayle. He was smiling. He said: "Well, is that right or is it?"

Quayle said: "That's right, Mr. Foden. It's quite obvious to me that you know what you're talking about." He walked slowly back to the fireplace. "Tell me this," he said. "Could you give me in a few words some idea of the extent—the scope of your information?"

"I could do that very easily," said Foden. "My information extends practically to the complete German organization in Morocco, and when I say organization I mean not only the organization which existed a year or eighteen months ago, but the organization they prepared and had ready to leave behind in the event of any success-ful Allied landing." He grinned. "I could go on talking for hours," he said. "You've got to realize, Mr. Quayle, I'm no fool. I've spent years thinking about this job. I've spent years watching it happen under my nose. You see, I'm a sailor and nobody takes very much notice of a sailor. He's always supposed to be cockeyed when he's ashore."

Quayle said: "I'm taking you very seriously, Mr. Foden. Don't worry on that score. Now tell me this: Supposing I was to ask you to give me a résumé of all the information you have—everything in your power—with such maps as you care to draw—details as you care to give us; supposing you could promise us that you could give us sufficient information to wipe out this entire enemy organization? Do you think you could do that?"

Foden said: "I don't think. I know. I'll tell you something. When I was in that camp they gave me a pretty bad time, but it improved a little when they discovered I was first-class at mixing cocktails. Eventually I became a sort of bar steward in the camp officers' mess. On my way from the bar to the store-room where the reserve stock of liquor was kept, I had to pass the commandant's room. All right. During the day he used to lecture to three or four young officers who were attached to the camp. They were German Panzer officers in fact, and he used to use a map. It was stuck up on the wall. It was a map of one sector of the system."

Foden grinned. "I used to pass that room a dozen times in an afternoon," he said. "Just on the left of the doorway, the mud wall was broken down. There was a hole I could see through. Every time I had a look, I looked directly at that map. I could draw it with my eyes shut."

Quayle nodded. "That, however, would only be one sector," he said.

Foden grinned. "Don't you believe it," he said. "You know what the Germans are. They love repeating things. The whole thing is a repetition of that sector, according to the geographical situation of the country and physical nature of the ground. You know what the Germans are."

Quayle said: "I see. In other words, having memorized the organization for that sector, you're pretty certain that you could duplicate it for any sector that we liked to put in front of you."

"I'm not pretty certain," said Foden. "I'm absolutely certain, and I'll prove that to you. I expect you know something about the fighting that's going on in Tunisia. Well, you know that every time the Allies come up against any sort of tough resistance, when they eventually get forward, they invariably find a destroyed signals station—the usual stuff—short wave wireless, heliograph, and all the rest of the German field stuff. Always there is another one—a duplicate one—concealed, and invariably somebody gives this away to the British or Americans for a bribe."

Quayle nodded.

"Whenever this happens," Foden went on, "that stuff is part of the scheme. Naturally when the authorities find the second place—the secret place which is given away to them—they're quite satisfied." He grinned. "Well, there's always *another* one," he said. "Maybe you've found that out in one or possibly two places?"

Quayle said: "You know, Mr. Foden, I'm beginning to believe that you really and truly know what you're talking about."

Foden said: "I'm no bluffer, Mr. Quayle. I don't know what's been going on during the last month or two, but you do. You know whether what I've told you is right or wrong. You know what's happened. I know what was planned to happen. So you can check on me every time."

Quayle said: "I've no reason to doubt anything you say, Mr. Foden. Tell me, if you place the whole of your information at our disposal, what would you expect us to pay you?"

Foden said: "I think it's worth five thousand pounds."

Quayle pursed his lips. "That's a lot of money," he said.

Foden grinned. "It's a lot of information. I don't think five thousand pounds means a lot on a job like this, but I want to get out of here. Mr. Quayle. I've had a tough time during the last year. I want to get away."

Quayle said: "I understand. I expect you've got some plans?"

"Plenty," said Foden. "Nothing very exciting. But believe it or not I want to be through with hanging around places. I want to have some-

thing solid behind me. I reckon there'll be a future in Morocco. I want
to get back there as soon as I can and start a business of my own."

Quayle said smilingly: "Once a sailor always a sailor."

"To hell with that part of it," said Foden. "I'm going to park myself
ashore and watch somebody else do the work. With five thousand
pounds I could get my hands on two or three light coast-trading
vessels, and keep myself in velvet for the rest of my days. You see,
I know the ropes."

Quayle said: "I understand. Incidentally, Mr. Foden, if you went
back to Morocco, you might be of great use to our people out there
now." He smiled. "And they might be inclined to treat you more kindly."

"Maybe they would," said Foden.

Quayle said: "Mr. Foden, I'll tell you what I propose to do. I
propose to make you an immediate advance of one thousand pounds.
To-morrow evening I'm going to ask you to meet one of my people—a
man who knows the Moroccan side pretty well. I want you to talk to
him. I want you to give him the fullest possible information. I know
you'll do that. You needn't worry about the balance of the money.
He'll hand you that to-morrow night. You can put it in your pocket
before you do any talking at all."

Foden said: "That's fine."

Quayle went to his desk. He wrote on a piece of paper, put the
slip of paper in an envelope, sealed it. He opened a drawer, took out
some banknotes. He came back to the fireplace. He gave the banknotes and the envelope to Foden. He said:

"There's the thousand. Inside the envelope is the name and
address of the man I'd like you to talk to. You'd better see him at
his place. It's nice and quiet. Nice and quiet and out of the way." He
smiled. "We don't want anybody to get wise to what you're doing,
Mr. Foden. We'd hate anything to happen to you."

Foden got up. He was smiling. He said: "I bet you would—until
after you've got this information. Then you wouldn't give a damn."

Quayle smiled pleasantly. He said: "Well, life's like that, isn't it?
We all want something. We're prepared to give anything for it until
we've got it. When we've got it—" He shrugged his shoulders.

Foden said: "Don't worry, Mr. Quayle. I can look after myself."

Quayle said: "Have another cigarette. When you've seen my
colleague—when you've had your talk and he's sucked you dry of

every particle of information you've got—then perhaps you and I might meet again. I think we shall have done a good job."

He held out his hand. Foden took it. He said:

"You're all right, Mr. Quayle. I can get along with you. You talk my language."

Quayle went to the door, opened it. He said:

"Well, *au revoir*, Mr. Foden. The messenger will see you out. Give them your pass on the way out. And good luck to you."

"So long," said Foden.

He walked down the passage on the heels of the messenger. He was smiling.

Things were coming his way.

II

At six-thirty Greeley walked up the carpeted stairs, tapped at the door on the first landing, pushed it open, went in. Foden was standing on the opposite side of the room with his back to the fire, his hands in his pockets. He was smiling.

Greeley thought you're a damn' good-looking feller and you hate yourself like hell! I don't think I like you. I don't think I like you a bit. He smiled. He said:

"Well, how did you get on, chum? Did you pull it off?"

Foden said: "You bet I pulled it off."

Greeley said: "You don't mean to say you collected? You don't mean to say they gave you all that bleedin' money?"

Foden said: "I got a thousand. I'm getting the rest to-morrow. I made it quite obvious to Quayle that I knew what I was talking about."

He took some banknotes out of the breast pocket of his jacket. He looked at Greeley. He was still smiling.

"I suppose you want your bit?"

Greeley grinned. He said: "I've never said no to money in my life. I think this is money from home. There's only one thing I don't like about this. Every time I think of poor old Zilla I think maybe it was my fault for bringing her into this."

Foden shook his head. He said: "It wasn't your fault, Horace. It was nobody's fault. You thought you were doing her a good turn." He held out two fifty-pound notes towards Greeley. "There's the hundred I promised you," he said. "When I collect the rest there'll be a bit more."

Greeley threw his cap on to the sofa. He stood fingering the notes, making them crackle in his fingers. He said:

"Do you know I've never had a fifty-pound note before. Now I've got two of 'em. Wonders will never cease!"

He took out a box of Players cigarettes; threw one to Foden who caught it expertly.

He said: "What's Zilla's boss like?"

Foden said: "Like you'd expect him to be—tough and hard-bitten. And he knows what he's talking about. By the way, it's O.K. about Zilla. He says neither of us is to worry about her. Somehow or other I don't think he was too surprised about that happening."

Greeley shook his head. "She always was a one for taking chances." He sat down in the armchair. "I suppose you're all fixed up now?"

Foden said: "I'm going to see somebody to-morrow—one of the men who works for him. I've got his name and address in my pocket. He's going to give me the balance of the money to-morrow night, and I'm going to say my piece."

He took the envelope that Quayle had given him out of his pocket, slit it open, took out the sheet of paper that was inside. Greeley was watching him. Foden's expression had not changed, but he was looking hard at the piece of paper in front of him.

He said, almost to himself: "Fells! Did Zilla ever talk to you about anybody of that name?"

Greeley shook his head. "She never mentioned any names to me," he said. "She used to talk a bit sort of generally sometimes, but she was too clever to trust anybody very much. Anyway," he went on sadly, "I don't think she thought a lot of my brains. I should think that I'd have been the last person for Zilla to trust."

Foden put the envelope back in his pocket. He said: "Cheer up, Horace."

Greeley grinned. "You're dead right," he said. "It's no good worrying about Zilla. We've all got to die sometime, and there's a hell of a lot of people died in this war already. You know what we ought to do?"

Foden said: "Well, what ought we to do, Horace?"

"We ought to have a celebration," said Greeley. "I could do with a drink." He grinned. "I'm so well off," he said, "I could almost buy a couple of bottles of brandy."

Foden said: "Well, why not? I've got an idea that after to-morrow I shan't have much time for celebrating."

Greeley drew on his cigarette. He said: "Why do you think that?"

Foden said: "I've got an idea in my head that this Quayle bird means to make as much use of me as he can. Well, that suits me all right."

Greeley said: "What's the arrangement? Maybe there'll be even some money more in it."

Foden said: "Who knows? I'm going to talk to this fellow Fells to-morrow. Possibly that's the end of it as far as I'm concerned, but somehow I don't think it will be. Quayle asked me what I wanted that money for and I told him I wanted to get back to Morocco. That interested him. I think there's still going to be a lot of trouble in Morocco," said Foden. "It's an odd sort of country. Maybe Quayle thinks I might be useful to him over there."

"You never know your luck," said Greeley. "It looks to me as if you're on a good thing. Funny you runnin' into me like that in that pub the first night you came over here. It's just as if there's a sort of luck, isn't it—some fellers have it and some don't?"

Foden said: "Well, you haven't got any grouses, Horace. You've got two fifty-pound notes in your pocket now anyway."

Greeley said: "Yes. It makes me feel as if I'd almost chuck that bleedin' job I got with the munitions squad. Maybe I'll do a bit of branching out myself." He got up. "Let's go and have a drink," he said. "I know a swell place I went to one night with Zilla. She knew all the classy places around London."

Foden asked: "Where is it?"

"It's a place called The Silver Boot just off Albemarle Street."

"All right," said Foden. He went to the wardrobe, got out his overcoat, began to put it on. Greeley watched him.

He said: "That's not a bad overcoat—for one off the hook."

"I was lucky," said Foden. He lit a cigarette. "I got one to fit me, and it's not a bad bit of cloth."

He stood in front of the fire, drawing the tobacco smoke down into his lungs, smiling at Greeley. Eventually he said:

"Don't make a fool of yourself with that money, Horace. If you're wise you'll put it by as a sort of nest egg. You might need it one day."

"What's the good of thinkin' about the future?" said Greeley. "As far as I can see it's no good to anybody thinkin' what's goin' to happen to-morrow or next week. Anyway, you're a fine one to talk."

He took out a fresh cigarette; lit it from the stub of the old one. He said: "It's funny how you an' me have sort of palled up, isn't it? Life is a bit of a joke when you come to think of it. But I suppose when you've got that big dough you're expecting I shan't see much of you?"

"Why not?" asked Foden. "You can take it from me that I'm going to be pretty careful with that money. That's my capital for the future. And you'll probably see quite a bit of me. I expect I shall be hanging about London for a while. Shall you be around to-morrow night—late?"

"Yes," said Greeley. "Why?"

Foden said: "I thought I'd run round after I've seen this man of Quayle's and tell you what happened. I expect it'll be late though."

"What does that matter?" said Greeley. "I'd like to hear. Come round to my place after you get through with him. I'll be interested to know what happens."

"All right," said Foden. He stretched. "Well . . . let's go." He picked up his hat. "Let's go and investigate The Silver Boot. I haven't had a real drink for a long time. I feel like one to-night. . . ."

He walked to the door. Greeley followed him. He thought maybe you'll get a drink you don't expect. He began to think about Mayola Green; to wonder about her. As he followed Foden down the stairs he thought about the different women he had met during the past two years . . . women who were working for Quayle.

Quayle certainly knew how to pick them. Greeley grinned.

Foden saw the grin. "What's the joke?" he asked in the hallway.

"Nothing much," said Greeley. "I was thinkin' of some girl I met once in Huddersfield. She was a cute one, that one . . ."

He told Foden the story as they walked down the street, making it up as he went along.

III

Quayle sat in an armchair in front of the electric fire in his bedroom. He was smoking an old briar pipe, thinking about Fells.

He, who had spent a considerable portion of his life in endeavouring to assess and analyze the characters and personalities of his fellow-man, found himself unable to be mentally definite about Fells. Quayle was quite sure of Fells. But he was not so sure of Fells *plus* Tangier. Fells, who had been single-minded about his job, who had never thought of much else—mainly because there was little else to think about—might easily be inclined to go off the rails now that this extraordinary thing called love had come into his life.

Quayle could visualize Fells and Tangier as an entity. They would be good. They were two people who would suit each other perfectly. They were of the same type in the main, differing in minor attributes to a degree that would prevent boredom. They would be very good for each other, thought Quayle—but not now. Definitely not now.

If Quayle had been the type of man who admitted sorrow for others he would have admitted that he was sorry for Fells. Fells was up against it. One way or the other he was badly up against it, and Quayle did not see what he could do about it. A job had to be done and only Fells could do it. There was no way out of that.

Quayle cursed quietly under his breath. Everything had been going rather well. Everything had gone according to plan until Zilla had got herself rubbed out. That was damned bad luck on her. But it was damned bad luck on him too—and even worse luck on Fells. Now, with Zilla gone, there was only one way to play it and that way was not even a good way. It was taking a hell of a chance and it might not even come off. And if it did not come off . . . well, it was going to be too bad for Fells, and that was that.

Quayle bit on the mouthpiece of his pipe. Life could be tough, he thought. He felt tired. He wished sometimes that other people could make his decisions for him.

The clock on the mantelpiece struck seven. There was a tap on the door. The blonde girl from the office came in.

She said: "Mr. Fells is here."

Quayle said: "All right. I'll see him in the sitting-room."

She said: "Very well, Mr. Quayle."

She was going, when he asked suddenly: "How long is it since you had a holiday?"

She looked at him. She smiled. Quayle realized for the first time that she was very pretty. She said:

"Mr. Quayle, don't say you're being concerned about *me.*"

"No, I'm not particularly concerned about you," said Quayle.

"I had a week's leave just over two years ago," the girl said.

Quayle grinned. "Quite enough too. But I think you'd better have a week off fairly soon."

She said: "That would be very nice, Mr. Quayle."

She went away. Quayle got up; knocked out the ashes from his pipe into a bowl on the mantelpiece. He went out of the bedroom, down the corridor, into the sitting-room.

Fells was sitting in an armchair looking at a magazine.

Quayle said: "Hello, Fells. How are you?"

"I'm all right," said Fells. "As a matter of fact I'm feeling particularly well."

Quayle pulled up a chair. He said: "Look here, I'm going to talk pretty straight to you. I want to talk to you first of all about Tangier Lawless."

Fells said: "Yes?" He raised his eyebrows. Then he smiled. He said: "You know everything, don't you, Quayle? I often wonder if you ever have time to sleep."

Quayle smiled. He said: "To tell you the truth, Fells, I don't think I've had a complete night's rest for the last six months. But that's neither here nor there. I don't want you to think that I'm butting into your private affairs, but I've got to talk to you about Tangier, and it's much better that you should know the truth about her."

Fells said: "I've got complete confidence in you. I know there's a good motive behind most of the things you do."

Quayle said: "Thanks. The point is this: You think you met Tangier—who is an old friend of mine—by accident. You didn't. You might as well know that it's been a habit of mine to put someone to have a look at important operatives who are working for me just to see how they are getting on; what their nerve's like; whether they're slipping. Tangier used to do that for me. That's how she met you. In fact," Quayle went on, "that was the last job she did for me. I wasn't particularly keen on her going on with that type of work, the reason being—" He grinned wryly—"I was inclined to think that I was getting to be a little too fond of her."

Fells nodded. He said: "I understand."

Quayle continued: "She's been to see me. She told me about you two. Well, in one way I was rather glad to hear it. I think it's a good thing. You two people would suit each other very well. But not at the moment."

Fells said slowly: "I see. You don't think it's indicated at the moment?"

"No," said Quayle, "definitely not—and for a reason which you'll understand. Your job is going to be a little difficult, and I know you wouldn't want Tangier implicated in anything like that. So the idea is that we get the job done first. Is that all right?"

Fells said: "That's all right. As a matter of fact," he said, "I've had a note from her. She's going away for a bit. Perhaps that's a good thing."

Quayle nodded. "I suggested it," he said. "Believe me, Fells, it *is* a good thing."

Fells said: "All right. Well, that's that."

Quayle got up. He put his hands in his trouser pockets; began to walk about the room. He thought to himself: I wish I could tell him the entire truth, but I daren't. If I told him the truth it *might* affect his point of view. He *might* slip up. He *might* lose his nerve. I don't think he will, but I can't chance it.

He said: "I want you to put everything you've got into this job, Fells—the job I'm going to explain to you now. The thing is this: Some little time ago a man called Foden arrived in this country from Morocco. We picked him up. We've maintained close contact with him. He professes to have a great deal of information about enemy action in Morocco. He seems to have a very good idea of their underground lay-out there. I've given him certain money already. It's arranged that he shall see you to-morrow night at your place. He'll talk to you. He'll probably draw maps. It's fairly certain that quite a lot of the information he'll give you will be correct. You understand that?"

Fells said: "I understand. That seems simple enough. But how shall I know whether this information is correct or not?"

Quayle said: "That doesn't matter. When he comes to your place, before you do anything else give him four thousand pounds—I'll give you the notes before you leave here."

Fells raised his eyebrows. "That's a lot of money for information," he said.

Quayle said: "It doesn't matter. I'm not really concerned with his information. Foden *might* be a German agent. I've been on to him from the start."

Fells said: "I see. So that's how it is. They're awfully good tryers, aren't they?"

Quayle said: "Yes, they are. The point is this: You remember Schlieken—your German boss—for whom you worked so assiduously?" Quayle grinned sarcastically. "Now it's probably struck you—as it has me—as being very funny that ever since this war's started Schlieken has laid off you. Not one of his people who have been over in this country—and God knows there have been enough of them—has tried to contact you. Yet we know that Schlieken trusts you. We've had ample proof of that. Understand?"

"I understand," said Fells.

Quayle said: "There's just a chance that this Foden *might* be one of the Schlieken boys. There is just a chance that Foden's picking this time—and it's an ideal time—to contact you. There's a chance that this Foden has been put over here specially for that purpose. See?"

Fells nodded. "I see," he said. "You're not certain about him and you've no way of checking."

"That's right," said Quayle. "So you see how it is? It's not at all an easy proposition. If Foden was all right we could do all sorts of things with him. But we don't *know*. If he's one of Schlieken's crowd he'd be on to everything we did. He'd know what we were at before we did it."

Fells said: "This might be a little difficult, mightn't it?"

"It might be damned difficult," said Quayle. "First of all you've got to be on your toes from the minute you meet Foden. He may not know you. He may not know who you are. He may even be just one of the routine sort of agents put in by one of the German army 'I' branches to pick up what he can get and out with it. But on the other hand," said Quayle, "he may be one of Schlieken's super-trained Nazis on the look-out for *you*. Remember, you've had ample opportunities of seeing all sorts of things in this country. You'd be invaluable to them now."

Fells said: "Well, I'm in Foden's hands, aren't I? He's either going to talk or he's not."

"That's just it," said Quayle. "He may carry on with the set-up he's used up to date. He may go on being Foden; giving you this information about Morocco, not knowing that you're the man who was working for Schlieken. On the other hand he may know all about you. You've got to be ready for anything."

Fells thought for a moment; then he said: "The situation seems fairly simple, doesn't it? If he goes on being Foden; if he believes that I'm working for you; that I've been deputed to receive his information about Morocco, he'll give it to me. He'll take his money and he'll fade out. On the other hand if he's one of Schlieken's bad boys, if he recognizes who I am, the probability is he's going to come straight out with it. You know that the Schlieken mob are very tough—I don't have to tell you that."

Quayle said: "No, you don't. And this Foden is one of the toughest propositions I've met. He knows what he's doing. He's quite ruthless and he's very clever."

Fells said: "If he goes on being Foden—if he gives me the Moroccan information—all I can do is to make a note of it and bring it back to you; give him his money. I presume you'll have somebody looking after him when he leaves me?"

Quayle nodded. "I'll look after that," he said.

"The thing is," said Fells, "what am I going to do if he plays it the other way? What am I going to do if he admits who he is, recognizes me and puts something up to me—some scheme he's had in his mind all along?"

Quayle said: "That's where the situation becomes a little difficult. I'm afraid you'll have to play along with him. You'll have to go back and start working for the Germans again." He smiled wryly. "And in that case you must be careful," he said, "not to make any contact whatsoever with me or anybody else."

Fells said: "How do I account for being put in to receive this information from him?"

Quayle said: "That's easy. Quite obviously a man like you, who'd been working for Schlieken, would have tried to get himself grafted somehow on to one of our departments here during war-time. Even if we hadn't trusted you very much we should still have used you. On the other hand if you'd remained loyal to Schlieken, and you've got to persuade Foden—if he's wise to you—that you *have* remained loyal to Schlieken, then it's going to be a great feather in your cap that you've been able to work yourself right in next to me in such a position of trust that I actually put you in to receive this secret information about Morocco. That's common sense."

Fells said: "Yes. I understand that."

Quayle went on: "The ideal situation will be this. The ideal situation will be that Foden recognizes you, discloses who and what he is, trusts you and proceeds to put you wise as to what he's really doing over here. That will be the ideal situation. You play along with him. You'll have to go to *any* steps to establish your loyalty to Schlieken. You'll have to assess the situation. If necessary you'll have to give away the fact that we've been on to him from the start. Use that as a last resort, because if you do that he'll *have* to trust you. That would look so good that he'd believe anything. If you play it that way you mustn't make any attempt to contact me. You'll have to play it on your own, leaving me to get in touch with you by some means or other as soon as I can."

Fells said: "I understand perfectly. There is just one point. Supposing for the sake of argument that Foden, whose entry into this country was successfully planned, *is* working for Schlieken, and has an exit plan worked out. What happens then?"

Quayle said slowly: "Well, if he's going to get out and wants to take you, you'll have to go with him, won't you? It would be marvellous if Foden took you out of this country—back to France or Germany— if Schlieken gave you still more work to do. It would be wonderful. Consider how good it would be if he actually sent you back here working for him as you were before."

Fells nodded. His face was very grave. He said: "Yes, it would be. Then you could play both ends against the middle."

Quayle said: "That was the idea."

There was a pause. Quayle took out his cigarette case; offered it to Fells. They began to smoke. After a little while, Fells said:

"Now I understand about Tangier. Now I see why you wanted to break that up—at any rate for the moment."

Quayle said: "I'm glad you understand, Fells. You know I'm damned sorry, but I've got my job to do, and you've got to do yours."

Fells got up. He said: "Well, there's nothing more to talk about, is there? I'll wait till Foden comes to-morrow night and then I shall know what I've got to do. And if he recognizes who I am I'll do the best I can."

"That's it," said Quayle. "And even if you go out of this country, I'll get someone in touch with you somehow—sometime."

He went to his desk; took out some banknotes. "Here's the pay-off for Foden," he said. "I arranged that you should give it to him before he starts talking. It breaks my heart to hand over so much money but it may be worth it."

Fells said: "It's a lot, isn't it?" He smiled. "You're after something really big, aren't you, Quayle?"

Quayle nodded. "I'm after Schlieken," he said. "If we could find out where Schlieken is. If we knew where he was; whether he was in France or Germany or where we could get him—somehow. . . . And if we got Schlieken we'd break up their English espionage branch in six months. . . ."

Fells said: "I see. If Foden's working for Schlieken; if he's got an exit scheme planned, he'll take me with him. Then you'll rely on one of our European people getting a contact with me, and then . . ."

"That's about it," said Quayle. "Damned good luck to you, Fells."

Fells said: "Thanks." He picked up his hat. He went to the door. He hesitated for a moment; turned.

He said: "You know, Quayle, it's been good fun. I'd like you to know that I've always been very grateful to you."

He went out.

Quayle stood in front of the fireplace looking at the fire. He took his cigarette out of his mouth and threw it into the grate. He said:

"Grateful—my God!"

CHAPTER 10
THE MICKEY FINN

I

THE Silver Boot Club is an ornate institution, situated on a first floor near Albemarle Street. It is just another of those places. It has existed for some years and the best accountant would be hard put to it to decide exactly how it makes its profits. It is furnished in pale grey and black with lots of chromium, and the young woman behind the bar, whose equilibrium was in permanent danger from the height of her French heels, had an air of almost aristocratic Bohemianism. She exuded charm, a spurious hauteur and "*Toujours à Toi*" perfume.

Foden and Greeley sat at the end of the bar furthest from the door. They were the only customers. Before them on the counter stood large whiskies and sodas—the fourth set-up since their arrival.

Greeley said: "This is a bit better than kickin' around pubs in the Midlands. This is class."

Foden said nothing. He was watching the girl behind the bar. Greeley was about to speak when the door opened and a girl came in.

She was quite startling. Although she was quietly dressed in a well-cut black coat and skirt, a silk shirt and a tailor-made hat, she presented a picture that was almost shattering in its intensity. Her hair was dead black. Her eyes large and brown. Her face very white. She had a beautiful mouth that was made up with the exact shade of carmine. She moved quickly, with an urgent vitality in every step. When she spoke she radiated energy. When she smiled her parted lips showed beautiful teeth.

She came straight to Greeley. She said: "Well, I'll be damned! If it isn't Horace!"

Greeley swung slowly round on his stool. He said: "Jeez—Mayola!"

Mayola laughed. Her laugh cut through the room. It was quite carefree. Foden had the impression that her life had been made by this sudden meeting with Horace.

She said: "Well, what do you know about that? And how's Zilla? I haven't seen her for weeks."

Greeley said, after a moment: "Neither have I. She hasn't been very well or something. I believe she's got some leave. She's away in the country somewhere. You know what she is."

"Don't I know?" said Mayola—"the old mysterious Zilla. Well . . . well . . . well . . .?"

She turned and looked at Foden. She looked at him long and carefully. She started with his shoes, then her eyes travelled upwards to his fair hair. She showed undisguised admiration. She said softly:

"Oh, boy . . . oh, boy . . . what a man! Who is it, Horace? I can hardly wait."

Greeley said: "This is Mr. Foden—a pal of mine. This is Miss Mayola Green. She's a friend of Zilla's. I met her here with Zilla in the old days."

Foden said: "I'm very glad to meet you, Miss Green."

Mayola said: "I'm very glad to meet *you*. It's a long time since I've seen a man who looks as good as you do."

Foden raised his eyebrows. "You're trying to flatter me," he said.

"Don't you believe it," said Mayola cheerfully. "I never flatter men." She swung herself on to a stool, the graceful movement giving Foden a chance to admire the suppleness of her perfect figure. She said: "Well, is anybody going to buy me a drink or do *I* have to buy one?"

Foden said: "I'd like to buy you a drink. What will you have?"

"The biggest drink of the most expensive thing they've got," said Mayola. "Brandy, I think. I feel like a lot of brandy."

Foden gave the order to the high-heeled guardian of the other side of the bar, who said with dignity: "You can only have one double brandy. We're running short."

Foden grinned at Mayola. He said: "I'm sorry you can only have one."

"One's better than nothing," said Mayola. "And if I want another one I know where I can get it. This place always has been stingy with liquor. They keep it for their friends."

The barmaid said: "I resent that. We're rationed; *you* ought to know that."

Mayola said: "You keep your hair on, ducky. And don't get annoyed; otherwise you'll fall over. You ought to get a boy friend to carve those heels down a bit."

The barmaid gave a little gasp. She put the double brandy in front of Mayola; turned, went to the other end of the bar with great dignity.

Foden said: "Miss Green's quite a personality, isn't she?"

Greeley chuckled. "A personality! My God!" he said. "She's a bleedin' whirlwind. You wait till you get to know her a bit better."

Foden said: "I'm looking forward to it."

Mayola picked up her glass. She drank off the double brandy quietly and consistently without a pause. She put the glass back on the counter.

She said: "That's better. Now, what's going on around here? What have you boys been up to?"

"We haven't been up to anything," Greeley answered. "We've just been having a few drinks—a sort of little celebration."

"Celebration, hey?" said Mayola. "What have you been celebrating? Has something good happened to somebody?"

"Just a little bit of business," said Greeley. "You know how it is these days. It's difficult to pull anything off. If you do, you're more than lucky."

"That's right," agreed Mayola. She said to the girl behind the bar: "I suppose it's true what you said about not having any more brandy?"

"It's true enough," the barmaid said. "And whether you believe it or not, it's true as far as *you* go."

"There's no need to be rude," said Mayola. "You ought to think yourself very lucky to be serving behind a bar. I expect most of the customers wonder why you're not in the Services. But I expect they haven't got around to your age-group yet."

She got off the stool. "Look, children," she said. "I'm sick of this dump. Any time I get in here I feel repressed."

Greeley grinned. "You're a one, Mayola," he said. "You don't alter a bit."

She looked at him impertinently. "D'you think you'd like me better if I did alter?" she said.

Foden said: "I don't think so." He looked at her out of the corners of his eyes. "I think I like you just as you are." Mayola smiled appreciatively. "Well, that's fine. Let's get out of here. We'll go around to my place. Believe it or not I've two or three bottles of *real* brandy, and some other stuff too. Besides, the atmosphere's better there." She looked at the girl behind the counter and laughed. "Well, how does that go?"

Greeley said: "It suits me."

Foden said: "I'm game for anything."

"All right," said Mayola. "Let's get out of here and get downstairs and see if we can get a taxicab. It's almost impossible but it has been known." She said to the girl behind the bar: "Good-night, Sourpuss!"

They went out.

Greeley's head was aching. He lay back against the soft corner of the settee. From out of the corners of his eyes he could see Foden on the other side of the room finishing his brandy and soda. Greeley thought: You must have a stomach with a steel lining. I thought I was pretty good but you take the cake!

A cuckoo clock on the mantelpiece began to chime. A little door on one side opened and a cuckoo came out. Mayola, who was perched precariously on the piano stool, bent down to take off her high heeled shoe. As she did so, the velvet dressing-gown into which she had changed when they arrived at the flat, flapped open and showed a long expanse of silk clad leg. Foden saw it. He grinned at Greeley.

The cuckoo clock was still chiming. By now Mayola had removed her shoe. She hurled it at the clock. Her aim, though wild, was lucky. The clock bounced on to the carpet and lay face upwards still chiming.

Mayola said: "Some clock! But it's a good one. How I hate that goddam clock. Every night just as I'm going to sleep it wakes me up, and when I want to wake up I never hear it."

Greeley said: "You should worry." He was surprised to find he was speaking a little thickly. He wondered how many brandies and sodas they had drunk. He looked at Foden.

Foden was lying back in his chair—relaxed and happy. He seemed quite sober. Only his eyes were a little bright.

Mayola said: "I don't know about you boys, but I'm beginning to be the tiniest bit high. Not cockeyed, mark you—just a little high."

She swung round on the piano stool. She began to play: "You Made Me Love You and I Didn't Want to Do It!" Then she began to sing. She had quite a good voice and she sang with a delightful air of abandon. She ogled Foden theatrically.

When she had finished, Greeley said: "What about the neighbours? Somebody's going to kill you one of these fine nights."

Mayola said: "There aren't any neighbours. Underneath this flat there's a shop, and above me it's all empty. I just reign in solitary state."

She began on another song. It was a hot plaintive number. Greeley thought: This woman could have made a lot of money on the stage.

Foden got up. He walked over to the piano. He said: "Did anyone ever tell you, Mayola, that you're very beautiful?"

She winked at him. She said: "You'd be surprised! But I don't believe most of 'em." She looked humorously serious. "You know what, Fodie-Wodie," she said, "whenever a man tells me that I look beautiful I always wonder what he's after."

Foden said: "I'll give you two guesses." He went on: "You've got very nice legs, Mayola."

She said: "Yes? I've heard that one before somewhere too. Let's have a drink."

She got up; walked a little unsteadily towards the sideboard. Greeley thought: Either she *is* a bit cockeyed or she's a damned good actress. He lit a cigarette.

Mayola knelt down and opened the doors of the sideboard. She poked her head inside. After a moment she began to swear. She swore very comprehensively. She said:

"Believe it or not there's no brandy." She produced an empty bottle. "What do you know about that?" she said. "Look at it—bone dry."

Foden said casually: "You ought to lock it up."

"You're telling me," said Mayola. "It's that cow who comes in to clean for me. I suppose she's been having nips. God—how I hate that woman!"

"Well, why don't you get rid of her?" Foden asked.

"Don't be silly," said Mayola. "You're lucky if you can get anyone to come in and look after you these days. Didn't somebody tell you there's a war on?"

Foden said: "Yes—I heard about it!"

Mayola began to examine the interior of the sideboard. She said: "You know, you boys, this is very, very serious?"

"What is?" asked Greeley.

"This liquor question," said Mayola. "I don't believe I've got any more drink. Hey, wait a minute . . . what's this?" She produced a bottle.

She stood up; stood looking at the label, her head on one side. After a moment she said dramatically:

"No, not that—anything but *that*."

"What's the matter with it?" asked Greeley. He thought: She's going to start something. I wonder how she's going to play it.

"What's the matter with it?" said Mayola. "Listen, Horace, I'd rather drink poison."

Foden walked over and took the bottle from Mayola. He began to laugh. "This is all right," he said.

Mayola said: "All right! Do you know what that stuff is?"

Foden said: "I ought to. I've drunk gallons of it. It's Araki."

"Don't you believe it," said Mayola. "It's just pure poison. I had another bottle of it. I had two drinks out of it about six months ago. It took me nearly a week to get over it."

Foden laughed. He put his right arm round Mayola's waist. He stood there looking down at her, the bottle in his left hand. He said:

"I've drunk gallons of this stuff. You can get lots of it where I come from—even if we don't keep it in pretty bottles like this. It's just got a kick, that's all. It won't hurt you."

"Won't it?" said Mayola. "Well, as far as I'm concerned you can have it."

Foden said: "It's really not very much stronger than whisky or gin. It's just an odd mixture, that's all."

"Maybe," said Mayola. "But it does things to me."

Greeley said: "What the hell is the matter with you two—quarrelling over liquor? *I* can drink anything that comes out of a bottle."

Mayola disengaged herself. She came over towards Greeley. She said: "Look, Horace, do you fancy yourself as a drinker?"

Greeley said: "Well, I'm not so bad. I'll drink with anybody."

"Yes?" said Mayola. "And how much can you drink without getting drunk?"

Greeley said: "I don't know. I can't remember when I was drunk."

Mayola was twiddling the rather large cameo ring on the third finger of her left hand. She turned it over. She turned it over so that the cameo was underneath.

Foden, who was leaning against the sideboard with the bottle in his hand, said: "You don't mean to tell me, Horace, that you can't get drunk?"

Greeley said: "I don't know about that. I just can't remember the last time I was drunk."

Mayola said: "Perhaps he doesn't mix his drinks. That's what does it—that and the cool night air."

"Hooey!" said Greeley. "I'll mix anything."

Mayola winked at Foden. She said to Greeley: "Look, you beautiful beast. I'll tell you what I'll do. You try a shot out of this bottle of mine—a good shot—and if you're sober ten minutes afterwards I'll eat my best hat in public."

Foden picked up her shoe from the hearthrug. He brought it over to her. She put her arm round his neck and supported herself while she put the shoe on.

Greeley said: "What is this? I believe you two are tryin' something on me. I think you're tryin' to get me cockeyed. Well, look, I'll drink level with you. I'll drink anything if anybody else will."

Foden said: "Don't you worry, Horace. This stuff couldn't hurt you. Mark you, it's not made for little girls, it's a man's drink." He squeezed Mayola.

Mayola said: "All right, you can have it. But leave me out."

Foden said: "Now, Mayola, you're not ducking, are you? You'd better have just a little drop—about a quarter of what we have." He winked at Greeley.

Mayola said: "You know, Fodie-Wodie, I think you've got designs on me, and I think you think that just one out of that bottle would just about make me right for you. Is that it?"

Foden grinned at her. He said: "I wouldn't do a thing like that."

"I bet you wouldn't," said Mayola. "You're one of those men that I'd just trust anywhere in any circumstances. Like hell I would!"

She took the bottle from Foden; went back to the sideboard; opened the drawer; took out a corkscrew. She put the bottle between her knees; extracted the cork.

Foden said: "You know, Horace, Mayola has very nice knees."

Greeley said: "You're tellin' me."

The corkscrew came out with a plop. Mayola dived into the sideboard; produced three glasses. She poured out two long shots and one little one. She picked up two of the glasses; gave one to Greeley—the other to Foden. Then she went back and got the third glass. She said:

"Well, I ought to know better, but here goes!" She put the glass to her lips.

They all drank. The liquor was potent in an odd sort of way. It burned the back of Greeley's throat. He thought it tasted a little like Vodka. He put the glass down.

"It's not bad," he said. "Anyhow, it's better than nothing."

Foden said: "I like it as well as brandy, if not better. Maybe that's because I'm used to it."

"All right," said Mayola. "Have some more. But I tell you I'm not feeling so good now. That stuff does something to me."

She re-filled the men's glasses.

Greeley said: "Well, here's how!" He swallowed his in one gulp.

Foden looked at him and grinned. He said: "You know, Horace, you're an extraordinary fellow. I've never seen anybody drink like you do. How much had you had to-day before I met you?"

"Not much," said Greeley. "Just a few beers."

Foden swallowed his drink. Then he began to walk towards the sideboard. He put down the glass and turned; then, without any warning, he collapsed on the rug with a crash. He lay there like a log.

Mayola said: "And that's that!"

Greeley got up. He went over to Foden; stood looking down at him. "He's out all right," he said. "How did you do it?"

Mayola held up her left hand—the palm towards Greeley. He saw that the big cameo ring on her finger was open. Inside the cavity there still remained a few grains of white powder.

Greeley said: "How long's he goin' to be like this?"

She shrugged her shoulders. "It depends on him," she said. "But he's tough and fit. He'll be coming out of it in about an hour." She put her fingers to her hair; arranged the waves. She said casually: "But don't let that bother you. I'll keep him under as long as you want."

Greeley threw his cigarette stub away. He took a box of Players from his pocket; gave one to Mayola. They stood smoking, looking at Foden.

Greeley said: "I'm sorry it had to be done this way. This one's a leery one. He's not goin' to like this when he comes round. He's goin' to be goddam suspicious."

She said: "I don't think so—not if we play it the right way."

"How's that?" asked Greeley.

She said: "You do what you've got to do and get back here; then I'll give you a mild dose of that—the same as he had. You can both come out together. Maybe I'll have a little myself too." She sighed. "The things I do for England," she said.

Greeley grinned at her. "You're a one, Mayola," he said. "I believe you like this."

"Like hell!" said Mayola. "This is just my hobby. What do you think?"

Greeley bent over Foden; straightened him out. He began to go through his pockets. On a ring in the left-hand trouser pocket he found two keys. He straightened up.

"That's what I want," he said. "This is the outside door key and his room key at the place he lives at. I'm goin' to take a look round there."

She said: "Well, I hope it keeps fine for you. And don't make a noise or you may find yourself knocked off for bein' a burglar."

Greeley said: "You teach your grandmother to suck eggs, Mayola."

She said: "All right. And what do I do with this gorgeous thing while you're away? Do I just leave him there?"

"Oh, no," said Greeley. "You get busy on him. Go over every inch of him—laundry marks—markings on underclothes—everything. And don't waste any time about it. I'd hate him to come round while you were working on him."

Mayola laughed. "You're telling me," she said. "He might get the wrong idea."

Greeley put the keys in his pocket. He went out into the hallway; took his cap from the table. She came after him.

She said: "Haven't you got an overcoat?"

Greeley said: "I never wear one. I don't feel the cold much. Well, so long, Mayola."

She asked: "When will you be back? Don't forget we've got to finish this little comedy in the right way."

"I know," said Greeley. "With luck I'll be back in an hour. And don't forget—" He nodded towards the sitting-room. "Go over the boy friend with a fine-tooth comb. I'll be seein' you."

He opened the front door; went out.

II

The blonde girl who worked in Quayle's office rested her head on her hands and gazed blankly in front of her. She was very tired.

By turning her wrist over and screwing her blonde head sideways she could look at her wrist-watch with the minimum amount of exertion. It told her that it was two o'clock.

She thought this is a hell of a time to be at work—two o'clock in the morning. But in any event she shouldn't be so tired. She had had six hours off in the afternoon and evening. If she hadn't rested that was her fault.

She wondered what Quayle was doing. She listened. No sound came from the next door flat, but anyway Quayle never made any sort of noise when he walked about. And he was always walking about. Pacing about the place restlessly like a tiger. She wondered if he ever went to bed and slept properly. She thought not.

That leave would be pretty good if she got it. She probably would get it. She would go away somewhere where it was quiet and think about nothing at all. She would try and forget Quayle and the long list of names and telephone numbers that she carried in her mind. She would merely think about herself and Eustace.

She began to think about Eustace and wonder where he was. He was in a torpedo boat somewhere or other. Eustace who was going to be an architect and was now an A.B. Anyhow, he looked damned nice in his uniform (she realized she should have said "rig" not "uniform"—Eustace would have pulled her up about that) and he was a pretty good sailor. But then he was good at anything he did.

Quayle would give her the week's leave all right. If he could. Unless something blew up. And you never knew when something was going to blow up. The blonde girl knew little about Quayle's organization but she had sense and she guessed a lot.

He must be pretty tired of it, she thought. Dashing about meeting people, plotting, planning, scheming. Trying to keep one jump ahead of the other side, trying to make up for all the time that the German Intelligence and external espionage services had had at their disposal during the years between the two wars when we were asleep and they were working night and day.

She yawned. She began to think about some of the people with whom Quayle used to keep in touch—people who used to telephone through to the office and who, for some reason or other, had ceased to ring up. There was that rather nice man Massanay, and the girl— the brunette—Dufours, and the little grey-haired woman named Swetham. The blonde girl knew about her. They had found her in a ditch near St. Albans in a fearful state. She had been terribly knocked about. The police thought that she'd been knocked down by a car and dragged along the road. There was a picture of the body in one of the filing cabinets. She'd seen it. It looked as if someone had taken the trouble to run over Mrs. Swetham several times—as if they'd rather liked doing it.

And Quayle had been fearfully fed up with that bit of business. His language had been terrible for a whole day.

She wondered what Eustace would say if he knew what her job *really* was. Of course he wouldn't believe it. Anyhow, it was none of his business. Next time she met him she'd wear her uniform. That would knock him for ninety. But she'd have to make up something about that. She couldn't very well inform him that she held the rank of Squadron Officer in the W.A.A.F. simply (as Quayle put it) so that she should be under discipline and forced to keep her mouth shut whether she liked it or not.

Well . . . she kept it shut. If you worked for Quayle you kept it buttoned up. She thought it probably wouldn't be so good for you if you didn't. Quayle could be kind but he could be damned merciless too if he wanted to be. She'd noticed one or two things; been able to put this and that together. . . .

And now there was something on with Fells. The blonde girl liked Fells. He was nice. You liked him instinctively. She was rather curious about him. And something was on. Whenever they came up to the office and actually saw Quayle—as Fells had done—then it was serious business.

She'd noticed something else too. Very often when people came up and saw Quayle they didn't come any more, and they didn't come through on the telephone. Probably, she thought, Quayle sent them off somewhere. She hoped they came back all right. She wondered where Fells was going. She knew that Quayle had lots of people in France. Perhaps he was going to send Fells there.

The telephone jangled suddenly. The blonde girl jumped. She took off the receiver. It was Greeley.

He said: "Hello. Mr. Quayle there?"

She said: "That's Mr. Greeley, isn't it? Hold on. I'll put you through."

She rang through to Quayle's bedroom. She said: "Mr. Quayle, Mr. Greeley's on the line."

Quayle said: "Put him through."

She plugged in the line. She put her head back on her hands and thought about Eustace.

Quayle asked: "Well, Greeley. How is it?"

"It's not so good," said Greeley. "We went round to The Silver Boot. We met Mayola. Then we went on to her place. That part of it's O.K. I've just left Foden's place. I've been over it with a fine-tooth comb."

Quayle asked: "Did you get in and out all right?"

"It was easy," said Greeley. "I used his keys."

"Did you find anything?" asked Quayle.

"Not a thing," said Greeley. "Not a goddam thing. Mayola may have found something on him. I'm going back there now."

Quayle said: "She won't find anything on him. Everything he'll have on will be new—bought in England. She'll draw a blank too."

Greeley said: "I expect you're right, Mr. Quayle."

Quayle asked: "Anything else?"

Greeley said: "Well, I had a talk with Foden to-night round at his place before we went out to meet Mayola. He told me he was meeting Fells to-morrow evening. He asked me if Zilla had ever mentioned the name. I said no—she didn't trust me enough. He told me Fells was going to give him the balance of the money when he saw him. He gave me a hundred and promised me a bit more. He said he'd come round and see me to-morrow night; that he might be a bit late. He *might* do that of course."

Quayle said: "Yes, he might. And he might not. I wonder what's the latest time he'd come round to you."

Greeley thought for a moment. "Well," he said, "if his business with Fells is going to take him a long time, they'd talk for a couple of hours or so and then fix to go on the next day. That would be the sensible thing to do, wouldn't it? In that case he'd be round at my place by ten or half-past."

"Yes," said Quayle. "He wouldn't make it later than that. If he was going to have a very long session with Fells they'd arrange to meet the next day, as you say."

Greeley asked: "Anything else, Mr. Quayle?"

Quayle said: "Not much. You'd better go back to Mayola and tie the ends up there. And there's just this. If Foden doesn't get to your place by ten-thirty to-morrow night ring me up here."

"Right," said Greeley. There was a pause; then he said: "Excuse me, Mr. Quayle, but wouldn't it be an idea to put a tail on Foden to-morrow; then you'd know what he was doing. You'd get some idea of what he was playing at."

Quayle said: "Perhaps I *know* what he's playing at. Thanks for the suggestion, Greeley, but I daren't put a tail on him. Foden's damned clever. If he got the slightest idea that we were tailing him it wouldn't be so good. It might make things even worse than they are."

Greeley said: "I see. Well, so long, Mr. Quayle."

"Good-night, Greeley," said Quayle.

Mayola opened the door. She was smoking a cigarette.

She said: "Come in, Horace. The exhibition is still on."

Greeley dropped his cap on a chair in the hall.

She said: "Well, did you find what you were looking for?"

Greeley said: "No, I wasn't very lucky."

She took the cigarette from her mouth. She said: "What's all this excitement about anyway?"

Greeley said: "Have you worked for Quayle for long?"

She said: "About three years. Why?"

He said. "It's long enough for you to know better than to ask questions."

"All right, snooty," said Mayola. "High hat, hey? I'm a woman you know, and therefore curious."

"Curiosity killed the cat," said Greeley.

They went into the sitting-room. Foden was stretched out on the settee.

Greeley said: "Well, I'll be damned. You must be a strong one. How did you get that big lug on there?"

She laughed. "You'd be surprised," she said. "I've lifted heavier ones than that before now." She went over to the sideboard; stood looking at Foden. "He's a tough bird, that one. Would you believe it, he started coming round about half an hour ago? He must have an inside like a battleship."

"What did you do about that?" asked Greeley.

"That was easy," she said. "I know all the answers. I put the fluence on him. I've got some stuff in a bottle."

"Nice work," said Greeley. "What is it?"

She shrugged her shoulders. "I wouldn't know," she said. "Quayle gave it to me."

Greeley said: "So you've done this stuff before. I thought you looked as if you'd had a lot of practice."

She said: "That's my business. Who's getting curious now?"

Greeley grinned at her. "I like you, Mayola," he said.

She said: "Look, Horace, don't tell me that you're picking a time like this for a love scene, because I don't think I could bear it."

Greeley grinned. "All right," he said. "Let's keep to business. Have you been over the boy friend?"

She nodded. "There's nothing on him. Everything he's wearing is new. He's got some money in his pocketbook, and the identity card they gave him down at his port of arrival. What did you expect to find—the Crown jewels?"

Greeley said: "Whatever we expected to find, we haven't found it, have we?"

Mayola went to the table. She picked up her own and Greeley's glass. She said:

"Well, this is where the nasty business starts. We've got to be artistic."

Greeley said: "You mean I've got to drink some of that damn' hooch with a Mickey Finn powder in it, hey—in order to make the game look all square?"

She said: "I'm not worrying about you, but I'll have to do it too, won't I—otherwise he might smell a rat? He saw *me* drink some of that stuff."

Greeley said: "O.K., Mayola. You're a heroine. They'll give you a medal one day."

"Like hell they will," said Mayola. "But I know that goddam dope. To-morrow my complexion will be yellow and my eyes like balls of fire. Anyhow, let's stop talking about it."

She poured out two small drinks from the bottle. Then she went out of the room. When she came back she had in her hand a small cardboard box. She dropped a few grains of the white powder in the box into each of the glasses.

She said: "I'm only giving us a little shot, but that'll be bad enough."

Greeley said: "What does it do to you?"

She shrugged her shoulders. "You feel very sick and fearfully giddy," she said. "And then you go out."

Greeley picked up his glass. "Well," he said, "here's to you, Mayola."

"Chin-chin!" she said.

They drained the glasses. Greeley sat down in a chair. Mayola, rather artistically, sat on the rug and leaned up against the side-board. Greeley looked at her. He thought she was very pretty. In a way she was nearly as pretty as Zilla. Life was a scream, he thought. Zilla Stevenson had sailed casually into his life and then sailed out again. And here was another one—another pretty woman. Gree-ley expected that after to-night he would never see her again. He thought it was rather a shame. He thought that all the women who worked for Quayle had something. They would probably improve on acquaintance.

Unfortunately for him the acquaintance never lasted for long. He felt very tired.

The room began to go dark.

CHAPTER 11
BETWEEN FRIENDS

I

IT WAS just after seven o'clock. Fells sat at the desk in the corner of his sitting-room. He began to write a letter:

"Dear Tangier,

"Thank you very much for your letter. Of course you're absolutely right. I had a talk with Q. yesterday. He told me all about you. He's given me a pretty good idea as to why he advised you to get away from London. I think he was quite right.

"He was right in thinking that it would be good if, just now, you and I didn't see very much of each other. He thought that my attitude of mind towards the job I'm on might be affected by the fact that I'm in love with you. But he was wrong there.

"I have spent so many years at this work. I've got so used to it, and I realize so strongly how much depends on Q. being successful, that I shouldn't allow anything to interfere with his plans.

"But Q. never takes a chance. One is never quite certain what's going on in his mind. He's very wise and very much braver than any of us are because although he takes many risks himself he spends most of the time thinking and worrying about the people who work for him.

"I won't say any more now. I hope I'll be able to finish this job the way Q. wants it finished. If I can there might be a chance for us."

Fells signed the letter, put it in an envelope, stamped it, went out. He posted the letter in the pillar box on the corner of the street.

When he came back his landlady was standing in the hallway. She said:

"That gentleman you were expecting has come, Mr. Fells. I've shown him upstairs."

Fells said: "Thank you." He walked up the stairs.

Foden was standing in front of the fireplace. His hat was on a chair. His overcoat was open. His right hand was in his overcoat pocket. He held a cigarette in his left.

Fells closed the door behind him quietly. He stood looking at Foden, smiling.

Foden said: "Hello, Fells. I'm glad to see you."

Fells said: "Why don't you take your coat off?"

"Thanks," said Foden. He took off his overcoat, put it on the chair with his hat. He went back to the fireplace. He said quietly: "You know, I think we might cut out a lot of frills, don't you? I expect you know who I am."

Fells said: "I don't. But I might make a pretty good guess."

Foden nodded. "Your guess would be right," he said.

"I'm Emil Reinek—very much at your service. I think I might describe myself as Herr Schlieken's personal assistant." He held out his hand.

Fells came across the room. He was smiling. He shook hands. He said: "That makes it easy, but I'd better go on calling you Foden, hadn't I?"

The other said: "Why not? It's an amusing name. It's certainly served me well. So until I shake the dust of England from my feet, I'll go on being Foden."

Fells said: "Your English is perfect. I've always admired the way Schlieken trains his people."

Foden shrugged. "My English *ought* to be perfect. I suppose altogether I've spent about ten years in this country. You know," he said proudly, "I can even speak with a Manchester accent if I want to."

Fells said: "There's another thing about you. You seem to have a sense of humour. That's more than a lot of Schlieken's people have."

Foden said: "Candidly, some of the Schlieken group take themselves much too seriously. To do a job like mine successfully one must be prepared for anything, and if one is going to be prepared for anything it's absolutely essential that one has a sense of humour. This situation, for instance," he went on, "is most amusing, don't you think?"

Fells said: "It's damned amusing. It's the sort of thing that seems absolutely impossible."

"Quite," said Foden. "Yet it's so simple. Shall we sit down? I would like to do a little explaining. That, at least, is due to you."

Fells said: "Of course. Will you have a cigarette?"

He produced the box. Foden took one. They sat down—one on each side of the fire.

Foden said: "Briefly, here is the position: It will appeal to you. You know, the war came a little suddenly for us. We did not think that the English would mean serious business for at least another two or three months. When war was declared I was in Berlin with Schlieken. We checked up on our people in the Department. Quite a lot of the external espionage and intelligence sections had not time to get back. They were all over the world. Most people in Schlieken's shoes would have tried hard to get them back. In the process he would have lost half of them. He would have got fifty per cent back and what good would it have done him?"

He drew appreciatively on his cigarette. He continued: "That is where Schlieken has genius. We were sitting in his office on the Frederickstrasse, drinking a glass of brandy. He said to me suddenly: 'Emil, I have an idea. We will leave every operative we have in any foreign country just where he is. All the people that we know and trust we will leave. We will not even make an attempt to contact them.' Of course it was a brilliant idea."

Fells said: "Was it? I think I know Schlieken's system as well as anybody. How was it clever?"

Foden blew a smoke ring. He said: "It was brilliant. Schlieken's idea was this: An operative is left in a foreign country. Of course he has adopted some other personality. Well, he's there. He can't get back to Germany and no contact is sent over to get in touch with him. Well, what's he going to do? No expense money is coming through. His lines of communication are cut and in any event even if they weren't he would be a fool to try and use them." He shrugged his shoulders. "One or two idiots over here tried to use them," he said, "with the result that the English got them. Schlieken expected that. People who were foolish enough to do things like that deserved what happened to them."

Fells nodded. "And the others?" he queried.

"Figure it out for yourself. Schlieken's argument was that the others would do one of two things. The mediocre ones would try and merge themselves into the identity of the country in which they found themselves. They'd get work of some sort. They'd manage to live somehow, always with the idea that one day they would be able to get back to Germany. But the clever ones, what would they do? Most of them had good identities established. They were supposed to be Englishmen or Frenchmen. Well, if they had intelligence, if they had really taken notice of their early training, they would obviously have got themselves in touch with one of the Intelligence Departments here. They would put up some story. They would work themselves in somehow, knowing that if ever they got back to the Reich they would be in possession of invaluable information."

Fells nodded. "I see," he said.

"When we came to your name on the list," Foden went on, "Schlieken said: 'I know what Fells will do. Fells hates the English. They haven't been at all kind to him. They kicked him out of the army. They put him into prison. They made his name stink. All the energy and loyalty which he had put into his service as an English soldier has turned into a hatred that is working for us. Fells will be very clever.' "

Foden drew on his cigarette. He drew tobacco smoke down into his lungs; expelled it slowly. He continued:

"Schlieken's idea was that some part of the English Intelligence—some Department—would find a use for Fells. They would think that Fells would be glad to have a chance of doing any dirty work. They would not know of course that you had been working for Schlieken. You understand?"

Fells said: "Schlieken is a most brilliant man. There's no one quite like him. Not only does he understand his job but he understands people."

"Exactly," said Foden. "You realize he understood you. I remember that conversation perfectly. He sat looking at me across that big glass-top desk of his with his eyes shining behind his pince-nez. You remember those little shining eyes—that sharp, razor-edged nose? I can remember him looking at me and smiling and saying: 'All we have to do is to leave Fells there for a year—two years—give him a chance to work himself in. Give him a chance to get himself a job. Give him a chance to get himself trusted. And then—then, my dear

Emil, when the time is ripe I think we will send you in to see our good friend Fells.' "

Fells said: "Very clever. That was nice work, Foden."

"It was," agreed Foden. "I came in here from Morocco. I've been playing a game with the English for years. I went to their people and tried to give information against the Germans twice. It was good information, too. They knew it when I went there. That's why they knew it was good. Afterwards, when I pretended to have something very big for them, I knew they would be only too glad to get the mariner Foden—the second officer who had been serving for years on Moroccan coastal ships—into England.

"But," Foden went on, "if we've thought that Schlieken was brilliant, we've still not yet realized *how* brilliant he was. Listen to this."

He leaned forward. His eyes were shining. Fells realized that this man loved his work; that excitement and danger were tonics to him.

"I said to Schlieken: 'Supposing you are wrong? Supposing Fells goes bad on us? I might be walking into a trap in one or two years' time when you decide to send me in.' Do you know what he said?" asked Foden. "Can you imagine what he said?"

Fells shook his head. "I can't," he said. "But I'll bet it was something pretty good."

"It *was* good," said Foden. "This is what he said: 'Supposing for the sake of argument that Fells *has* gone bad on us. Supposing that in an excess of misguided patriotism, or because of money, or because of something, Fells decides to go back to being an Englishman again—to work for those damned people. Supposing he tells them what he knows of us. All right, what will happen? Anybody that I put in—anybody who professes to have first-class information for the British, such as you will profess to have, Emil—that man will be certain to come up against Fells, because the information which he will profess to have will be information bearing on those things which Fells learned while he was with us.

"'Very well then, we will imagine,' Schlieken continued, 'that you meet Fells and that Fells has gone bad on us. They will still let you out and they will still let Fells out. Because consider—if Fells is working for them they will think it possible for them to contact him. They will think it possible to use him. *We* shall be working for them they will think. *We* shall be taking Fells out of England and putting him into Germany. They will think that one of their many agents operating in Germany will be able to contact him.' "

Foden said: "Well, is that brilliant or is it not? More importantly"—he smiled at Fells—"is it correct?"

Fells said nothing for a moment. He thought whatever you do, Fells—whatever you say—you're in a trap. Whatever they think, your number's up. Schlieken is very clever. They're going to use you as a sort of hostage. In any event you're for it.

He said: "Herr Schlieken does not flatter me, does he? I imagined he knew me. How could he think that I could ever do anything for the English after what they did to me?"

Foden nodded. "Precisely," he said. "That is exactly what I said. And that is what he knows. At the same time I think you will agree that his theory showed us that we're not taking many chances."

Fells said: "I shall be glad to get out of here. I've had enough of this country. Schlieken knows what I think of it—all of it—everybody in it."

Foden smiled amicably. He said: "My friend, you shall have your wish." He got up, stretched. "This is really a rather marvellous situation," he said. "Our good friend, Mr. Quayle, imagines us closeted together with me giving you all sorts of information—information for which he was paying the sum of five thousand pounds."

"Exactly," said Fells. "Incidentally, I've got the balance of four thousand here for you."

Foden grinned. He said: "Well, I don't think we shall have any use for it. But it *is* amusing, isn't it? Instead of my giving you all sorts of information to go back to him, in a couple of days' time you will be in Germany. You will be giving Schlieken the benefit of three years' experience of war in this country. You must have information enough to make a book."

Fells said: "Enough to make half a dozen books."

He helped himself to another cigarette. He was glad to notice that his fingers holding the lighter were quite steady.

He asked: "What are your plans?"

Foden said: "We must be quick. Everything is ready. Everything is arranged. We have a very good exit route which is still unknown to our English friends. We shall use it. We shall use it late to-night. In the meantime we will leave here. There is just a chance that Mr. Quayle might be curious. I don't think so. I think he would be too clever to do anything that would cause me to have any suspicions. But one never knows. So I suggest you get your hat and coat and then we will go for a walk, and then a cab drive so as to lose any curious people who *might* be tailing us." Foden heaved a great sigh. He said:

"I shall be glad to get back to Germany. The places I want to go to—the things I want to do—the women I want to see again! Schlieken works us very hard you know. This time I expect him to give me something really big. I deserve well at his hands. Incidentally," he went on with a smile, "so do you. You'll find him very generous to a man who has played the game with him."

Fells said: "I know. Schlieken always treats his people well."

"Precisely," said Foden. "He has always been very good to *loyal* people in his Department. Shall we go?"

Fells said: "Why not?"

He went into the bedroom; put on his overcoat and hat. Foden was waiting for him in the sitting-room. He said:

"It seems a pity to leave all these cigarettes. I think we'll take them with us, don't you?" He smiled charmingly at Fells. He began to fill his cigarette case from the box on the table.

Fells said: "You're quite right. You think of everything, Foden." He said to himself: So we're going to stay under cover until we move out of England. We're going to lie low. We're not even going into a shop to buy cigarettes. That's why he's taking these.

They went down the stairs. When they were in the hallway, Fells's landlady came up from the basement. She said:

"Will you be late, Mr. Fells? And do you expect any telephone calls?"

Fells said: "I shan't be very late to-night, and I don't think there'll be any phone calls. If there are any say that I expect to be back before eleven."

She went back to the basement. Foden opened the door. He stepped to one side. He said pleasantly to Fells:

"After you, my dear Fells."

Fells said: "Thank you."

As he went out he looked over his shoulder up the stairway. He had been very comfortable in that place. He had an idea he would never see it again.

II

Greeley sat by the side of the fire in his bed-sitting-room. An unlighted cigarette hung from his lip. He was reading *The Evening News*. He thought that the boys in the desert army must be having a hell of a time. Greeley thought he would like to be there. It would be colourful—exciting.

He looked at his wrist-watch. It was thirty-two minutes past ten. He thought: Well, that's that! He went over to the telephone. He dialled the number.

The blonde girl in Quayle's office answered: "Is that you, Mr. Greeley?"

Greeley said: "Yes, it's me all right."

She said: "Have you any message?"

Greeley said: "No, nothing at all."

The blonde girl said: "All right. I'll be getting on to Mr. Quayle in a minute. He should be round to see you very shortly. Perhaps you'd like to open the door."

Greeley said: "All right. I'll be waiting for him."

He lit the cigarette. Then he went downstairs; took the door off the latch; stood inside the dark hallway. Five minutes later Quayle came. Greeley led the way upstairs to his room. When they were inside the room he took a quick look at Quayle. He thought Quayle looked worried.

Quayle put his hat on a chair. He took out his cigarette case, lit a cigarette. He said:

"So there's been no sign of Foden—nothing at all?"

Greeley shook his head.

Quayle said: "Well, that means they're going out." There was a tone of finality in his voice.

Greeley sat down in the chair by the fire. He thought: I wonder what the hell's going to happen now. It looks as if he hasn't got anything up his sleeve. It looks as if somebody's played a trump card on him. He felt vaguely unhappy.

Quayle asked: "Exactly what happened last night?"

Greeley went through it in detail. When he'd finished, Quayle said:

"Well, it doesn't tell us a lot, does it? But I never expected we'd find anything at Foden's place. I never expected we'd find anything on him. He's too clever for that."

Greeley said: "This Foden bird seems pretty smart."

Quayle said: "Yes, he's smart enough. He ought to be."

"Why?" asked Greeley.

Quayle smiled a little. He began to walk up and down the room. He said: "Foden is one of the best men in the German Intelligence Service. He's a hundred per cent, dyed-in-the-wool Nazi. He's an absolutely first-class man." He looked at Greeley. "Look how he speaks English," he said. "He speaks three other languages as well as that. I wonder if he ever even *thinks* in his native tongue."

Greeley said: "Struth! So he's a Jerry!"

"That's right," said Quayle. "He's German all right. He's been playing it off the cuff all along, and it looks to him as if it's come off. A wise bird, Foden."

Greeley said nothing. He wanted to ask questions. Quayle went on talking. He said:

"There's no reason why you shouldn't know something about this now, Greeley. I haven't told you much about it before because you know it's my rule to tell agents only as much as they ought to know. My experience is that if you tell an operative too much—give them too big a picture to think about—they are inclined to go off the rails. I don't believe in that."

Greeley said: "I know that, Mr. Quayle. I don't think you ever let your left hand know what your right hand's doing. Maybe you're right."

"In our peculiar profession I'm definitely right," said Quayle. "But this time is perhaps an exception. Foden's been very clever about this business. He was put in by Schlieken—the biggest shot in the German External Intelligence Service—to work in Morocco. Foden was in the German Navy once. It was easy for him to get a job as second officer on some coasting boats. What he didn't realize was that Estalza—the man who owned those boats—was working for me."

Greeley whistled. "So you've been wise from the start?" he said. There was a gleam of admiration in his eyes.

"Oh, yes," said Quayle. "I've been wise from the start. I've been on to Foden through every move in this game."

Greeley said: "You know, Mr. Quayle, I think sometimes we aren't half as bad as people think we are."

Quayle smiled. "That's a matter of comparison," he said. "We'll know before this war's over. Well, Estalza was wise to Foden. Even then Foden was preparing for the big job—getting over here. He went twice to our people in Morocco with information about the Germans. Of course the information was true—but unimportant. He was annoyed with them when they wouldn't listen to them. They wouldn't listen to him because they knew all about him. Estalza had seen to that. So Foden began to be a little suspicious of Estalza. Soon after that Estalza got himself killed. Foden thought that somebody—if they were wise enough—might get the idea—and quite rightly—that he had something to do with this, so he arranged to get himself sent to the Vichy Internment Camp. He was still building up his story. But unfortunately something happened in that camp which hasn't done him any good."

Quayle stopped pacing. He drew on his cigarette and looked at Greeley.

"You remember that photograph he showed you," he went on, "the photograph of the group taken in the internment camp?"

"I remember," said Greeley. "He showed it to me down at the port. And you found it behind the dressing-table in Zilla Stevenson's flat."

"That's right," said Quayle. "It was rather unfortunate for Foden that he didn't know I had a duplicate of that picture. When that picture was taken in Morocco, one of my people bought a print of it. He wanted to get it back to me. He got it back to me. He identified on the back of the picture the people in it, and he said just who and what Foden was."

Greeley sighed. "What do you know about that?" he said.

"That's why Foden had to kill Zilla Stevenson," said Quayle. "When he went to her flat he was doing that act about Morocco; telling Zilla the story he told you. He took that photograph out of his pocket and showed it to her. I can imagine what happened.

"She recognized that photograph because the man who got that picture back to me was her husband. She was very fond of her husband, and now she knew who Foden was. *He'd identified himself to her.*"

Quayle sighed. "Poor old Zilla," he said. "You can guess what happened, can't you, Greeley? He gave her that picture. She looked at it. They were probably standing in front of the fire—she nearest to the door of her bedroom. How she must have hated Foden—the man who was responsible for her husband's death." He shrugged his shoulders.

"She probably thought that Foden was getting away with it. She probably thought that I didn't know who he was. She lost her head. She went into the bedroom and she came out with the picture in one hand and her automatic pistol in the other. Her idea was to hold Foden up, telephone through to me and get him picked up. Poor Zilla. . . ."

"I get it," said Greeley. "He took a jump at her; got hold of her hand with the pistol in it and turned the gun on her?"

"Yes," said Quayle. "Well, that was all right. He thought he'd cleared that one up. I imagine that during the struggle Zilla threw that photograph into the bedroom. It fell behind the dressing-table. Foden didn't worry about it, because it didn't mean anything to him. He probably thought that Zilla was a come-on girl working for one of our Intelligence Departments; that she suspected him and was going to turn him in. So he didn't worry about the picture."

Greeley said: "He must have had the breeze up. He must have known he was skatin' on thin ice."

Quayle shrugged his shoulders. "Foden's used to skating on thin ice," he said. "I believe he likes it. In any event he wasn't worrying about Zilla. He knew we wouldn't do anything about that."

Greeley nodded. He was beginning to understand.

"Well, to go back to Morocco," Quayle went on, "when he got away from the Internment Camp, Foden waited a bit; then he got in touch with one of our people in Marrakesh. He thought it was time to get moving. His instructions were to get into England, and he thought he was on a good wicket. He put up a very good story—the story being that he'd had his information turned down twice. This time he'd got some really big stuff and wanted paying for it.

"Our people in Marrakesh made out they'd fallen for this—hook, line and sinker. They put him on to somebody in Suera and this some-body put him on to a Mrs. Ferry." Quayle smiled reminiscently. "Mrs. Ferry," he said, "is a woman of great perception. She's been working for me for years. It was through her that Foden got over here and when he got here you were waiting for him."

Greeley said: "Pretty neat that. You're no fool, Mr. Quayle."

Quayle said: "I don't know about that. We'll see." He resumed his pacing. "Foden still thought he was on a good wicket," he went on. "He looked at it this way. He knew that sooner or later he'd get in touch with somebody who mattered. That story of his was too good for him not to. Well, they were either going to believe him or they weren't. He really didn't mind very much because he knew this: Supposing we *did* suspect him? The obvious thing for us to do would be to let him get out just to see how he *would* get out. He would reason that we must know that if he had a way into England—and he'd found a pretty good way—he'd have a way out. He reasoned that if we suspected him we would know he was working for Schlieken—the idea being that if we came to this conclusion we would most certainly put him in touch with Fells.

"When we do that," said Quayle, "what's he going to do? The obvious thing for him to do is to tell Fells the truth; to arrange to take Fells out with him; to arrange to make use of Fells. He thinks we're going to let them both out because that puts Fells in touch with Schlieken."

Greeley said: "I've got it."

"But what you don't know," Quayle went on, "is that Fells was working for Schlieken before this war. I put him in to do that. He worked very hard for them for quite a while," said Quayle with a smile. "They'd be able to find a use for Fells even if they didn't exactly trust him. He'd still know a lot that they could make use of."

Greeley said: "I've got it. Foden reckoned that if Fells was working for you you'd let him take Fells out just on the chance of making a contact with this Schlieken in Germany. He reckoned that if Fells wasn't working for you—if he was still prepared to play along with Schlieken—he'd have information for those boys that would be worth a million."

Quayle nodded. "That's right," he said. "And in any event you realize that they have ways and means of making people talk even if they don't want to."

Greeley said: "I know. I've heard about it. I wouldn't like to be Fells."

He took a box of cigarettes out of his trouser pockets; lit one. He was thinking that it was pretty tough on Fells.

There was silence for a little while; then Quayle said: "It's a tough game this."

Greeley grinned. He said: "You're telling me. Well, I suppose this is the end of the story. It was nice of you to tell me about it. It makes it very interesting. I've sort of got the whole picture now, which is a thing I've never had all the while I've been working for you, Mr. Quayle."

Quayle smiled. He said: "Well, Greeley, I thought it was about time that you might actually know something—not that it'll do you any good."

"No," said Greeley. "I don't suppose it will."

Quayle stopped his pacing. He threw his cigarette end in the grate. He walked to the chair. He picked up his hat.

Greeley said: "Well, I suppose if you want me you'll get in touch with me, Mr. Quayle?"

Quayle nodded. "Yes. You'd better stay here for a bit. If I want you I'll call you."

Greeley got up. He said: "It's tough luck on Mr. Fells. I was thinking—"

Quayle stopped. "What were you thinking, Greeley?" he asked.

"I was thinking it might have been *me*," said Greeley.

"Yes," said Quayle, "it *might* have been you. If you'd been Fells—if you spoke German as well as he does—if you'd taken the chances he's taken—if you'd done all he's done—you might have had the great reward of—" His face was grim. He shrugged his shoulders. "Goodnight, Greeley," he said.

He went down the stairs.

III

Mayola Green opened the door of her flat; closed it quietly; walked across the dark hallway; switched on the light in her sitting-room. She was tired. She looked at herself in the wall mirror. She thought this is a hell of a life. Won't it be nice when this war's over? You won't know yourself, Mayola. I wonder what you'll do when it is over. I should think you'd make a pretty good actress. But I think you'd be bored being an actress. She sighed. Her head was aching. She realized she'd drunk a lot too much the night before. She thought that it wasn't very much fun to drink too much when you didn't want to; having to play parts; to be somebody else all the time.

She lit a cigarette. She was physically tired, but her brain was not tired. It was revolving like a squirrel in a cage. The trouble with life is, she thought, that you never know from one day to another what you're going to do, my girl. Perhaps you'll stay here in this flat for two or three weeks or a month before anything else happens. Then Quayle will come on the line, or that blonde girl of his. You'll have to go somewhere, pretend to be something that you are not, behave in a way that's quite foreign to you. All for what? Something you'll never even know about.

She stretched. She walked across the room into the bedroom. The bathroom door was open. The idea of a warm bath appealed to her. She switched the light on in the bathroom; turned on the taps.

The door bell rang. Mayola thought for a minute. She turned off the taps, quickly closed the bathroom door, switched the light off in the bedroom, closed the door behind her, walked across the sitting-room, opened the door. She opened it just a little way.

Quayle was standing outside. He said: "Good evening, Mayola."

She held the door open. Quayle entered, put his hat on the chair in the hall.

Mayola said: "Wonders will never cease—a visit from the boss himself. My! This must be important. Would you like a drink?"

Quayle said: "No, thanks. I'll smoke a cigarette if I may."

She brought him one.

He said: "What did you think of last night, Mayola?"

"Candidly," she said, "I didn't think it was very good. I thought it was rather amateurish. I don't know anything about your boy friend Foden, but he'll be an awful mug if he doesn't suspect. It was rather like a scene in a film."

Quayle smiled. He said: "He'll suspect all right. But what does that matter?"

Mayola asked: "Did you really expect to find anything on him?"

Quayle shook his head. "No, Mayola. Tell me something: What happened? Did you give him the usual dose?"

She said: "I gave him the dose you advised—a small one. It was too small for him. That man's as fit as a horse. He was coming out of it in about half an hour."

Quayle nodded. "And then?" he said.

"I did what you said," said Mayola. "I gave him a little sniff out of the bottle you gave me."

"I see," said Quayle. "And what happened then?"

"He just went off again," said Mayola. "He was muttering and grumbling and writhing about the place. Some anæsthetic, I must say, that stuff of yours!"

Quayle said: "I suppose you took the trouble to listen to what he said?"

She laughed. "I tried to," she said. "He said a hell of a lot of stuff. You know how they talk. It never means anything."

Quayle nodded. "I know," he said.

"It's easy to see he was a sailor," Mayola went on. "He was talking about the tides, and he did a little bit about latitude and longitude. That was all Dutch to me. Then he said something about a hell of a joke. Then he said some foreign sort of name."

Quayle said: "Was the name Schlieken?"

"That's right," said Mayola. "That's what he said—Schlieken."

"What else did he say?" asked Quayle.

Mayola said: "He was obviously thinking about ships of some sort. He was talking about boxing the compass. Tell me, how do you box a compass? What does that mean?"

Quayle was smiling. He said: "It would take a long time to explain that, Mayola, and I've got to be going."

She said: "It's been an honour, I'm sure. It's a long time since you were here last. What's going to happen to me now? Do I just stay around and wait for the telephone to ring?"

Quayle said: "No, you can have two weeks off, Mayola. I think things are going to be quiet for a bit."

She said: "Do you mean that?"

Quayle nodded.

"All right," she said. "You won't see me for smoke. To-morrow I'm off to a little quiet spot in the country, where nobody thinks of cocktails and the most exciting thing is looking at a cow in a field."

Quayle said: "I envy you. That sounds good to me." He got up. "Good-night, Mayola," he said. "I'll be seeing you."

"Good luck," she said.

She followed him into the hall; closed the door quietly behind him. She went back to the sitting-room. She said to herself: Mayola, my girl, you've got two weeks' leave, and you can put a lot of bath salts in your bath. You've earned it!

CHAPTER 12
EXIT

I

THE moon was full. Fells thought it must be somewhere around three o'clock. It was a quiet and beautiful night.

In front of them the road stretched up over the hill, between the woods on the top of the hill, like a twisting ribbon. Through the open window of the car the breeze came. It brought in the salt tang of the sea. Fells wondered where they were.

Sitting beside him, hunched back in the corner of the car, was Foden. His cigarette tip was glowing. It glowed regularly as Foden drew on it. He was breathing quietly, without haste. Fells thought it would take a great deal to disturb Foden's equilibrium.

In front of him he could see the slim back of the girl who was driving the car. Fells thought: They're pretty hot having women working for them over here. I suppose she's a German. She's pretty good. And she can drive.

He lit a cigarette. Quite obviously, he thought, there was a very good organization over here. This car, for instance—a big touring car with a Hackney carriage plate on it. Somehow, with all the regulations and restrictions about cars and petrol, they could run a car like this, and have a girl to drive it. Nice work, thought Fells; then qualified the thought with the idea that in all probability Quayle had a similar service somewhere in Germany. Why not?

The girl certainly knew her stuff. During the last half-hour she had twisted and turned that car all over the countryside. Fells, who had tried in the beginning to note the direction, had become quite bemused now. He had not the slightest idea where they were.

Foden said suddenly: "A penny for your thoughts, my friend."

Fells grinned. "They're not worth that," he said. "I was just thinking that this girl is a damned good driver. By the way just where are we?"

Foden asked. "Does that worry you?" He went on: "She's a good girl. Schlieken found her about six years ago. She was a maidservant working for a family in Berlin. I don't know how he came across her. He trained her for three years. Now look at her. She speaks two languages and"—he laughed quietly—"she's been over here for eighteen months. She works for a car-hire firm—a very good operative!"

Fells asked: "Does she get her stuff back to Germany?"

Foden shook his head. "No," he said. "That's the old system. It creaks. She waits over here till someone comes over here to get it from her. Too many good people have been lost by trying to work that antiquated post office system of getting information out of a country. It's old-fashioned. We don't do that any more."

Fells asked casually: "Do the English?"

Foden looked at him sideways. "Of course," he said slowly, "you wouldn't know. You've probably been out of touch with that sort of work for some time. Candidly, we don't quite know what the English are doing." He threw his cigarette stub out of the window. "You know," he said slowly, "the English are not fools. There's always been this idea that British Intelligence Services are bad—this sort of ridiculous Colonel Blimp idea. As a matter of fact many of these English Colonel Blimps are very much more clever than the people who decry them know. In any event there are quite a lot of things to be learned from the English." He smiled. "We have been learning them," he said.

Fells said: "It's a surprise to me to hear that Schlieken has anything to learn from the English."

Foden said: "My dear Fells, that's where you make a great mistake. Schlieken will learn from anybody. That is his great virtue. There are two great things about Schlieken. One is that, as you probably know, he is a very brave and cunning man. Secondly, he is a man who has always the most open mind. He's always seeking to find some better way of doing something."

Fells nodded. He said: "I know. Schlieken is a man of many surprises."

"How right you are," said Foden. "And I'll guarantee you something, my dear Fells. I'll guarantee that he will give you an even greater surprise than you've ever had before."

"That's going to be very interesting," said Fells. "When do I get surprised?"

Foden looked at his wrist-watch. He said: "Any minute now."

The car had mounted the hill. Now they were driving along a road which ran between two small woods. As they descended the hill on the other side, the breeze came through the car windows with added vigour. Fells realized that they were near the sea.

The trees were thick on each side of the road. The car began to slow down. Then it stopped. The girl who was driving looked over her shoulder. She pushed back the glass panel. She said, with a little smile:

"I think this is the place, Mr. Foden."

Foden said: "Yes, this is the place." He said to Fells: "Shall we get out?"

Fells got out of the car. Foden followed him. They stood on the grass verge at the edge of the road. Everything was very quiet except for the noise of the night breeze in the trees and the rustling of dead leaves. Somewhere near them Fells heard a rotten twig snap. He turned towards the noise.

A man came out of the shadows. He walked towards them. It was some time before Fells could see his face.

Foden said: "Here is your surprise, Fells. This is a meeting of old friends."

The man was quite near to them now. He was smiling. Fells could see little eyes behind the pince-nez. He said under his breath:

"My God! Schlieken . . . !"

Foden heard him. He said: "I thought that would surprise you."

The man said: "Congratulations, my dear Foden. You have done very well." He put his hands out and patted Fells's shoulders. "How delighted I am to meet you once again, my dear Fells," he said. "This is indeed a happy meeting. Excuse me one minute."

He moved towards the car. He said to the girl very softly: "I have very good reports of you, Karla. You are doing very well. One day, when you return to the Fatherland, you will find a decoration waiting for you."

The girl said: "Thank you, Herr Direktor." Her face glowed.

Schlieken came back. Fells said to him:

"You're the most amazing man I have ever met in my life. I don't think there's anybody quite like you."

Schlieken shrugged his shoulders. He said: "You make a mistake, my dear Fells—you who so seldom make mistakes. I am not at all amazing. I do the obvious, simple things. Figure to yourself," he said, "it is quite obvious to me that our delightful—our very brilliant—friend Quayle believes that I am sitting somewhere in my office in the Frederickstrasse controlling my organization." He laughed softly. "I wonder what the delightful Quayle would say," he went on, "if he knew that for the last nine months I have been living in a charming little house in the country about seventeen miles outside London, controlling my small but extremely good organization in this country."

He stopped speaking. He said abruptly to Foden: "What is the time? How long have we to wait?"

Foden said. "About ten minutes; then we can move."

"Are the other two here?" Schlieken asked.

Foden nodded. "They will meet us a little further along," he said. "They will be waiting now."

Schlieken said: "Good." He turned to Fells. "My dear Party-comrade here," he went on, "may have told you my idea which we put into operation three years ago. For six months before the war the English were getting very panicky. They took all sorts of precautions so I conceived the idea of leaving all my operatives in England, cutting them off from headquarters, letting them stew in their own juice, as you English say. One or two of them I knew were all right. I knew where I could get in touch with them. The rest of them—I let them go. The English got some. Quayle got at least a dozen and I don't think he was at all happy about it. He could not conceive how it was that these men—well-trained and, as he thought, well organized—were just left here with no channels of information or communication for them to use. I think it worried him a great deal."

Fells said: "It must have worried him."

Schlieken went on: "But I knew that of that number there were fifteen or so who were much too smart to worry about not being able to communicate with the Fatherland. I got in touch with them for the first eighteen months by sending people over and getting them out afterwards. We used a little scheme which was planned originally by Foden here. It worked excellently. I do not believe that, except in perhaps one or two cases, the English have ever realized just what we were doing.

"Then," Schlieken continued, "when the time came I paid our friend Mr. Quayle the supreme insult. I decided to come here myself." Schlieken laughed. "Really," he said, "I would like to know what he would say if he knew that at this moment I was standing here with you and Foden discussing this business so amiably."

Fells said: "You took a hell of a chance, Schlieken."

Schlieken shook his head. "No," he said. "Shall I tell you why I didn't take a chance. Listen, my friend: Always I have been a man who likes to have a way of escape. I am a man who always looks for the back door in case I have to get out quickly. You understand? It occurred to me before I came here to England that possibly our good Quayle and his colleagues might have a little more intelligence than they usually show. I had to think of some water-tight scheme for making my exit from England a certainty. I thought of one."

He laid his hand on the lapel of Fells's coat. "You!" he said.

Fells said: "That was *very* clever."

"It was intelligent," said Schlieken. "I looked at it from this point of view: When I wanted to get out we should get Foden in. You know how we got Foden in. He's probably told you. His background was perfect. His service in Morocco was perfect. Years ago he went to the English. He gave them information which they did not want, because they knew it already. But the fact made them trust him. Then he was interned in a Vichy camp. He then arranged to come to England, because he had important information to give the English—true information," said Schlieken, "but information which we did not *mind* giving them. We knew Foden would get in. The thing was would he get out? Then," said Schlieken, "I thought of you. It seemed obvious to me that if Foden could get next to Quayle—if he could work himself into a position in which any superior branch of British Intelligence came in contact with him, it was a certainty that he would be passed on to Quayle. And what would Quayle do? Quayle would most certainly put him on to Fells—his expert on Morocco."

Fells said nothing. Schlieken's smile was charming. He continued: "How did we know that? We knew it because we knew Fells was working for Quayle." He put his hand on the lapel of Fells's coat again. "Do not misunderstand me, my dear friend," he said. "Don't think I am accusing you of any disloyalty to me. You were left here by me at the beginning of the war—you who had worked so loyally and faithfully for me for sometime before the war. It was quite obvious that as a good servant of the Reich—as a good servant of myself—you would naturally endeavour to become employed by some branch of the

British Intelligence, so that when the time came we could have the benefit of your knowledge and experience. Is that not so?"

Fells said: "You are always right, Schlieken." He thought: God help you, Fells. They know all about you. Your number's up!

"Very well," said Schlieken. "So I concluded that Quayle would put Foden on to Fells; that Quayle would believe that Foden's one idea would be to get Fells out of England into Germany—back to Schlieken. So that he, Quayle, would know that he had near to him in Berlin—near the hub of the Reich external intelligence department—a man in whom he is foolish enough to have confidence. He would believe that at least one of those very brave and clever Englishmen that he has operating in the Reich—and unfortunately we have not got all of them yet—would be able to make a contact with you. In other words, he deluded himself that he would actually start an information service from my central office back to him in London." Schlieken sighed. "Such impertinence!"

Foden said: "Excuse me, but the time is getting on. I think we should move."

"Very well," said Schlieken. "Just as you say, Foden. This is your party."

Foden said softly to the girl: "Good-bye, Karla. Be good. Work hard and bravely for your Fuehrer. When the time comes we shall take you back to Germany."

The girl made a little movement with her hand. She said very quietly: "Heil, Hitler!" She turned the car. In a minute its rear light had disappeared over the brow of the hill.

Foden said: "Herr Direktor, I regret that you will have to walk a little way."

Schlieken said: "Why not? You always tell me that I never get enough exercise, Foden. Let us walk."

They began to walk down the hill. The trees began to thin out. The road narrowed into a path. Two men came out of the shadows of a little thicket.

Foden said: "Here they are—Valetz and Kuhler. Good evening, gentlemen."

The two men said good evening. One of them was wearing a suit of plus-fours and no overcoat. The other looked like a city man. He had a dark-blue overcoat and bowler hat. They followed a few paces behind.

By now the footpath had disappeared. They were walking through bracken. Fells could see the line of the cliffs descending on his left, terminating in what looked like a plateau. Away in the distance in the moonlight he could see a lone house. They walked for a few minutes. They were within a hundred yards of the cliff edge.

Foden said: "I believe we should walk carefully here. The cleft is narrow."

They entered a cleft which ran down through the cliffs to the beach.

Then Fells remembered. The lone house he had seen at the bottom of the hillside was the public-house where he had met Greeley and the other two—the Box of Compasses! He smiled bitterly.

They walked down the cleft. As they neared the bottom the cliff walls rose on each side of them. In front the shingle and sand—white in the moonlight—sloped down steeply to the sea. The tide was high. The white horses on the sea—blown up by the gale—came in towards them on the wave-tops.

Fells leaned against the side of the cleft. He breathed in the air deeply. His mind for some odd reason was concerned with all sorts of *little* things that had happened to him in his life. Not the great things—only the little things. He thought it odd that the mind should run in such strange grooves at a time like this.

He began to think about Tangier. . . .

They stood on the shingle at the mouth of the cleft. Schlieken and Foden in front, with Fells just behind them, and Valetz and Kuhler between the cliff walls still further back. Foden shaded his eyes with his hand and gazed out to sea. He muttered to himself angrily, for although the night was fine a sea mist hung over the water a hundred yards out. Beyond that one could see nothing.

Schlieken asked: "Is this the time? How long do we wait, my friend?"

Foden said: "They have to be careful—very careful. There are those cursed Coastal Command planes and the naval patrol. Still, they should be all right." He turned to smile at Schlieken. "They are using a boat like a British 'E' boat," he said. "That makes it a lot easier for them."

Schlieken nodded. He turned to Fells. He said: "Our friend is good, is he not? A good workman, our Mr. Foden."

Foden said: "Ah, listen!"

From beyond the mist came the sound of a gull calling. Twice . . . three times. . . .

Foden ran back into the cover of the cleft wall. He brought out a flash lamp. He flicked it on and off three times. He said: "Good . . . they are here!"

Schlieken looked at Fells. He smiled.

The boat came suddenly out of the mist. It was headed straight for them. It came on at a terrific rate, its bows cutting up the sea into a white foam.

Valetz and Kuhler came out of the cleft.

The boat was fifty yards from the shore. Then, as the engines were reversed, and she slowed abruptly, almost under the shadow of the shelving beach, the white beam of a searchlight broke from the boat's bows, blinding the watching men on the shore.

"*Achtung!*" Foden's voice was almost a shriek. Schlieken began to blaspheme horribly. Then Fells saw the Mauser pistol in Foden's hand and flung himself flat on the shingle. Foden started to shoot, shouting in German.

A tommy-gun began to chatter. Fells, raising his head, saw in the side beam of the searchlight, sitting in the bows of the boat, swaying with the bucking of the tommy-gun—Greeley . . . Greeley grinning.

He pushed his head down into the shingle. Now Schlieken was almost beside him, both hands to his stomach, writhing, drooling at the mouth, making unintelligible sounds. . . . Near him Foden lay still. The tommy-gun was silent. Fells could hear the bows of the boat on the shingle. He looked up.

Quayle was on the beach, splashing through the water. Behind him, the tommy-gun under his arm, came Greeley, his shirt soaked with blood.

Fells got up. He began to walk down the beach. He walked fast. He could feel his hands trembling.

He said: "Quayle . . . you've got Schlieken . . . you've got Schlieken . . . !"

Quayle said: "I know . . . I'm damned glad. I had to play *you* to get *him*. See?"

Fells nodded.

Quayle smiled. "Nice work, Fells," he said. "I'm much obliged to you."

Fells walked with Quayle across the scrub in the direction of the Box of Compasses. The night breeze was freshening. Fells drew the air into his lungs gratefully. He said:

"I suppose the greatest moment of my life was when I saw Greeley in the bows of that boat."

Quayle said: "So you were surprised. It wasn't so difficult as I thought. I think I know most of their ways in and out of this country; I ought to. But I wasn't certain as to whether they'd take this one or another one and I had to be very careful. I daren't have people watching." He laughed.

"I'm awfully sorry Foden didn't live long enough for me to tell him that *he* gave it away."

Fells said: "Foden gave it away . . . ?"

Quayle said: "Horace Greeley and Foden had an evening with a young woman called Mayola Green. She gave Foden a Mickey Finn—a very weak one. Before he had quite come out of it she put him to sleep again with a little mixture I have"—he smiled wryly in the darkness—"held under the nostrils. You know an anæsthetic usually makes people talk, and Foden had been repressed for such a long time; he's been playing the part of Foden for so long; that I guessed he'd *have* to talk a little."

"And he talked?" Fells asked.

"Enough," Quayle went on. "He talked about Schlieken. He talked about the tides, and then Mayola Green said he talked about 'boxing the compass.' She misunderstood. Foden said 'The Box of Compasses.' "

Fells said: "Poor old Foden."

"Then I knew it had to be here," said Quayle—"that and the remark about the tides. You realize that the tide has got to be right here in order to get a fair-sized motor-boat right up under the shelf of the beach. We had their boat dealt with by the naval patrol, and we slipped in a little late."

They were half-way across the scrub: On one of the pathways they passed Foden's hired car. The girl stood beside it. Two men were with her.

Quayle stopped. He said in German: "Too bad, Karla . . . the Herr Direktor wasn't quite as clever as he thought."

Her mouth worked spasmodically. Then, as Quayle began to move away from her, she spat in his face.

He took out his handkerchief. He said to Fells:

"Such a nice little thing, isn't she?"

Fells said: "What about Greeley?"

"It's nothing," said Quayle. "Foden's first shot hit him sideways—straight across the stomach. It's taken out a nice little ridge. A lot of blood but nothing that really matters. Greeley will be all right in a fortnight."

He took out his cigarette case, offered it to Fells. They stopped to light their cigarettes.

Quayle said: "Tangier will be pleased about this, won't she?"

He looked at Fells sideways . . . smiling.

II

Fells sat in the big armchair by the side of the sitting-room fire. He was half-dozing. The clock on the mantelpiece told him it was seven o'clock, but he felt disinclined to move. It was a bad night. He could hear the rain pattering on the windows. He put his hands behind his head and stretched.

He began to think about Foden and Schlieken. . . .

There was a knock on the door. Fells's landlady came in.

She said: "If you're not going out to dinner, Mr. Fells, I thought I'd better bring you some coffee and some sandwiches. And here's a letter for you. I didn't bring it up before. I thought you were asleep."

She put the tray down on the table; went away.

Fells picked up the envelope. It was a large important looking envelope. He slit the flap. Inside was a letter from Quayle and another envelope with *O.H.M.S.* on it. Fells read the letter. It said:

"My Dear Fells,

"I think the time has come when you and I must part company, the reason being that I think you deserve a little promotion.

"Quite candidly, you've served your purpose with me. Although we've got rid of our two friends F. and S. the other people will be much too wary after our last exploit to enable me to make any real use of you.

"I have therefore arranged—and I think this may please you—that you shall join one of the Military Intelligence branches.

"I have talked to them and they will be very glad to have you with them under your own name and in your old army rank. The official letter is enclosed herewith. You report to them after a couple of weeks' leave of absence.

"So once again a military career stretches before you. Incidentally, with reference to your little trouble in India years ago—a little trouble for which I am very grateful because it brought you in touch with me originally—the idea has been circulated in the Department in which you will work, and generally, that that Indian business was a frame-up against you, put on for the benefit of our German friends, and that they fell for it.

"When you start work and when you're all dressed up in your new uniform you might give me a ring. We'll have lunch together. But not during the next four weeks.

"Yours ever,

"W. V. S. Quayle.

"P.S.—You might remember me to Tangier."

Fells sat looking at the letter. He found he had difficulty in seeing the words.

The blonde girl in Quayle's office was trying to answer two telephones at once. She was also trying at the same time to talk to Quayle through the doorway. She put her hand over the transmitter of one telephone. She said:

"I've got your Scottish call, Mr. Quayle."

Quayle came into the room. He picked up the telephone.

He said: "Is that you, Hewlitt? Right. Now, listen. He'll come in on the boat to-morrow night. His papers are in order and the police won't interfere with him. Give him his head. You understand? Let him get through. Unless I'm very much mistaken he'll gravitate in the direction of Surrey. They had an organization there that we've succeeded in breaking. Just keep on his tail. When you've got something to say come through and let me know. Do you understand?"

He hung up. He said to the blonde girl: "I'm going now. I ought to be back in four or five days' time."

She said: "Your suitcase is packed, Mr. Quayle. It's in the hallway."

He said: "Thanks. You can have your leave when I get back."

"Thank you, Mr. Quayle," she said. "And good luck to you."

Quayle went out.

The blonde girl unstopped the other telephone. She said:

"Is that Mrs. Greeley—Mrs. Horace Greeley? Oh, Mrs. Greeley, I'm secretary to Mr. Edmundson, the Managing Director of the Midland Smelting Company. . . . Yes, we're a munitions firm. . . . Your husband, Mr. Horace Greeley, was slightly injured last week in an accident in the ammunition testing shed. . . . No, it's nothing at all serious, Mrs. Greeley, and you needn't worry a bit—just a very slight flesh wound, and he'll be up in a few days' time. Mr. Edmundson, our Director, asked me to tell you that if you want to see Mr. Greeley, he's in the Good Samaritan Hospital at Finchley. He's very keen to see you. Of course all your expenses will be paid and your hotel expenses while you're up here. . . . Yes, I assure you it's nothing, Mrs. Greeley—nothing for you to worry about. Good-night."

The blonde girl hung up the telephone. She yawned. She rested her chin on her hand, and sat waiting for the telephone to ring.

THE END

24994036R00111